Edited by:

Lura Lee Genz

Mia Manns

Rachel Weaver

Avenstar Productions

ISBN: 0990331431 (ISBN-10)

978-0-9903314-3-8 (ISBN-13)

Realms of Time

A SCRAPYARD SHIP NOVEL

Written By

Mark Wayne McGinnis

Preface

Here's where we left things off in the previous book (*Space Vengeance*):

...Keeping to his promise, Captain Jason Reynolds takes The Lilly to Allied space and returns the rhino-warriors to their home world. Jason quickly discovers the Craing fleet, of fifteen hundred warships, has returned, with the intention of destroying everything that remains of the Allied worlds.

...A possible new Caldurian ally, Granger, offers up new and advanced wormhole travel technology to the Earth Outpost, for the United Planetary Alliance (EOUPA) fleet —but at what price?

...Nan and Mollie are back on Earth and trying to make something of their scrapyard living conditions. With the help of an advanced drone Mollie has named Teardrop, Nan constructs a remarkable prefab home, with all the bells and whistles.

... Captain Stalls is still causing mayhem and taking his fleet of pirate ships, as well as his cloaked, weaponized, luxury liner, Her Majesty, to Earth. He's looking for some payback with Captain Reynolds and destroying Jason's home planet will be top on his list. But first he must find Nan, and make her his own.

...Having had his fleet decimated before, Admiral Reynolds is looking for some retribution of his own. Now, with hundreds of recently commandeered Craing warships, as well as the remnants of the Allied fleet, and, of course, The Lilly, a ferocious battle with

the Craing fleet ensues. The very survival of the Allied worlds is at stake. Things are looking promising for the Allied forces until the Caldurian, Granger, arrives, with a highly advanced vessel, named the Minian. When the ship enters the fight, on the wrong side of things, The Lilly pursues her back to Earth space.

...Brian and Betty (and a being called the hopper) have just escaped from an embattled, and adrift, space freighter in a small craft, called a bin lift.

... Captain Stall's pirate fleet arrives in Earth's solar system but does not fare well against Earth's remaining EOUPA, and the Craing's warship forces. Stalls escapes by the skin of his teeth, in a shuttle. With the information he had earlier tortured out of Brian, Jason's brother, Stalls finds Jason's home, in San Bernardino, CA.

...Nan and Mollie barely have a chance to enjoy their newly built home, when Stalls makes his appearance. In the end, the home's security measures aren't defensible against Stalls' ship. But Nan and Mollie didn't give in without a desperate fight. Near death himself, Stalls shoots Nan in the head. It was only with Mollie's help that Mollie, and mortally wounded Nan, were able to escape out the back of the house. Stalls, barely conscious, had Nan in his gun sights—if he couldn't have her, no one would.

...Apparently, there's no easy way to land a freighter bin lift craft. Brian's indiscriminate crash, landing on top of Nan's newly constructed home, and Captain Stall's head, was indeed timely.

Chapter 1

"What the hell is it doing?"

"Circling, sir," Perkins replied, now standing beside Jason.

"We're being hailed, Captain. It's the *Minian*," Perkins said.

Jason didn't respond as he continued to stare at the Caldurian vessel on the overhead display.

"What's our damage?" Jason asked, looking about *The Lilly's* fully staffed bridge. Ricket was moving between several stations, Gunny Orion was on tactical, and McBride was at the helm and looking back for further instructions.

Perkins, the only one who had been thrown to the deck, stood and turned his attention to his virtual notepad. "No fatalities; a broken wrist in Engineering. No outer hull breaches. Miscellaneous minor damage to all decks. Repair drones have been dispatched."

"That ship just took *The Lilly's* shields down in what, two plasma strikes?" Jason queried out loud. Hell, if they hadn't phase-shifted into the *Independence* when they did, they would have been destroyed.

Now, as *The Lilly* hovered within the Dreadnaught's main corridor, Jason had an uneasy feeling. Something told him the *Minian* had no intention of destroying The Lilly, but could have quite easily.

The battle raged on in open space. Under the direction of his father, Admiral Perry Reynolds, and the combined forces of

EOUPA and Allied fleets, along with the addition of nearly four hundred Mau warships which felt her pull had become recent allies, they were now getting the upper hand on the Craing. Until recently, the Craing's two thousand strong fleet was considered unstoppable, indestructible. But no longer. Less than eight hundred of their enemy's ships remained, and Jason expected the Craing's forthcoming surrender within moments. That is, if the *Minian*, with its highly advanced Caldurian weaponry, stayed the hell out of this battle.

"Captain, we're being—"

Jason cut Seaman Gordon off. "I know, the *Minian*—"

"No, sir. It's the admiral."

Jason, nodding his assent, pointed to the display.

"What in God's name is going on?" His father's voice filled the bridge. "We're detecting massive energy spikes coming off that foreign ship."

"We're fine, in case you're interested, Admiral," Jason voiced back sarcastically. He instantly regretted his quick retort. Definitely an offense, if he were still in the Navy.

The admiral let it pass with only a mild reprimand. "We know you're fine, that's what sensors are for. Tell me about that ship."

"It's the *Minian*. The limited information we have is it's a new Caldurian vessel. Travels the multiverse as easily as we do our own solar system. They've been hailing us for the last few minutes."

The admiral stared at his son with an incredulous expression. "So answer the damn hail and let me know what they want." The display segment showing the admiral's face disappeared.

"Go ahead and acknowledge the hail from the *Minian*, Seaman."

Not totally surprising Jason, Granger's smiling face appeared on a new segment.

Jason nodded toward Orion as she entered the bridge, returning from Dreadnaught One. Together, four recently clustered Dreadnaughts composed the ten-mile-long Meganaught. She took her seat at the tactical station.

"Jason," Granger said, "I do hope you and your crew have not been harmed."

"No, no harm at all. Although I would like to know why you fired on our vessel."

"I am but a low-level emissary. That was not my doing. Let's just say it was a cautionary signal from my superiors. A warning, if you will, concerning your recent use of wormhole travel."

"Wormhole travel that you went out of your way to provide to us?"

"Regrettably, that was a mistake. A decision intended to level the playing field against the Craing has brought you within reach of advanced technologies for which your society simply is not ready."

"You want to put the genie back in the bottle? I'm not sure that's possible. We have our own relationship with the interchange."

"I'm sorry, Jason, the decision has already been made. Although we cannot stop you from contacting the interchange directly, we can make it unpleasant enough for you that doing so won't be worth it."

"What is it you're really afraid of, Granger? I know when someone's bullshitting me. We're no threat to you, with or without the ability to travel throughout the universe."

Granger's eyes shifted to someone off screen and then came back to Jason. His smile was gone and he was clearly agitated.

"We are not a violent people. But we are not opposed to taking steps that will ensure the security of our society."

"From what you've told me, your society no longer inhabits our same space and time. Why would—"

Jason stopped himself mid-sentence. He knew why. "The multiverse. This technology also allows us to move within the multiverse, doesn't it? You don't want us moving into your neighborhood."

Granger stared back but held his tongue. Again, he looked off screen—he spoke guardedly to someone near him.

"I'm sorry, Jason. Please just do as you're asked; don't tempt fate."

About to reply, Jason was startled to see another segment added to the overhead display. It was of Earth.

"No doubt, Jason, you are viewing twenty-first century Earth on your display?"

Jason nodded; the seriousness of the situation was elevating to a new level. What were the Caldurians willing to do to make their point? Wipe humanity from the planet? Destroy Earth?

"Captain, a new wormhole is spooling," Orion said.

Jason wasn't going to sit back and watch their home world face annihilation right before their eyes. He turned his attention to Ricket, sitting at his station toward the front of the bridge.

Jason caught his eye and Ricket nodded his head.

A second wormhole began to form, just as the *Minian* disappeared into the first one.

"Helm, phase-shift us to that wormhole!" Jason barked.

Less than ten seconds behind the *Minian*, *The Lilly* was back in Earth space.

"Cap, the *Minian* is three thousand miles off our stern," Orion reported.

"On screen."

"Detecting energy spikes. Not sure what. She's firing, sir. Five missiles headed toward Earth."

"Can you take them out?"

Orion shook her head. "No time, Captain."

Jason watched as the five projectiles continued on a singular trajectory and then, as they suddenly separated apart, changed to five individual courses.

"Not missiles, Captain," Ricket said, moving to another station. "More like drones. Drones being fed an incredible amount of data. One minute to contact, sir."

"Where?"

"Multiple continents: Asia, Africa, Europe, South America, and North America, Cap," Orion interjected.

Jason looked from the feed of Earth to the view of the Caldurian ship.

"Gunny, any weaknesses you've been able to detect on the *Minian*?"

"No way—not a one. It's *The Lilly* on steroids, Cap. She's as close to indestructible as—"

"Helm, phase-shift *The Lilly* directly into the bridge of the *Minian*."

McBride nervously glanced back at Jason.

"Now, Ensign. Do it now!"

Chapter 2

After a bone-jarring phase-shift into the forward section of the *Minian*, everything went black. Anyone standing now lay on the floor unconscious. Those who were seated found themselves on the floor as well. Jason tried to rise, but thought better of it when spikes of pain shot through the back of his head. *Where are the emergency lights?*

"Captain, are you all right?" Jason recognized Orion's voice. She sounded scared.

"I'm alive, Gunny. What's your status?"

"I'm OK, I think."

Jason heard people begin to move around. A few moans and several expletives. Orion was at his side. In the blackness, he felt her hands moving around his body, checking him out for injuries. When she reached the back of his head, her hands moved with more care.

"Cap, you have blood on the back of your head. A gash, two or three inches in length."

Dizzy, Jason tried to sit up and felt a wave of nausea engulf him. "Thank you, Gunny. Check on the others. And see if you can get some lights going."

The Lilly shook, seemed to fall or slide for several moments, and then resettled at a different angle. Wherever they'd landed, presumably somewhere inside the *Minian*, the location was unstable.

Jason leaned forward and touched the back of his head. It felt sticky and, sure enough, he felt an open gash, easily an inch wide and several inches long. It throbbed, but the bleeding seemed to have slowed to a trickle.

Slowly, he got to his knees and, like a blind man, groped—trying to get his bearings as to where he was actually situated on the bridge. His left hand brushed against something solid to his left. Reaching in that direction, he realized it was the command chair. Fighting off another wave of nausea, Jason blacked out.

He had no idea how much time had elapsed. Somewhere there was a faint light moving in the distance. Someone was sobbing. Then more hands were on him, feeling around his body.

"I'm fine; check again on the others," Jason urged.

"The others have been taken care of. "Dira's lightly accented voice was close to his ear. She'd found his injury and was wrapping a bandage around his head. When finished, her hands continued to check his body. Then they were on his face, her fingertips gently checking his skin. Dira leaned in close and he could smell her familiar fragrance.

"You've been out for close to an hour, but you'll be okay. You have a concussion. Don't move around too much until I've had a chance to treat that gash."

"Dira, where's Mollie? Is Mollie all right?"

"She's with me, standing right in front of you."

"I'm sorry ... so dizzy. We need to get the emergency lights turned on."

"Definitely a concussion. The lights are already on, Captain," Dira replied. But there was something different in her voice.

"So, I'm blind?"

Jason felt Mollie pull herself onto his lap and hug him close. He reached for her, taking her small face into his hands and felt her tears. She had been the one sobbing. Now, uncontrollably shaking, she cried into his chest.

Hugging her tight, he leaned over and whispered, "Come on, I'll be fine, Mollie. It's all going to be fine." He felt her pull away, trying to speak, to say something between sobs.

"Daddy... Mommy's... dead."

"What? Oh no. Please no."

Dira's voice was soft and sympathetic, "It was an unstable, nearly catastrophic phase-shift. It sent multiple power spikes throughout *The Lilly*. Many systems went offline. I'm sorry to say, Nan's MediPod shut down before she could be saved. There was no way to get the MediPod up and running again fast enough..."

Jason reached again for his daughter, trying to pull her in close, but the blackness pulled at him, engulfing him. Fighting now to stay with his daughter, consciousness gave way to deeper darkness and utter silence. He desperately clung to his final thoughts. *I'm coming, Nan. Wait for me.*

* * *

Mollie crawled into the MediPod even before its clamshell lid completely opened. Jason, coming awake, took in a deep breath as realization of recent events flooded his mind. Dread coursed through his body as he put his arms around his daughter and held her tight. *Oh God, Nan is dead.*

He kissed Mollie's forehead and she shifted her position so she could better look at him. Her eyes were puffy and red ... and questioning. She didn't need to speak to convey what was going through her mind: *How could this happen? How could Mom be taken from me?* More jostling around and Mollie pulled one of her arms free. Gently, she wiped away the tears beneath Jason's eyes.

"I'll take care of you, Dad."

"We'll take care of each other, sweetie." They hugged each other tight. Jason saw Dira standing alongside the MediPod. Her face showed concern and something else. "Captain, I'm sorry. We need you. Things are happening—"

"Help us out of this thing," he said, lifting Mollie up to Dira's outstretched arms and sitting up. With another deep breath, Jason climbed out and was on his feet. Mollie, now standing near Dira, looked up at her father. Jason took a quick look around Medical and realized all the MediPods were occupied, as were the hospital beds in the next room. His eyes lingered on the MediPod where Nan had lain, seeing instead another crewmember's face through the small observation window.

"I've got to go to work, Mollie. I'm sorry. I'll be back as soon as I can."

Dira nodded and attempted a weak smile. "She'll be here with me. Go, they need you."

* * *

Jason left Medical and walked into a crowded corridor. Brian was the first to greet him. He'd obviously spent time in a MediPod himself. The MediPod had gone to work, replacing Brian's eye in the process. The bandage he'd seen around Brian's head was gone and he seemed miraculously no worse for wear. His face showed concern when he stepped toward Jason and the two brothers hugged.

"I'm so sorry, Jason."

Jason nodded. Before he could comment, Perkins nudged him on the elbow. "Captain, we have a situation."

Jason hurried down the corridor after Perkins, nodding back towards his brother before disappearing into the bridge.

"Captain on deck," announced the AI as Jason moved to the command chair. The bridge showed some damage, and several stations were unoccupied.

"Status, XO?"

"*The Lilly* is situated within a forward section of the *Minian*."

The overhead display showed a high-resolution perspective of the *Minian* from several miles off her port side. Distorted and venting from multiple locations along her hull, she appeared to be a dying ship. The XO continued, "The result of our phase-shifting into the *Minian's* hull was devastating. She's obviously no ordinary vessel. While *The Lilly* is in relatively good shape, the displacement of matter from the phase-shift process was nothing less than cataclysmic to the *Minian*. Her bridge and numerous other sections of the ship are now history. Subsequent explosions resulted, forcing multiple hull breaches; the ship's atmosphere has vented into space at multiple locations. Billy is currently heading up a rescue team to locate any survivors. We're not optimistic that there will be any."

Jason brought his attention to the display and there, bright blue and perfect, Earth slowly rotated in the distance. The loss of Nan filled his mind and he longed to see her again. There were things left unsaid, things incomplete. It took all his will to push the vision of her aside. Jason gestured toward the blue planet above them on the display.

"And the result of those five missiles fired from the *Minian*? Earth seems to be in one piece."

Perkins didn't answer, waiting for Ricket to slowly make his way across the bridge. He was limping and seemed to be in some pain. "Captain, those five projectiles were actually targeting transmitter drones. Each hit its intended target and was in the process of a massive data download when the *Minian* was struck."

"What were the targets?"

"Spread out over five continents around the planet—the specific locations allow for optimal communications dispersal between transmitter drones."

"So, what were the Caldurians planning to use those drones for?" Jason asked.

"I believe they were following up on their promise. Setting the time reference of Earth back one hundred years."

"So we stopped whatever the Caldurians were attempting?"

Ricket and the XO glanced at each other. Ricket continued, "The transmitter drones were able to connect, basically network between themselves and generate a continuous, overlapping, relay system. The Caldurian intent was to blanket the Earth, within the shifted time/space reference, back to the beginning of the twentieth century."

"That would have been devastating. We stopped it, right?"

"No, not entirely, Captain. When we phase-shifted onto the *Minian*, the data stream was interrupted. From what I've been able to piece together, this caused the transmission drones to compensate, or at least try to compensate. Corrupted information was propagated across the drone network and replicated itself, until finally stabilizing at its current time reference."

"And what time reference is that?" Jason asked.

"It depends on the specific location. There doesn't seem to be any one single timeframe, Captain. The planet is in chaos—multiple time references, or realms of time, are coexisting. One, two, or even three completely different time references can be found within a one hundred mile radius."

"How do we turn them off? Is there something on board the *Minian* that can do that?"

"There was," Ricket replied, matter-of-factly. "Not now. I can't stress this enough, Captain. How we proceed is critical. Tampering with any one of the five transmitter drones could make this time imbalance permanent. Only by destroying the five drones simultaneously can we enable our present day timeframe to be reinstated."

Chapter 3

Phase-shifting into open space, *The Lilly* was finally extricated from the *Minian*. Jason, running from one emotional fire to the next, tried to keep his grief in check and still be present for his little girl. Mollie was sleeping now, which gave Jason the opportunity to check in with his father and the fleet's ongoing battle with the Craing, some sixty light years away.

"I'm sorry, son. I wish I could be there for you. I'm ever so sorry."

With a subtle nod, Jason acknowledged the sentiment. "Well, I'm sorry I had to leave you to fight the Craing on your own, Dad. But I understand the Craing have surrendered."

Jason saw the life return to his father's eyes. "I can't tell you how good it feels to finally turn the tables on those ..." the admiral let the words trail off as he shook his head.

"Dad, Earth as we know it is gone. Ricket believes there's a remote chance things can somehow be returned to normal. But he warns us we should be prepared for the worst."

The admiral saw the pain and guilt on his son's face. "You did the right thing, Jason. Earth, our home, was undergoing an alien incursion, and you used the only means available at the time to strike back."

"To what end, Dad? Nan is dead. Life on Earth is a living hell. Wouldn't things be better if I'd—"

"Fuck no! We'd be at the mercy of those pinch-faced

Caldurians while they held our world hostage a hundred years in the past. No, you did the right thing. Now, I need to get back mopping things up here. And by the way, thanks for the mess you dumped on the Meganaught. We have Scrapins, trolling pill bugs shooting acid from their asses, and a wide assortment of every man-eating creature you could possibly think of—yeah, thanks a lot for leaving us to deal with all that," the admiral added with a wry smile.

Jason appreciated his attempt at humor and smiled back.

"Oh, and have Ricket coordinate the spooling of a wormhole for tomorrow. I'd like to be there for Nan's service, son."

* * *

The flight deck was open on both sides, *The Lilly*'s shields invisibly holding back the black void beyond. Shuttles and fighters were moved closer to the bulkheads, leaving room on the flight deck for the simple pod of brushed-chrome metal. Positioned at the starboard side of the deck, Nan's pod sat mere feet from the open vastness of space.

Jason held Mollie's hand. She wore a simple dress—one her mother had previously configured and stored on a replicator. Jason wore his captain's dress whites. Behind them stood the crew, family and friends. Rhino-warriors stood tall at the perimeter of the flight deck, their hides painted black, their horns a contrasting bright white.

The admiral, then Orion, and lastly Jason, shared warm remembrances of Nan Reynolds. Tears fell, not a dry eye to be seen. He looked out at family members, and those who'd become his shipboard family. Brian looked pained and uncomfortable. Ricket, standing near the front, was wearing officer's whites. Unaccustomed to the spectrum of emotions he had been feeling over the last few days, Ricket seemed to have taken the loss of Nan particularly hard. His eyes were moist and he repeatedly blinked and wiped at his cheeks.

Earlier, Jason had asked Mollie if she wanted to select the music, or a special song to play at the end of the service. She had spent hours alone listening to her mother's iTunes library. In the end, she selected *It's So Hard to Say Goodbye to Yesterday* by Boyz II Men. Now, as the familiar song filled the flight deck, Jason felt as if his heart was being torn from his chest. His eyes never left Mollie, standing beside him, looking so brave. Brave and something else ... She looked determined.

As the song was ending, Nan's pod rose and hovered several inches above the deck. Slowly it moved forward, eased off the flight deck, through *The Lilly*'s shields and out into open space. The gathering moved forward and watched. In a bright flash the pod shot forward, streaking toward the sun. The final verse of the song echoed off the bulkheads.

And I'll take with me the memories

To be my sunshine after the rain

It's so hard to say goodbye to yesterday.

* * *

What remained of the day belonged to Mollie. After conciliatory hugs and best wishes, Jason and Mollie returned to his suite and changed clothes. Together, they made their way down to the Zoo. Mollie inputted the code to enter HAB 4 and they stepped into the lush, humid world that Nan had come to love and often escaped to when she needed some time alone. Green and vibrant, the jungle was alive with sounds and movement. Within moments Raja, an Indian elephant, made her way toward them. Mollie ran forward and hugged one of Raja's thick front legs. The end of Raja's trunk gently probed Mollie's face—a gesture that seemed profoundly touching to Jason. The sounds of the jungle increased and then quieted as a distant rustling closed in on them. Alice, running full out, broke from the dense foliage. Her six legs strode forward in a mismatched rhythm that added to her quirky, lovable nature. The drog, as Mollie had named her species, leapt and caught Mollie off guard, knocking her to the ground. Alice relentlessly licked her face until giggles erupted.

Jason found the low wooden fence where Nan would sit for hours reading a paperback book. This was her spot. Now, sitting on the top rail, he watched Mollie and Alice play. He rubbed the wood beneath his hands and felt a splinter. To his right, the top of the vertical post where Nan would rest her book had been marked. Leaning in close, Jason realized it had a familiar symbol scratched into its surface. There, plain as day, was a heart with two names etched inside it: Nan + Jason.

He let his fingers follow the contours of the etched, weathered wood. A gentle breeze rustled the treetops and, like a soft caress, touched his face.

Chapter 4

"Why can't we simply destroy them from up here—from high orbit?" Jason asked.

Ricket pursed his lips and said, "It's because they are droids. That makes it more difficult. They're mobile and will detect and evade a barrage of synchronized incoming missiles. They are programmed to hide; they'd either dig into the Earth's crust or simply find sufficient cover elsewhere. They also have shields, making plasma strikes too unreliable—again, they all need to be destroyed simultaneously."

Jason looked around the captain's ready room conference table. No one offered up any suggestions until Billy spoke up. "We handle this like any other mission. We engage them one at a time."

Jason was about to interrupt him.

Billy held up a hand, "I didn't say destroy, Cap, I said engage. One at a time we locate the drones, then disable or incapacitate them."

Jason thought about that and slowly nodded, adding, "We attach our own explosive munitions, along with a transmitter and triggering device."

"That could work," Ricket said, then added, "but we cannot underestimate Caldurian technology. The droids may be equipped with a self-destruct mechanism. One that overrides any programming when captured or, as you said, incapacitated."

Orion, sitting to Billy's right, raised her eyebrows as if something else occurred to her. "The *Minian*'s not completely destroyed, right? Maybe there's more of them lying around we can test?"

"No, they would have been constructed on the fly, much as *The Lilly* does with her own JIT phase-shift munitions," Ricket interjected. "But if the *Minian*'s own phase-synthesizer unit is still operational, we may be able to fabricate one."

All heads turned to Ricket as he brought up a virtual 3D representation of the *Minian* and expanded it out over the conference table.

"The areas that are black have been destroyed and are not accessible."

Jason watched the model slowly rotate. Much of the forward third of the vessel was completely blacked-out and numerous areas farther back were either black or dark grey.

"If we use the configuration of *The Lilly* as a possible example, the *Minian*'s phase-synthesizer would be situated here, or maybe here." As Ricket spoke, the corresponding sections of the virtual model changed color.

"Billy, did you see anything like our phase-synthesizer when you were searching for survivors?" Jason asked.

"You're assuming that I'd know what that was. I probably wouldn't, even if it bit me on the ass."

Chuckles erupted from those seated around the table, including Jason. "Have environmental and gravitational systems been restored?" Jason asked, turning to Ricket.

"Yes, well, for the most part. Obviously some areas are closed off—areas that are still open to space."

"Why don't we go take a look? I'm itching to get a good look at that ship anyway."

For the first time, Dira raised a hand to speak. "And you're sure there are no more bodies, no deceased crewmembers?"

Billy shook his head. "No guarantees, but I believe we found them all. Since most of the crew would have been positioned forward, they were either vented out to space, or displaced with any matter *The Lilly* came into contact with."

"Battle suits and multi-guns; let's not take any chances," Jason said. "Give me thirty minutes to take care of some business. We'll meet in the mess."

Jason was the last to emerge from the conference room. Brian was waiting in the corridor.

"Hey," Jason said.

"Hey. Listen, I was wondering if I could hitch a ride back to Allied space?"

"Don't want to stick around for a while?"

"No, it's not that. I promised to get Betty back home. She saved my life—least I can do."

Jason listened to his brother and watched his face. "You got a thing for her?"

"What are you talking about? Thing? Me?"

"Yeah, you. It's been a few years since we've spent much time together, but I do know when you have a thing for a girl," Jason said.

"Whatever. I'd like to get her home, that's all."

"Dad's still here. Go back with him."

"He hasn't spoken to me since we arrived."

"I'll talk to him. He's leaving within the hour, so you, Betty, and that hopper creature need to be ready."

Brian shrugged and turned to leave.

"Oh and Brian, thanks again for what you did to save Mollie. I won't forget it."

"Think *everything* of it," he replied with a smile.

Two doors down, Jason was at his father's cabin door. A moment later, the door disappeared and the admiral stood in front of him. Mollie was on the floor playing a virtual game of some sort.

"Come on in."

"Thanks."

"That was a beautiful service, son."

"I think Nan would have appreciated it," Jason said. "Listen, Dad, I was wondering if you could set your differences with Brian aside for a while and let him return to Allied space with you."

"I don't have a problem with that. I was meaning to talk to him after the service, just didn't get to it."

"I'd appreciate it. He seems to have ... I don't know—perhaps matured somewhat?"

"I'll believe that when I see it," the admiral said.

Mollie looked up from her game and scowled.

"What's up with you, Mollie?" Jason asked, returning her scowl with his own.

"I've asked three times for someone to bring Teardrop to me."

"Teardrop? Is that a game from your cabin?"

"No, it's my drone. The one that saved my life, Dad. I told you all this."

"Yes, I remember now. I owe that drone my appreciation. It's being repaired up on 4B. Ricket's tending to its repairs himself—as time permits."

There was that face again: determination. She held two fingers to her ear the same way he typically did, and a moment later she was speaking to someone.

"... is he ready yet? No. Okay. Okay, good bye."

Jason raised his eyebrows. "What was that all about?"

"Ricket says he'll bring Teardrop down in a few moments."

Jason exchanged a glance with the admiral and sat down next to his daughter. "What's this game you're playing?"

"I don't know what it's called. It's something I made up. Not everything has to have a name, Dad."

Jason was well aware that Mollie would be going through a rough patch for an indeterminate period of time. He knew her emotions were churning inside her like a blender, and right now she was angry. Later, it might be grief, and even something else beyond that. All he could do was be there for her. He watched her as she positioned hovering geometric three-dimensional puzzle pieces together. Some gave the appearance they would fit together just fine, only to discover when they were flipped over they were not the right shape.

A melodic sound pinged from the door. Mollie rushed over and provided access to Ricket, with Teardrop following close behind. Mollie pulled the drone inside, hugging its reversed pyramid-shaped torso in close to her. Its painted-on face stared straight ahead, mute, saying nothing.

"You're going to live here now, Teardrop. Did you bring everything you need?" Mollie asked.

This was news to Jason. How had the drone so quickly taken his own place as the one to console his daughter? Jason stood up and he, Ricket, and his father stepped to the other side of the room, away from Mollie and Teardrop.

"I need to know, is Mollie safe with that thing? I'll be away from the ship off and on over the next week or so, and I need to know I can count on that drone."

The admiral placed a beefy hand on Jason's shoulder. "She's obviously bonded with the thing. We should all be so lucky to have something, anything, to connect with at such a profound time of loss. She'll come around. Right now, let her dictate the terms of what she needs."

"Since when did you become an expert on parenting?"

"I guess when I became a grandparent," the admiral replied, squeezing Jason's shoulder.

"Captain," Ricket said, "the drone, Teardrop, would sacrifice its own existence to protect your daughter. Caldurian technology is not something to take lightly. This drone is practically a sentient being. I believe she's in good hands."

Chapter 5

Jason, suited up and armed with a multi-gun, entered the mess and joined Ricket, Billy, Orion and Dira. They too carried a multi-gun with the exception of Dira, who wore a sidearm holstered on her hip and a medical pack on her back.

"I know what you're going to say, Captain, but I'm not convinced there aren't some survivors over there. And I'd like to take a look at their Medical."

"I wasn't going to say anything. You are, of course, more than welcome to join the team." Dira's face brightened somewhat behind her visor and her posture visibly relaxed.

"In fact, why don't we start there," Jason continued, looking down at Ricket and indicating he should alter their phase-shift coordinates.

In one flash, the team phase-shifted into the *Minian*. He wasn't sure what he'd been expecting, but this sure wasn't it. Their Medical, two to three times larger than the one on *The Lilly*, was in pristine condition and though more technically advanced, its overall atmosphere created just as soothing an environment. As on *The Lilly*, indirect lighting and soft-cushioned surfaces made it seem a comforting, almost inviting, space. Jason counted thirty MediPods of various sizes and configurations. And there were other devices: six large glass booth-type containers, each one over ten feet tall, and filled with some kind of clear liquid. Two of them had something in them: some biological form—definitely not human.

Both Dira and Ricket moved to virtual consoles to access the *Minian*'s medical database.

In moments Dira threw her hands up in defeat. "I'm locked out. It was worth a try anyway," she said as she stepped away.

Ricket stayed at his console a moment longer. Virtual displays around the room came alive, along with some characteristic beeps of medical devices being initiated. Hearing the familiar sound, Dira grinned and turned back to her console, starting to scroll curiously through several screens of information. "Ricket, you're brilliant, as usual." Turning to Jason she said, "This technology is amazing, Captain; we need to get this ... all of this over to *The Lilly*," she urged.

"As long as things are compatible," Jason said.

Jason stepped from Medical out into the corridor. So similar to *The Lilly*'s, but newer bigger. Uneasy, he had a feeling of trespassing into someone else's space, which, of course, was exactly what they were doing. But they needed to hurry. How long before the Caldurians came looking for their ship? What would their reaction be, seeing it in its current condition?

"Orion, Billy, I need you to check out the *Minian*'s weapon systems. Go see what is still operational. Operational without a functioning bridge."

"Aye, Cap," Billy replied.

"Let's keep in contact. Check in every ten minutes."

"Aye, Cap."

Billy and Orion headed off down the corridor, as Jason turned back into Medical. Dira, still at the console, was oohing and ahing over each new discovery.

"You going to be all right?"

Without looking up, Dira nodded at Jason and said, "Yes, sir, I'm fine. You don't mind if I hang out here for a while, do you?"

"No, but you too check in with me every ten minutes or so," Jason replied.

Ricket, who'd been watching Dira do research at the console, stepped away and joined Jason as he left Medical. As they headed toward the closest DeckPort, Ricket slowed.

"The *Minian*'s AI is still operational. It's staying quiet, in the background. But its many ship systems, ones that would require its functionality, are operational."

"So you're wondering why it hasn't taken hostile actions against us?" Jason queried him.

"Yes and no, Captain. There's little doubt that the AI is aware of our presence and where we've come from. After all, *The Lilly*, too, is a Caldurian vessel. As with the drone, Teardrop, artificial intelligence here has progressed far beyond that on *The Lilly*."

"How would that demonstrate itself?"

"No way to tell, at this point. But factors such as self-preservation may be an aspect." They both stopped before stepping through the DeckPort.

"How safe is this?"

"I do not know," Ricket replied.

"AI, are you there?" Jason asked, looking up and around the large corridor.

"Yes, Captain Reynolds, I am here," a female voice replied. It sounded extremely humanlike, even having personality inflections. There was a questioning nature to her simple response, as if saying *I am here, but I'm not quite sure what to do with you yet.*

"Is it safe for us to use the DeckPorts?"

"Yes, Captain. If you are inferring that I would use it to do you bodily harm, understand I would not need a DeckPort for that purpose."

That made perfect sense to Jason. "Lead on, Ricket. Let's go find the phase-synthesizer." They emerged into a slightly smaller corridor, exactly halfway between two circular cul-de-sacs at its opposite ends.

Ricket led the way, moving off to the right. They came to three separate eight-foot-high doors. Ricket approached one and it dissolved away, allowing them access. Jason followed Ricket inside and quickly realized the compartment was not what they were looking for. This was more like a laboratory, with rows of benches and a myriad of highly advanced test equipment. There was another door to their left and, like the first one, it dissolved away as they came near.

Jason could immediately tell they'd found it. The area was easily as large as the flight deck on *The Lilly*. The phase-synthesizer had multiple hatches and ports of varying sizes, some hundreds of feet wide and just as tall. While the phase-synthesizer on *The Lilly* looked like ad hoc equipment that was more of an add-on afterthought, here everything was integrated and of a much larger scale.

Ricket stepped to one of the virtual displays, a touchscreen, and seemed to know how to access what he was looking for. Jason was hailed.

"Go for Captain."

"Hey, Cap," Billy said, "we've taken a look at the ship's tactical capabilities, including any viable weapons."

"What have you discovered?"

"That this is one brute of a ship. Both plasma and laser cannons, big and mean-looking rail-guns, and something else."

"What's that?"

"Well, I'm not so sure it falls in the category of a weapon; probably has more to do with propulsion or helm control. Ricket should take a look."

"We can do that later. Why don't you and Orion head back to us. Your HUDs should show you the way."

"Aye, Cap."

Jason hailed Dira, surprised she hadn't called in yet. There was no response. He could see her life icon was still active.

"I'll be back soon. I'm going to check in on Dira," Jason told Ricket, and headed out of the compartment. Jogging down the corridor, he kept an eye on her icon, which was still active, but unmoving.

"Go for Billy, Cap."

"Billy, I'm on my way back to Medical. You two meet me there."

Jason hit the DeckPort at full stride and exited without slowing. Billy and Orion arrived from the opposite direction and the three of them entered Medical together.

Dira was not where he'd left her, though her icon showed her still in Medical.

"Dira?"

There was a scuffling noise behind the liquid containers, and he noticed Dira's legs.

Jason realized Medical was even larger than he'd first noted, seeing that it continued past the six clear containers another ten feet or so. Dira was on the ground—not moving.

Jason hurried to her side and unlatched her helmet, gently pulling it free. Her eyes fluttered open and she nervously looked around.

"She okay, Cap?" Orion asked.

"Yeah, she's okay. Right, Dira, you okay?"

"I shouldn't have touched it, I guess."

She gestured toward one of the ten-foot-tall glass enclosures. A stepladder was at its side and at its top the enclosure's lid was askew.

"There was something in the container; it started moving. It seemed to be trying to communicate. I guess I let curiosity get the best of me. I reached in and touched it."

The organism was moving within its enclosure and began to make noises.

"Is that what you heard? What you thought was a form of communication?"

Billy stepped over to the towering enclosure and tapped on its surface. In a blink, the organism moved next to Billy, its fifteen or twenty thick tentacle legs constantly moving and probing.

"Seems to be a cross between an octopus and something else, something definitely otherworldly," Orion said, making a face. "You actually wanted to touch one of these things, Dira?"

Dira, with Jason's help, slowly got to her feet. She shrugged.

"I don't know what I was thinking. Or if I was even thinking. More like I was compelled to touch it." Right then, the other five enclosures came alive with movement. Startled, Jason, Dira, Billy and Orion jumped back in unison.

"Shit, they're all occupied," Billy said. "They must have been lying flat along the bottom."

"And they can change their size," Orion said, stepping closer.

All four of them watched. The organisms not only dramatically changed their size, but their shape as well.

"This one here looks like a baby seal. Kinda cute," Billy said, back to tapping on the enclosure.

"I wouldn't do that if I were you," Jason warned.

Dira bent over to retrieve her medical pack. Startled again, Billy was the first to notice, and pointed. "Stand perfectly still, Dira."

She froze. Her eyes widened with realization of what had happened.

"Everyone just stand still while I take a look, "Jason said. "It's OK, Dira, I'm just going to move around to your back." Jason slowly moved to Dira's left and peered around her shoulders. He nodded his head, reached down and picked up her helmet. Slowly, he stepped in close and brought it up in front of her, positioning it so it would slide over her head. The escaped organism shifted and one of its arms extended out above Dira's right shoulder and probed at the helmet, exploring first around its exterior and then within the helmet's opening. Two more tentacles reached out and took hold of the helmet. Jason froze, and immediately felt his grip loosening. Unable to hold on to the helmet, he glanced over at Billy. Relieved, Jason saw that Billy had the muzzle of his multi-gun pointing at the creature.

"Say the word, Cap, and that thing's fried calamari."

Both Jason and Dira's eyes darted to Billy, unappreciative of his bad joke.

Startled for the third time, the organism shifted its weight upward on her shoulders. Now, holding the helmet directly over Dira's head, the multi-armed creature brought it gently down until the helmet seated into the cowling at her suit's neck. More arms extended, their tapered ends probed until they had found the latching mechanism. With a click, her helmet was secured.

Chapter 6

Perhaps even more impressive than the organism replacing Dira's helmet onto her head was its willingness to relocate itself from Dira's shoulders, maneuver back across the deck, and work its way up the side of its enclosure.

They watched as it used thousands of suction-cups, along the posterior of its arms, to pull itself up along the flat surface. At the top, one by one its arms, and then its thick shapeless body, fell into the clear liquid within the enclosure. Then, reaching up with one tentacled arm, it lifted the enclosure's lid and dragged it back into position, letting it fall into place.

Jason turned to Dira. "How do you feel? Did you get stung? Did it bite you?" She took her helmet off and checked her scalp, then her neck, with one hand. "Doesn't appear to be anything amiss. And it was more like a shock, anyway."

"Let us know the second you notice something. Anything at all. I don't need to remind you what happened to Morgan back on HAB 12, do I?"

"I wish you hadn't mentioned that. Now I'll be thinking about that all day ..."

"Sorry, I'm just saying—"

"I know what you're saying, Jason. I think I'm fine."

More noise came from the enclosures. Within four of them the organisms had changed shape. Dira brought a hand up to her mouth; the others simply let their jaws drop. Suspended in the liquid now were four human shapes; shapes that were an exact duplicate of their own bodies. The only exception—these forms were totally naked.

Billy's eyebrows shot up in an arc, letting his eyes linger a bit too long on Dira's twin naked body. Orion was already spinning him around and pushing him out of Medical. Jason pulled himself away and followed the other two. Dira was the last to leave and caught up to Jason in the corridor. He glanced over at her and they locked eyes.

"Well, I told you Jhardian girls are anatomically different," she said, and nervously laughed out loud.

* * *

They entered the compartment housing the phase-synthesizer. Seeing the device for a second time, Jason was just as impressed by its sheer size as he was the first time. The device had been initiated and now maintained a consistent low-level humming sound. Ricket emerged from behind a console and was startled by their presence.

"Captain!" he said, excitedly, "This device is quite amazing."

"What's it doing?" Jason asked, seeing something emerge from one of its mid-sized openings.

"Accessing the database took me some time, but I've located the same drone configuration that was dispatched to the five continents."

What began to exit from the opening was not what Jason expected. It was a sphere the size of a small automobile, matte black in color, with an irregular surface composed of varying-sized panels and small protrusions.

As if laying an egg, the phase-synthesizer expelled the spherical drone. The drone hovered a moment before quickly moving in the direction of the bulkhead. There it slowed and lowered itself several feet above the deck's plate flooring. Small panels moved aside and segmented support struts locked into place. The drone lowered itself the rest of the way down to the deck.

Ricket returned to the console and called up a virtual 3D model of the drone. He ran through a complicated list of menu items and selected a sub-category.

"As expected, Captain, once these drones have been fully activated, as those on Earth have been, they work autonomously. No way to deactivate them."

"What can we expect when we go up against them on Earth?"

Ricket continued to scroll until stopping on another group of menu items. He selected the first item and both the virtual drone, as well as its physical counterpart, changed configuration. Weaponry protruded through eight access panels, several of them located on the far side of the drone. Ricket stepped away from the console and approached the sphere. Seeming to track his movements, four separate muzzles moved in unison. Without turning away, Ricket signaled for Jason and the others to join him. Immediately, another panel opened and a stubby, significantly larger gun barrel locked into place with a definitive click.

Ricket took another step forward, now less than twenty feet from the drone. As if something was internally triggered, translucent light-blue shield segments, overlapping and constantly moving, hovered several feet around the black sphere.

"Dynamic shielding," Ricket said. "Very difficult to breech." He took another step forward and the shield segments repositioned themselves and added new ones, separating itself even more with Ricket's advance.

Jason continued to watch Ricket incite the drone to react in different ways. It obviously was a highly intelligent piece of technology, but something wasn't adding up. Why hadn't the Caldurians sent other ships to rescue the *Minian*? Perhaps the better question was, why no retribution?

"Ricket, is the *Minian* able to communicate with other vessels, ones that exist on other planes across the multiverses?"

"I do not believe so, Captain," Ricket answered, taking another step closer to the drone.

"Aren't you afraid of it firing on you, or the thing exploding?" Billy interjected.

"No, I've disabled those functions."

"So, in all probability then, the Caldurians are not aware of what has happened to the *Minian*?" Jason asked.

"I do not believe what we accomplished, utilizing phase-shifting as a weapon, would have crossed their minds. We are unique in that we have a Caldurian vessel of our own, *The Lilly*, that has phase-shift capability. I've noticed the Caldurians are overly arrogant and take pride in their unique technologies. To them, the *Minian* was impregnable; it is their latest, most-advanced vessel. We may still have time before they send another ship to look for her."

Jason let that sink in for a moment. *But how much time?* He turned three hundred and sixty degrees, not looking at anything in particular. "This ship, what's left of her, may be our best and only defense against them when they do come."

Ricket smiled and gestured toward the phase synthesizer. Jason hadn't noticed, but numerous items had emerged out of several ports. Some were small, no bigger than a cellphone; others were the size of a minivan. Hover drones, retrieving the items as they appeared, placed them off to the side.

"I anticipated this, Captain. As I mentioned, this device is quite amazing. Amazing enough to manufacture, replicate, everything required in rebuilding the bridge and other damaged areas of the ship. With the help of the hover drones, she can be completely restored."

"Timeframe?"

"Perhaps a week, maybe less."

"What's your estimate for finding a weakness on the drone we can exploit?"

"By tomorrow morning. That is if it's even possible."

"Do your best. We're in a lot of trouble if you can't," Jason exclaimed. "Also, you'll be part of the assault team that's going to Earth to disable those five drones. I'm not exactly sure what we'll be running into down there, but I have a feeling we're in for a wild ride. One that makes what happened to us on HAB 12 seem like a walk in the park in comparison."

Billy and Orion looked at each other and smiled. Dira crossed her arms over her chest. "Maybe I should sit this one out?"

"Sorry, we'll definitely need a medic."

"What about Mollie? She's going to need a lot of TLC over the coming days, perhaps even weeks."

"Already have something in the works for Mollie. She won't like it but my options are limited."

Chapter 7

"No! I want to stay with you."

"I'm sorry, Mollie. It's not safe where I'm going. You'll be with people you know, and Grandpa."

"Will Dira stay with me?"

"Not this time, Mollie. Think of it like you're going on your own adventure."

"Where's that?"

"To a place where there are other planets and different kinds of people."

"Can Teardrop come with me?"

"Of course. Teardrop is yours."

Mollie chewed the inside of her lip, seeming to weigh everything in her mind. He watched her as she scooted up in her bed. She had bed hair and a bad case of morning breath. Without her mother around, he'd need to help her stay on top of such things. Jason's heart froze, realizing with Nan gone, his little girl would now depend on him more than ever. Guilt tugged at his heart—of all times to have to leave her ...

"Will Uncle Brian be there?"

"Uncle Brian? Um ... I'm not sure. I guess I can find out."

"OK. If Uncle Brian is there, then I'll go."

Jason smiled and kissed the top of her head. "I need to make arrangements; why don't you hop in the shower. And don't forget to brush your teeth."

But Mollie was somewhere else. Her teary eyes glazed over and Jason knew she was thinking about her mother. She leaned forward for a comforting hug and Jason, wrapping his arms around her, kissed the top of her head a second time. "We'll be all right, little one. I promise."

* * *

The admiral ran his fingers through his own crop of disheveled bed hair. Jason had obviously gotten his father out of bed, and by the looks of things from sixty light years away, he wasn't too pleased about it.

"If you haven't forgotten, Jason, I'm the commanding officer for the entire Allied forces. Not a good time to make a play-date for me and Mollie."

Jason let his father's words hang in the air.

"But of course she can come," the admiral relented. "There's nothing more important to me than my granddaughter."

"She wants her uncle to be there, too."

"Brian?" the admiral asked, sounding amazed anyone would actually want Brian around.

"Probably something to do with him saving her life back at the scrapyard. Is there a problem? Has he already left?"

"No, although we've certainly tried to expedite that process." His father looked as though he regretted what he'd said and continued, "It's not so much Brian, but that creature, hopper thing. If it's not nonstop eating, it's shitting in the corridors. We were just hoping to get them off ship as soon as possible."

"Why don't you drop the hopper off on Trumach. Probably lots for him to eat down there."

"That was my first suggestion. Brian seemed open to it, but the hopper wouldn't go along. Seems to have developed a bond to your brother."

"To Brian?" Jason asked, not understanding how that would be possible.

The admiral shrugged.

"I'm sending *The Lilly* back to you, Dad. It's just a matter of time before the Caldurians come looking for the *Minian*. We're no match for their technology. How we overtook that ship was a fluke, and not something we should count on happening again. I don't want to jeopardize the crew, especially Mollie."

"And you'll be able to deactivate the drones on Earth?"

"We have the *Epcot* shuttle, as well as what's left of the *Minian* that we can use for a base of operations."

"Let me know prior to your spooling a wormhole. And son, I'm staying optimistic you'll be able to deactivate those drones. Seven billion displaced people are quite a burden for anyone to manage."

"Thanks for reminding me. I'm well aware what's at stake. Returning Earth to the twenty-first century is at the top of the list."

Jason cut the feed, turned in his chair, and saw Mollie coming down the hallway. Her hair was wet and she was all dressed, though barefoot.

"Well, is Uncle Brian going to be there?"

"Looks like it. Grandpa's going to talk to him."

"What should I pack?"

"Nothing. You'll be going in *The Lilly*. Things won't change all that much for you. You can even keep working in the Zoo, if that's what you want." Mollie brightened with that bit of news and even smiled. Jason heard noises coming from their kitchenette area: cabinets being opened and closed, the hum of the replicator, and silverware being laid out on the table. Teardrop hovered into view behind Mollie.

"Go get your shoes and socks on before sitting down to breakfast. Okay, kiddo?"

* * *

Why was the Minian*'s AI being so amiable* was a question still on Jason's mind, as Billy showed him a part of the ship that was very unusual; in fact, an entire deck that had no correlation to anything like it on *The Lilly*.

They entered another compartment similar to four others they'd exited from over the last few minutes. It, too, had rows of equipment, like generators or turbines; the ten-foot-high by thirty-foot-long items occupied every inch of the five compartments. Jason stood with his hands on his hips and looked up at the closest of the huge pieces of equipment. Black and heavy looking, they looked similar to early nineteenth-century locomotives. There seemed to be a layer of grease covering each mechanical component.

"Like I said, Cap. There are hundreds of these things," Billy said.

"It's a Zip farm," Ricket's voice commented as he entered from the far end of the compartment.

"What the hell's a Zip farm?"

"I've never actually seen one," Ricket said, stopping to take a closer look at one of the strange devices. "Only seen theoretical models. And certainly nothing of this scale."

"Are these used to support some kind of weapon?" Jason asked.

"No, these are referred to as Zip accelerators and are how the Caldurians cross over to other planes of the multiverse."

Jason nodded, his mind returning to the AI.

"AI, are these devices of Caldurian technology?" Jason asked, out loud.

"No, Captain. This technology was developed on Alurian, a planet in the Corian Nez constellation system, one hundred thirty light years from Earth. Caldurians only discovered this technology eighty-nine years ago."

"AI, can you tell me why you are assisting us?" Jason asked.

"Recent modifications to the *Minian*'s command structure subroutines necessitates my compliance with any and all of your requests."

"When were these changes made?"

"Four days ago."

"Who instigated these modifications?"

"That information is not available."

Ricket moved to Jason's side. "Can you provide the user's designation?"

"Only that it is designation BRSTL."

Jason shrugged and repeated the letters phonetically. "Bristol?"

Billy said, "Isn't that the name of that scrawny kid—the traitor on board *The Lilly*? Could it be the same person?"

"Where is he now, AI? Is he currently onboard this vessel?"

"Access to that information is provisional."

"What the hell is that supposed to mean? Provisional in what way?"

"Captain," Ricket said. "I believe your question, asking the AI why it is helping us, triggered this AI subroutine."

Ricket asked, "AI, what are the provisions?"

"Non-retribution."

Non-retribution? Jason's anger flared. It was Bristol's brother, Captain Stalls, who'd shot Nan, causing the wound that eventually led to her death.

Both Jason and Billy removed their helmets. Billy brought out a cigar but when he saw Jason's expression, he put it back away.

"AI, tell me where Bristol is."

"Access to that information is provisional."

"Perhaps we should hear him out, see what he has to say. Without his help, I doubt we would have survived on this vessel more than a few seconds," Ricket said.

Thinking, Jason paced up and down between two rows of Zip accelerators. With Stalls dead, revenge hadn't been an option. He'd buried his anger, his rage, until now.

"AI, the provision is accepted."

Chapter 8

"So where is Bristol?" Jason asked the AI. No answer came—the compartment was quiet with the exception of a low-frequency hum from the multiple Zip accelerators.

Bristol entered the compartment and stood at the far end of Jason's row. He wore an ill-fitting environmental suit and was holding an energy weapon. "Move and I'll shoot you. As you can see I'm armed and I can easily shoot all of you," Bristol said, his high-pitched voice revealing his nervousness.

Jason and Billy slowly turned toward Bristol at the same time.

"How'd you get here?" Jason asked.

"Shut up! I'm asking the questions now. Do you understand?"

"Sure, whatever you want. You're the one in charge, Bristol."

Ricket, the only one still with his helmet on, would have access to his HUD and phase-shifting capability. Jason had just begun to wonder if Ricket would take the initiative when the compartment flashed white. Ricket had phase-shifted to a new position behind Bristol. Realizing too late what had happened, and feeling Ricket's sidearm poking into his back, Bristol raised his hands.

"Crap!"

"Drop your weapon, Bristol. You know I don't need much of an excuse to shoot you," Jason said.

His energy pistol hit the floor with a metallic clunk. Ricket reached down and retrieved it.

Bristol swung around. "Push me like that again you little troll, and I'll—" Seeing Ricket's face through his helmet's visor, Bristol cut his rampage short. "Looks like someone's had a little corrective surgery."

"Shut up, Bristol," Jason said, striding down the row and stopping in front of him. "Again, how did you get here?"

"I have no fucking idea."

Jason raised his gun and placed the barrel to Bristol's forehead. "Then there's no reason for me to let you live."

"My brother's fleet was in Earth space and immediately we came up against some outpost ships. Even with close to one hundred ships of our own, we were no match for Craing technology. Anyway, I thought it was a stupid idea, but we faked surrender; we then used one of my phase-shift devices to allow the raiders and me to subversively board one of their cruisers. But we totally botched it. They were ready for us. The other raiders were killed, all except me. I got away and ran. But when I realized I had nowhere to hide, I jumped into the phase-shift void. I thought I was going to die."

"Okay, so you didn't die, obviously. How did you end up here?"

"I told you already. I have no fucking idea. One moment I was jumping to my death, the next I was sprawled out on this vessel."

"Where exactly?"

"Engineering. I was dangling half-off of a catwalk. I almost fell over the edge, but I swung my legs over it and was safe."

"Nobody saw you there?"

"That's the strange thing. Other than me the ship was pretty much deserted—like a ghost ship."

"Pretty much deserted, so there were others?"

"I'm just assuming there were. Like on the bridge. But no, I never saw anyone else."

"So, what have you been doing for the last four days?"

"Staying out of sight. The AI was hostile and took shots at

me from several defensive locations. Twice it tried to vent me out to space," Bristol added. "That's when I went to work at one of the Engineering consoles. I was familiar with the basics of the ship's programming, although this ship is far more advanced than *The Lilly*. But in time I was able to hack the core and grant myself administrator rights."

"You're a smart kid; too bad you've wasted it on being a pirate," Jason told him.

"We don't get to pick our families. My brother's a dick, but he's my brother."

Billy looked over to Jason, then back to Bristol. "Well, kid, hate to be the one to break the news, but your brother's dead."

Bristol nodded and smiled, "Uh huh, sure he is."

"Flattened to the size of my hand," Billy said. "That's what happens when a fifty thousand pound bin lift falls on your head."

Bristol stared at Billy with the same sardonic smile, then his face registered shock. His shoulders sank and his eyes filled with tears. He folded, dropping to the deck, and cried out loud, burying his head in his hands.

Coming down the row of Zip accelerators, both Orion and Dira heard most of the conversation with the young pirate. Dira went to Bristol's side and sat down next to him. Orion, now standing next to Billy, said, "Nice, real nice Billy."

Dira had an arm around Bristol's shoulders and pulled him close to her as he continued to cry. "I'm so sorry, Bristol. Let it out ... let it all out."

Jason held up a finger—unable to speak. He felt his rage build, increasing tenfold. "You do know what he and his brother have done, right? You know that Nan would still be alive if—"

"My brother didn't kill her, she died in the MediPod—"

Furious, Jason took a step in closer. Restraining himself, he turned and glared at Dira, turned, and walked in the opposite direction. "I'll be on *The Lilly*. Keep him off my ship."

* * *

Jason had called for an 0600 staff meeting in his ready room. Standing at his cabin's expansive porthole, he looked out at Earth. Looking bright and beautiful, it belied the reality of what was sure to come. How much time was there before individual time realms crossed into one another? Eventually the ensuing conflict and turmoil would progress on a massive scale. With hundreds, if not thousands, of different time references merging, the upheaval, deaths, and mass suffering on Earth would be in astronomical numbers. He needed to get down there and destroy those drones; every second wasted, lives most certainly will be lost. And what if the Caldurians returned before he had the chance to deactivate them? A scenario where the Caldurians took back the *Minian* and disrupted their attempts to remove the drones was unthinkable. Frustrated, Jason had to get down there today, right now. He heard people filing into the ready room and pulled himself away from the porthole. He entered the conference room and took his place at the head of the table.

"Some of you will be heading back to Allied space with *The Lilly*; others will be staying here as part of the assault team to deactivate the five Caldurian transmitter drones."

"Ricket, what's the status of your tests?"

"The drones do not have any inherent weaknesses. Their dynamic shielding can withstand an attack from multiple directions so there's no way for an adversary to sneak up on them."

"Are you saying they can't be destroyed?" Jason asked him.

"No. We may have come up with an idea."

"We?"

Ricket looked over to Billy and Orion, then back to Jason. "Actually, the idea came from Bristol."

"Bristol?"

"Yes, sir."

"And you trust him? Five days ago he was involved in a raid on outpost warships. Why on earth would we trust—"

"It's his idea or nothing, Cap," Billy said. "Look, I don't like the guy any more than you do. But he has a good idea and I think we should consider it."

Jason noticed out of his peripheral vision that both Orion and Dira were nodding their heads. He'd been avoiding looking in Dira's direction. "So? What's his idea?" he asked.

Ricket continued, "We replicate five identical transmitter drones. Similar to the one I replicated on the *Minian*. If we do this correctly, we'll position each one within several yards of a drone now situated on Earth. With luck, their presence won't trigger a combative response. Once all five drones are in suitable alignments, we activate a simultaneous phase-shift."

"Where will they go? Where will they phase-shift to?"

"Off-planet, somewhere into deep space. We were thinking about multiple programmed phase-shifts that will transfer them to the far reaches of the universe."

Jason thought about the idea and had to admit it sounded like it could work.

"There are a few kinks we need to work out, Cap," Billy said.

"Like what?"

"We have a general idea where the drones are located. They are stealthy, and we can't pinpoint their locations any closer than a mile. So each drone will require a fairly rigorous search."

"A search traversing multiple time references," Ricket added.

"And once we do locate the drones?"

"We relay our position to the *Minian* and she maneuvers to

within three thousand miles of our location. We then phase-shift each drone's mate down from the *Minian*, one at a time."

"Can't we just take the drones along with us?" Jason asked.

"The drones are heavy, and anyway there's isn't sufficient cargo room in the shuttle to carry all five of them."

"All right, we'll go with the plan. Now let's discuss our assault team. Billy, assemble ten of your best SEALs. Ricket, Orion, Dira, you're all on the team. We'll need rhino-warriors. Unfortunately, they've returned to Trumach, but I'll talk to Traveler and see if he'll join us one more time."

"I'll need two hours to produce and program the drones, Captain," Ricket said.

"I'll get to work on outfitting the team with multi-guns and upgraded battle suits," Orion added.

"Okay, in three hours we meet back on the *Minian*. *The Lilly* will head back to Allied space. If there's no more questions, let's get to it."

Chapter 9

Jason had to face reality. Nan was dead. Gone forever. And the feelings he'd tried to bury were catching up to him. His grief, masked in anger at both Bristol and Dira and the impossible drone situation on Earth, was quickly setting him up emotionally to explode like a powder keg. And with Mollie now sixty light years away, back in Allied space, his last true connection to Nan was gone.

Seconds after *The Lilly* disappeared through a newly-formed wormhole, an outpost Craing light cruiser emerged in its place. Earlier, Traveler and his rhino-warriors had returned to Trumach, their home world—a world free from the tyranny of the Craing. They'd returned to their mates and offspring. Now, with help from his father back on the Independence, Jason had tracked down Traveler. Happy to hear from Jason, Traveler explained how he had found Stands in Storm's mate and her offspring, several young rhino males. After delivering the news of Stands in Storm's honorable death in battle, Traveler had presented himself to her, as so obligated, to become her new mate, her provider. But the obligation was dismissed. Believing Stands in Storm dead, she had already found another mate to provide for them. And something else surprised Jason as he listened to the rhino's deep voice.

"This place is no longer my home. I miss the land where the Furlong bear hunts, where the wolf howls at the moon. Captain, would you allow me and several of the other rhino-warriors to return to that place, to the habitat on board *The Lilly*?"

"Of course. You can return there whenever you wish. I do have one request, though."

"Yes, Captain. The admiral has already spoken to me of your situation, the plight of your home planet. I would be honored to join you, to again fight at your side."

Now, with the outpost cruiser secured alongside the *Minian*, Jason and Billy watched their friend exit through a mid-deck airlock. Traveler greeted them, ready for battle: a heavy hammer hung from a thick leather thong at his belt, and an energy weapon strapped to his left wrist. He wasn't alone; Rustling Leaves followed close behind, and eight other rhino-warriors followed soon afterward.

* * *

Jason hadn't had the opportunity to check out the *Minian*'s flight deck previously. He was surprised to see a fleet of one hundred royal blue two-man fighters, similar to the *Pacesetter*, and numerous shuttles all symmetrically lined up in parallel rows. There were also hundreds of smaller un-manned drone fighters, secured, with their wings collapsed, mounted in rows high up along the bulkheads. Equipment began to load onto the largest of the *Minian*'s shuttles, one nearly twice the size of the *Epcot*. There was a flurry of activity: SEALs stowing their packs and multi-guns; Ricket maneuvering equipment into place; several rhinos carrying extricated seats; and Dira, who'd abruptly brushed past him, carrying several large medical bags. He heard her say something under her breath about him cutting Bristol some slack.

Ricket emerged from the shuttle. Jason noticed he wasn't wearing a battle suit. "We're scheduled to leave in ten minutes, Ricket. You need to get into your battle suit."

"Captain, deploying the drones from the *Minian* will be a fairly technical process. There may be a necessity to alter the code, or handle any number of issues on the fly."

"We may have similar needs on the ground," Jason replied.

"Undoubtedly, you will."

It was then Jason noticed an awkward-looking member of the team hovering nearby. "That better not be who I think it is," Jason spat. Both Dira and Orion, who had been conversing closer to the shuttle, turned to see what the commotion was about.

Ricket took a deep breath and brought his hands up in surrender. "I cannot be in two places at once, Captain. The only other person who has sufficient technical capabilities is Bristol. Please understand, these advanced drones are programmed not to be detected. Even with specialized equipment, you'll need to get in close—even then, it will be hit or miss locating them."

"I don't want him on my team."

"Would you trust him alone on the *Minian*, which will be operational within the next few days? I would be happy to switch places with him, but I don't think that is the best course of action."

Dira glared at Jason; behind her helmet's visor, he could see her furrowed brow. Jason looked around and spotted Rizzo coming out of the shuttle.

"Rizzo!"

The young SEAL jogged over to Jason's side, "Aye, sir?"

"See that guy over there? That's Bristol."

"Yes, sir. I know who he is."

"You're responsible for him for the duration of this mission. Where he goes, you go, and visa versa. Do you understand?" Jason could see Bristol was listening. "One more thing. If he does something to compromise this mission, or exhibits harmful action to another team member, you have my permission to shoot him."

"Aye, Cap."

That brought a laugh from Billy, taking hold of another seat being passed down to him from Traveler up in the shuttle. "Cap. Another small problem," Billy said, making his way across the flight deck. He took a soggy stub of a cigar out of his mouth and looked at it.

"What's that?"

"Even with the larger shuttle, there's not enough room for everyone on board."

Jason raised his eyebrows and gestured toward Bristol. "Leave the kid."

"Still wouldn't be enough room," Billy replied. "Two people."

Jason walked toward the other side of the flight deck and laid a hand on one of the fighters. "Other than Bristol, who wants to ride with me?"

Dira spun on her heels and walked in the other direction.

"I'll ride with you, Cap," Billy responded, still finding the situation funny.

"Huddle around, everyone," Jason ordered. He waited for the team to move around him in a semi-circle. "AI, please provide a holographic representation of Earth." When it appeared, Jason added, "Good, now expand it to four times that size." He took a step forward and gave the now ten-foot-diameter projected model of Earth a gentle swipe, causing the planet to rotate on its axis.

"AI, show the five drones approximate locations." One by one, their locations were indicated, by small expanding red rings over five continent positions.

"We'll start here, the drone located in the southern part of the African continent. A few days ago the terrain would have been flat, fairly open—small trees and brush. Don't expect that to necessarily hold true now. Anything is possible."

Ricket made his way to the front of the crowd and looked up to the virtual model. "Your battle suits have been upgraded. HUDs have time-reference indicators."

"What does that mean? How does that affect us?" Billy asked.

"It means you'll always know the time period you're inhabiting, based on modern Earth's Gregorian Calendar—sometimes referred to as the Christian Calendar. You'll want to keep an eye on the HUD's displayed date. Things will change, depending on your specific location. And realize there isn't any one single timeframe. The planet is in chaos—multiple time references, or realms of time, may and probably will coexist within any one hundred mile radius."

Dira raised her hand and when Ricket acknowledged her, she asked, "So ... will the landscape change? Like between one time frame and the next?"

"Good question, Dira. The short answer is probably. Until we're actually down there, we won't know the variable spectrum of time. It could be millions of years or thousands. The time flux currently being generated by the five drones makes sensor readings impossible to read," Ricket added.

"Explain to them about the PTCC," Jason said.

"It's something I've developed and incorporated into your HUDs," Ricket said. "As the captain mentioned, we call it a phase-time-comparator circuit. Or PTCC. Sorry, rhinos, you won't have this functionality built into your wristband displays. I'm working on that."

"So, what's it do?" Billy asked.

"Go ahead and select PTCC from your main HUD sub-menu."

Jason watched as everyone did as they were told.

"What it will do is allow for playback of previous timeframe visuals, based on current optic references. For example, I have set the parameters to exactly twenty days in the past. Now, as you look around viewing the current timeframe, either a smaller window, or a direct visual overlay, will display the corresponding visual timeframe of twenty days ago."

"That's flippin' cool!" Rizzo announced, slowly turning around and, like the others, seeing the activity of the past displayed on his HUD. "I can see Caldurians. They're doing something to that fighter over there," he said, pointing to the fighter Jason stood next to.

"Understand this visual information may not be exact. It's Caldurian technology and the visual information is pulled from the multiverse. All right, you can play with that function later. Orion, let's talk weapons," Jason said.

"Yes, Captain. You each have a sidearm, including the rhino-warriors—we've switched out the wrist weapons. These sidearms are similar to your multi-gun rifles; both guns have settings for plasma fire, rail-gun, and tracking micro-missiles. I'll be spending time with each of you in small groups going over your sidearm and rifle weapon functionality. When I do, pay attention; your life and the lives of those who count on you will depend on it."

"Thank you, Orion," Jason said. "Your phase-shift belts function as they did in the past. Their phase-shift radius has been extended out to one hundred yards. Again, be mindful of where you're phase-shifting to. You don't want to phase-shift into the side of a mountain or into solid rock. Doing so would not kill you, since your matter would displace any other matter, but that might not be all that comfortable, as you'd probably be trapped, unable to move. Orion will be reviewing phase-shifting, along with weapon functionality."

"You mentioned there are five drones. You should mention

where else we are going," Billy said.

"In addition to Africa, one is to a location within the North American continent, another to the South American continent, another to Asia, and one to Europe. It's imperative that each one of you understands the importance of this mission. The drones on Earth need to be removed. Getting close to them is virtually impossible. So we're bringing in identical drones from the *Minian*. With luck, they'll be accepted by those other drones and allowed to saddle-up close. Once all five drones around the planet have been paired with a sister drone, they'll be simultaneously phase-shifted off the planet. Any questions?"

Jason waited but no one said anything. "Good, we leave in one hour."

Chapter 10

"I'm still uncomfortable with your being alone on the *Minian*," Jason yelled above the noise of the fighter's dual rear-mounted thrusters.

"*The Lilly* can be back here in minutes, or you can phase-shift via the shuttle or fighter in minutes, if necessary. There are multiple fighters on board, as well as drones. I believe I am safe here," Ricket said.

"If the Caldurians return, and we know they eventually will, it's still uncertain if the AI will take up a defensive position. After all, its original programming was developed to protect Caldurian interests."

"Understood. In addition to getting the bridge and other key systems back online, I'll have time to work on that aspect as well, Captain."

Jason triggered the fighter's canopy to close. Below, Ricket gave a short wave goodbye and headed off the flight deck.

"He seems to know what he's talking about," Billy said, from his seat behind Jason.

"I'm just uncomfortable having Bristol along on this mission. Who knows what his motivations are. Hell, he could kill us all in our sleep."

"We'll watch him, Cap."

Jason brought the fighter up off the flight deck and hovered there. The shuttle, which they decided to call the *Magnum*, was being piloted by Lieutenant Grimes. She'd been a last minute addition brought over from *The Lilly*. Other than, the fighter squadron's commander, she was considered the best; some thought an even better pilot than Wilson.

The *Magnum* rose off the deck and together both vessels moved toward the massive opening on the starboard side of the *Minian*. They emerged on the far side of the shields and continued on toward Earth. It felt good to be behind the stick again. Jason had hoped his nano-devices would have the necessary updates for piloting this more advanced, more sophisticated fighter. Now seeing he instinctively knew what each of the dash readouts meant, and how to configure the ship's navigation and phase-shift systems, he let himself sit back and enjoy the ride.

They entered the upper atmosphere and descended to a midpoint in the Atlantic Ocean. Jason watched the time-reference indicator on his HUD as it changed every second or two. The time spectrum seemed to be all over the place: some date readouts were millions of years in the past, some thousands of years in the future. They were flying at close to two thousand knots per hour, and the coast of Africa was quickly approaching. The first drone's location was in a remote area that had never been overly populated. But since recorded history only went back five or six thousand years, he was basically guessing the same held true now.

At twenty thousand feet, Grimes took the lead as they headed northeast toward the central part of South Africa. Less than a moment later they descended into a deep fog, with visibility extending only feet from the nose of the fighter. A holographic representation of the landscape below hovered several inches above Jason's instrument panel, and he saw a faint ring, signaling the rough location of the first drone, come alive. They were close. Although she was out of his sight, the *Magnum*, less than a mile ahead, was stationary after lowering to the ground. Jason brought his fighter to within fifty yards of the shuttle's position and landed. His time-reference indicator had settled on a single date era: two point five million years BC.

"Whoo. I guess we're not in Kansas anymore ... Am I reading this right, Cap?" Billy asked while activating his seatbelt's auto-release mechanism.

"I think so." Jason looked out through the canopy at a world two and a half million years in their past. They climbed down and stood with their back to the fighter. Both raised their multi-guns.

"We're not going to be eaten by a dinosaur or anything, are we?"

"No, that would require us to be in a time realm sixty million years farther back. We should be OK," Jason replied, sounding anything but confident. He took the opportunity to contact Ricket, to make sure all comms were still in working order.

"Go for Ricket."

"We're on the ground and starting our search for Drone One."

"What is the time-reference date there, Captain?"

"Two point five million years, BC."

"Interesting. Good hunting; all is well here."

Jason broke the connection and he and Billy headed off toward the shuttle. As they approached, the aft hatch opened and a gangway extended toward the ground. The first one off the ship was Orion, quickly followed by Dira. Rizzo was next with Bristol shuffling behind him. It became evident Rizzo and Bristol had been going at it. Voices were raised and, clearly, tempers were short.

"No, that's where you're wrong, Bristol. I *am* your boss. You'll do as I say, or you'll pay the consequences. Got that?" Rizzo barked.

"You sound just like your mother; she wanted it a certain way, too," Bristol replied, thrusting his hips in and out in a lewd gesture.

Rizzo raised his multi-gun, turned it over and was preparing to ram the stock into Bristol's mid-section.

"Hold up there!" Billy yelled. Then, looking over to Jason, he asked, "I'm taking it you wouldn't have stopped him, would you?"

"Probably not. I would have shot him."

Billy stood between Rizzo and Bristol. "Where's your equipment, Mister? Aren't you the science officer?"

Bristol gave a quick shrug and said, "I guess it's still on board the shuttle. Get one of those freaky monstrosities to bring it down."

Jason's temper was building, and he felt the heat increase in his ears. He checked the setting on his multi-gun. Dira, reading Jason's body language, moved to Bristol's side. Whatever she was saying to him, Jason couldn't decipher from this distance. Bristol nodded his head, then turned and disappeared back into the shuttle.

Over the next few minutes, the ten SEALs and ten rhinos exited the *Magnum* and were loosely assembling at a nearby rock formation. Eventually, Bristol appeared on the gangway carrying a backpack; a separate satchel hung from one shoulder. Rizzo was waiting for him and pointed in the direction of the SEALs. "Over there."

Grimes jogged down the gangway and joined Jason. "Cap, you want me to stay here, keep an eye on the shuttle and your fighter?"

Jason looked over at the fighter and thought for a moment. "Can you remote pilot that fighter?"

"Yes, sir"

"Send it back to the Minian. We can always call it back here if it's needed."

"Yes, sir"

Jason signaled for Billy to join them.

"Aye, Cap?"

"I'd like you to assign two SEALs to keep watch here with Grimes. And have them get several fires going."

"You got it, Cap." Billy spun on his heels and barked out two names: "Holloway, Donaldson!"

"I'll close up the shuttle, Cap," Grimes said, and headed off. Jason watched her leave, realizing he couldn't recall ever seeing the young lieutenant in one of their newer formfitting battle suits before. He had to admit, she filled it out in all the right spots.

"Excuse me, Captain."

Jason turned to see Rizzo approaching, with Bristol several paces behind. "What's up, Rizzo?"

"Bristol's got his instrumentation going. He may have a rough indication where the drone is located."

Bristol released the strap of his satchel and let the device slide down to the ground. Crouching over, he pressed a small indentation on the device's side and two long flaps on its top opened, revealing a holographic virtual landscape representation that was nearly identical to the one Jason had earlier accessed on the fighter. The landscape flickered and disappeared several times, breaking into tiny digitized blocks, then held steady for several seconds, before repeating the same process, over and over again.

Bristol looked up. "Um, the thing's freaking out, but if you watch ..."

Jason saw it. The third time a small red icon blinked on—then off—at the farthest eastern coordinates of the landscape.

"There. See it?"

"I saw it. You sure that's it?" Jason said.

"What else would it be? And it's coming up at that same

location each time. The drone's doing its best to stay undetectable."

"What's the distance from our current location?"

"Um, I guess around three-quarters of a mile. Close. But the terrain looks to be ridiculously uneven moving eastward. I cannot guarantee we'll find a more suitable campsite."

"Here's fine. At least it's close. Hell, this might be easier than we thought."

* * *

Local time was 2:20 PM. Jason, in the lead with Bristol and Rizzo, was followed by the rhino-warriors and SEALs. Orion and Dira brought up the rear. Life was abundant. Flocks of birds flew overhead, and small rodents crossed in front of them. More life than he would have thought possible. Several stubby-necked giraffes watched the team from afar.

Passing a large fresh pile of excrement, Jason wondered what kind of animal could produce such an ample load. He figured this would be a good time to play around with his HUD's phase-time-comparator circuit, the PTCC, and find out. He set the parameters for one hour earlier and watched the corresponding video feed. It took several seconds, and then he saw them: two horned, white rhinoceros. No less than twenty of them and they were big, easily five thousand pounds each. He watched as one of the animals stood at that same dump spot and dropped his load. Three others followed his lead and did the same ten to twenty yards further up ahead—as if making a line. Perhaps marking their territory? Jason fast-forwarded the feed and saw them retreat the way they'd come, behind them.

The scream echoed across the plains. Jason spun in time to see that one of their rhino-warriors had been pierced from behind. An African rhinoceros was attempting to dislodge the thousand-pound warrior from his embedded horns. Traveler, heavy hammer in hand, reached the carnage in two bounding steps. He gripped the dead warrior's leather breastplate and pulled the carcass free. The white rhinoceros charged again, his two bloodied horns missing Traveler's abdomen by inches. Unexpectedly, this time it was Traveler who charged, letting his heavy hammer fall free he caught the rhinoceros' horns in two hands. In what seemed like a long time, Traveler, down on one knee, slowly ratcheted the beast's massive head—turning it one hundred and eighty degrees until its neck made a distinctive crack. Traveler released his grip on the horns and let the animal fall free to the ground. By this time the other rhino-warriors had circled around. In unison, they all bent to one knee, scooped up a handful of soil and gently tossed it onto their brother's remains. Traveler, the first to stand, turned to face Jason. Jason had seen that expression before. Traveler was exuberant.

The nine remaining rhino-warriors brought their heavy hammers up high in the air, smacking them together, producing a sound so loud Jason took a reflexive step backward.

"Captain Reynolds, you have a fine planet. A place where one can fight with honor. And these beasts look like—"

"Yes, we've noticed the similarity, Traveler," Jason said, looking at the dead team member. "I'm sorry for the loss of your warrior."

"He died with honor against a formidable opponent. What more can one ask?" Traveler noted, retrieving his hammer and standing tall, looking proud.

Chapter 11

They continued on toward Bristol's flickering drone icon while maintaining a more acute vigil for what was behind them and to their sides. As the afternoon progressed, more and more wildlife came into view. First, an odd-looking grouping of stubby-legged antelope leapt by, then a pride of eight or nine lions. They looked identical to modern day cats, with one significant difference: They were easily twice the size.

"What the hell are those?" Bristol asked startled, as he looked up for the first time from his instrumentation.

"Lions."

"So, not friendly?"

"No. Not even close," Jason replied, taking a bit of pleasure in Bristol's uneasiness.

Jason glanced at Bristol's wide eyed expression behind his helmet's visor. His pimply face was shiny with perspiration and he looked to be on the verge of hyperventilating.

As if on cue, another antelope sprinted by mere feet in front of them. Seconds later, a lioness ran by in close pursuit. After several dodging and weaving maneuvers, the antelope seemed to fatigue and started to slow its pace. The lioness pounced; claws gripped and tore at the antelope's torso and her massive jaws encircled the prey's neck. With the antelope's carotid artery severed, blood sprayed into the air and onto the lioness's face.

"Oh God. What kind of fucking place is this?" Bristol screamed.

"Take it easy. They're not interested in you."

"How do you know that?"

Jason shrugged and kept on walking. "We're almost there. Keep your mind on your job."

Up ahead was a rocky rise in elevation. Jason turned around to see their team procession catching up behind them. Off in the distance, behind the SEALs and rhino-warriors, Orion casually waved that all was well. Dira, at her side, looked the other way.

Bristol was crouching down, looking at his equipment. "The icons a bit more steady here. The drone's actually below ground, subterranean." He stood up and looked toward the rocks a hundred yards away.

"Could it be a cave?" Jason asked.

"You're asking me?"

"Yes, I'm asking you. You said it was below ground."

"I guess that's as good a guess as any," Bristol replied. "So sure, it could be a cave."

Billy caught up and also looked at the rocky ridge in the distance. "That where the drone is?"

"Looks like it. But below ground," Jason said. "Let's set up camp here and investigate first light."

"You got it, Cap," Billy replied, and hustled off to join the other SEALs.

Within half an hour, three large fires were blazing. One by one their tent-like enclosures, called Retractable Camp Modules, or RCMs, unfolded and took position in a circular perimeter around the fires. No less than five SEALs and five rhino-warriors were assigned revolving four-hour sentry duty shifts. The rhinos were all business, first helping with the fires and then preparing the game to be cooked on the open fire. Jason hadn't noticed they'd been hunting along the way. Three antelopes, skinned, disemboweled, rubbed with oils and seasoning, then skewered from end to end, were being positioned over the centermost fire.

As the meat popped and sizzled, its juices dripping into the fire, dark smoke rose into the air. The aroma was spectacular and Jason felt his stomach growl. The rhinos had brought in large rocks for everyone to sit on. Everyone sat, helmets off but within easy reach. Jason was the last one to take a seat and found himself sitting between Bristol and Rizzo.

Rizzo gestured toward the distant rocky ridge. "Cradle of humankind."

"What's that?" Jason asked.

"Taung Child ..."

"I've heard of that," Jason replied.

"History major in college," Rizzo said, taking a bite. The meat's juices dripped off his chin.

Jason hadn't considered that Rizzo was academically oriented. "Where'd you go to college?"

"Columbia. Always loved anything to do with history and archeology."

"So what's this about the Taung Child?"

"This place is considered by many to be the birthplace of humanity. A child's skull was discovered in caves near Johannesburg somewhere around 1924. When it was realized the skull's characteristics weren't ape, and had divergent humanistic properties, this area, Taung, became a hotbed of activity for archeologists around the world."

Jason was handed a platter and began to eat. He already knew the rhinos were skillful at preparing game and he thoroughly enjoyed his first bite of antelope. He looked around to the others and saw Dira sitting across from him, mostly obscured by the blazing fire at the center of the circle. She was talking to one of the SEALs Jason didn't personally know and was animated, using her hands to describe something. When she noticed Jason staring at her, she furrowed her brow and turned her body to the side. She was obviously still mad about something—Jason couldn't even remember what.

Bristol was done eating and flung a large bone into the fire. Others followed suit and when Jason finished, he too pitched his bones into the blaze. As the sun disappeared below the landscape and darkness crept into the camp, the horizon began to brighten with fluctuating colors, not unlike an aurora borealis, but this night display was constantly moving, wavering.

Bristol said, "You're looking at the nearest time flux. Not visible during the day, they're like curtains separating realms of time. If we sit here long enough, we'd find ourselves in another time period."

Jason nodded and continued watching the sky. "It's beautiful."

Bristol glanced toward the anomaly, scratched at something on his back and abruptly stood. He stretched and said, "I'm beat. My bunk is calling." He fetched up his helmet and disappeared into one of the RCMs.

"Odd kid," Jason said.

"Oh yeah. Creepy loaner," Rizzo added.

One by one everyone left the warmth of the fire and made their way into their RCMs. Jason wasn't tired and walked the perimeter of the camp, every so often crossing paths with one of the SEAL or rhino sentries. A SEAL and rhino-warrior stood together in the distance, both looking out toward the dark plains.

As he approached, Jason asked, "What's caught your interest?"

The two turned toward Jason; both the SEAL and the rhino-warrior were unfamiliar to him.

"We're seeing movement, Captain," the stocky SEAL replied.

Jason glanced at the name tag on his chest. J. Parker. "Any signs of aggression, Parker?"

"Not so far, sir."

Jason replaced his helmet and was able to see what the two were looking at. Infrared heat signatures showed what appeared to be thirty men walking single file along the rocky ridge. Then, one by one, each heat signature was gone.

The rhino made a deep grunting noise, then cleared his snout with a misty snort. "They go beneath the rocks."

"Captain," Parker said, "this is Fast Like Wind. He says they were following us and were watching our camp."

Jason momentarily considered the rhino's name and wondered if he was in fact a fast runner. "Seems like they're turning in for the night. Let me know if anything changes."

"Yes, sir," Parker replied. The rhino grunted again.

As Jason turned toward the cluster of RCMs in the distance, a laughing cry from a distant hyena wailed mournfully into the night. The camp was quiet, with a flickering amber light moving along the back of Jason's camp module. Coming around to the front, he saw that the zipper-like flap was partially open. He pulled his sidearm and tentatively stepped inside.

"We need to talk," Dira said, looking up from her seated position on his cot.

She was out of her battle suit and wearing a spacer's jumpsuit with the top portion hanging loose, exposing a small white tank top. Her arms were crossed over her chest. The small overhead lantern cast a warm glow over her violet skin, accentuating her softness—her curves.

"I wouldn't recommend removing your battle suit in this environment, Dira."

She bit her bottom lip and raised her eyebrows.

"So what is it you want to talk about?" Jason asked, sitting down next to her.

"You know exactly what I want to talk about."

"I honestly don't," Jason replied, pulling his helmet off and placing it down at his feet.

"With what you're going through, Nan's death, feelings of loss ... I know you're angry. Angry at Stalls, his little brother, and probably everyone else. I want to be there for you, Jason. But you seem determined to push everyone away. I didn't expect to be one of those people."

Jason let her words hang in the air for several moments before speaking. "I am angry. Angry my little girl will grow up without a mother, angry that I can't be there for her right now. And I'm angry I won't be allowed some form of retribution against Stalls."

"At least, from the sounds of things, he went out with a bang," she said.

Jason's mind envisioned Captain Stalls as he was literally crushed to death beneath a goliath space vehicle. The ends of his mouth slightly pulled up, eventually giving way to a smile. "I guess that's one consolidation."

Dira pulled one of his hands free and intertwined her fingers with his. "You're an amazing man, Jason. I can't pretend to understand what you're going through. The loss that you feel. My heart aches for you."

She brought his fingers up to her mouth and gently kissed them. He watched as her lips brushed against his hand and he felt familiar emotions stir. Emotions he had buried deep beneath others, including those of anger and hatred. Now, looking at Dira's closed eyes and her long, spectacular lashes, he let his feelings for her reawaken. Overwhelmed, he abruptly stood up.

"You should go, Dira. We have a big day tomorrow."

Chapter 12

Jason awoke with Dira still on his mind.

Showering in an RCM's cramped bathroom enclosure was surprisingly effective. It actually didn't use water at all, but heated pulsating streams of cleansing nanites. After several minutes, when the nanites completed their task, they recirculated back to the nozzle above where they'd be used again when needed.

Jason emerged from his RCM in his battle suit and triggered the module's collapse. Most of the other RCMs were gone, stowed into individual's backpacks. Traveler and several other rhinos were scattering what remained of the three campfires to ensure there were no hot embers lying about.

Jason hailed Ricket to see how things were going on the *Minian*.

"Go for Ricket."

"Good morning. Status?"

"Good morning, Captain. All is quiet here. I have the first three drone pairs ready for you. Have you located the first one?"

"I believe we're close. From what Rizzo tells me, we're at a location referred to as the Cradle of Humankind. Early man evolved in this general location."

"According to my historical database, that very well could be true. At two point five million years in the past, yes—you're at a pivotal point in your species' evolution."

"Stand by. Once we have the exact coordinates of the drone, I'll contact you." Jason cut the connection and joined Billy and several other SEALs. They were again looking toward the rocky rise in the distance.

Billy's visor was up and a stub of a cigar filled the corner of his mouth.

"Our friends are back," Billy said.

Jason put his helmet on and used his HUD to zoom in on the distant ridge line. Thirty men, all naked and hairy, stood as if keeping vigil over the exact location Bristol had indicated the drone would be located.

"They're armed," Rizzo said.

"Spears. Basically sharpened sticks. That too much for you, Rizzo?" Billy asked with a smirk.

Rizzo nodded, then said, "Considering those few beings just may represent the birth of mankind, are you sure you want to kill even one?"

Bristol joined the group, his helmet held in the crook of his arm. His hair was oily and plastered to his head. Drops of perspiration glistened on the back of his neck. He huffed as he looked over to Rizzo.

"You obviously don't know what you're talking about. Once the drones are all paired and deactivated, time here will revert back to its relative *reality*."

Rizzo bristled, "How do you know? And by the way, you have a big mouth." Rizzo then shrugged and smiled condescendingly.

"Explain," Jason said.

Bristol turned and scowled—looking as if the energy needed to reply was more than he was willing to exert. "The drones aren't really time machines." He thought a few seconds and continued: "Their original purpose was to set the calendar back one hundred years, right? What they were doing in actuality was creating a network that projected a multiverse representation of how things were one hundred years ago in the past. But once the drone network is deactivated, time continues on from where it left off."

"So you're saying all of this, what we're experiencing, is nothing more than a multiverse projection? None of this is real?"

"No, that's not what I'm saying. This is perfectly real. It's just not our reality specifically. And that's what is important, isn't it? Kill those hairy bastards on the ridge, have the rhino-freaks skewer them up for lunch if you want; I don't care—it won't impact our own time reference. Got it?"

Jason didn't answer. He used Ricket's PTCC and rewound Bristol's commentary. Satisfied he had it all, he used his HUD settings to message it off to Ricket.

Bristol looked quizzically at Jason, "What? Do I need to talk slower? Maybe draw pictures in the sand?"

Before Jason could reply, Billy's fist caught Bristol on the chin. Now all arms and legs, Bristol cartwheeled ten feet backward and landed on his hands and knees. He grabbed at his jaw and started to weep.

"I think it's broken. You broke my jaw."

Ricket was hailing and Jason turned away from Bristol.

"Go for Captain."

"What you sent me, Bristol's commentary? It's basically correct, Captain. You're not impacting our *own* time while there, not in the least."

"Got it. Thanks"

Jason hailed Dira.

"Hi there!"

So much for comms protocol, he thought with a smile. "Can you bring your medical bag? Seems Bristol took a mean fall."

* * *

On the move again they approached the ridgeline. The hairy figures were gone and the South African plains were relatively quiet. Bristol, checking his instruments, was clearly on edge. Several times Jason saw Bristol out of his peripheral vision, watching him, assessing him. As long as Bristol kept his mouth shut, he'd live through the day, Jason thought. They moved up into the rocks, slowing their pace. Halfway up the ridge, a hidden valley dipped down into an area the size of three adjacent football fields. Jason's eyes were drawn to several caves.

ping, ping, ping.

"Yeah, it's definitely here. Like close," Bristol said.

"Can you tell which one?" Jason asked, now seeing four caves of different sizes—two against the hillside and two cavernous openings on the ground before them.

"Um, let me see ..." Bristol moved forward, stopping every so often to check his readings. "If this fucking thing would stop blinking out ..." Several steps later he moved off to the left toward one of the caves on the hillside. "Well, it's probably this one."

"Probably?" Billy said, not even attempting to hide his disdain.

Bristol looked up but held his tongue.

"All right, we'll check it out."

Jason turned and signaled for Traveler. As he approached, Bristol took a tentative step back.

"We're going in; we'll need several sentries out here. Same with you, Billy," Jason said. Billy and Traveler turned and gathered their teams.

Jason approached the cave and realized that it was the one most often used. Nearly all the hillside grass had been trampled away, leaving clear-cut pathways into the dark void ahead. Hearing running feet behind him, Jason turned to see Orion jogging up the hillside in his direction.

"Cap, I was thinking."

He waited for her to reach him and nodded for her to continue.

"Maybe we should set our multi-guns for stun or heavy stun. Just seems overtly cruel to come into their home and start killing everyone. Even if they do attack."

"Agreed. Go ahead and spread the word."

Orion opened a channel and spoke the directive. Each of the SEALs stopped and seemed to stare off in space, accessing their HUDs and making necessary changes.

Standing at the mouth of the cave, Jason realized just how immense it was—guessing it was one hundred fifty to two hundred feet wide. Turning, he saw five rhinos and five SEALs taking up positions around the valley. With one exception, the rest of his teammates were headed up to join him at the mouth of the cave.

"Bristol, you're going to have to move quicker than that. Get up here and help direct us."

The team cleared a path for Bristol as he made his way to Jason's side. Still looking at his instruments, he pointed. "In there."

"Really? You'll need to do better than that."

Bristol continued forward and veered off toward the right, eventually disappearing into the darkness. Echoes bounced off the rock and into the black void above. Their helmet lights came on and Bristol came back into view. Both Jason and Billy hurried to catch up. There was something in the far distance, something—a flickering light—a campfire. Billy communicated to the team to spread out. Jason thought it strange that he'd yet to see any cavern walls. This was even bigger than the cavern beneath the scrapyard. The ground was definitely sloping down now and he found himself having to check his forward momentum. They walked for close to an hour in the darkness.

He'd been aware of the growing number of red icons appearing on his HUD. Hundreds of them.

"Cap, I'm feeling uneasy about this," Billy commented.

"Just take it slow. So far I'm sure we're just a curiosity to them," Jason said, trying to sound calm.

The cavern they were in suddenly closed down to a ten-foot-wide roughly hewn archway. The area beyond was brightly lit and there were excited voices, some yelling. Jason and Billy stopped at the entrance and tentatively peered in. What Jason saw caused him to hold his breath. A cavern expanse, easily the size of a football stadium, had fires along its periphery and a larger one blazing in the middle. Groups of ape-like people were congregated. Some were holding spears, others baskets; some were bare-chested females. But it was what he saw above them that captivated Jason's attention. As high as the eye could see were switchback paths, like catwalks, angled upward toward some dark, unseen pinnacle above. Hundreds more of the apelike people were traversing the narrow walkways, some going up, some coming down.

Bristol stepped into the cavern still looking at his instruments. Jason reached for him, but he was already five feet ahead. Still looking down he held out an arm and pointed straight up. As if realizing he'd walked off by himself, he looked up and around. The hordes of apelike people had stopped and were now facing in their direction. Spears came up amid a growing sound of angry murmurs. Spears flew from all sides and above. Jason sidestepped one, only to walk into the path of another. Their battle suits easily shielded them from harm.

"Where's the drone, Bristol?" Jason asked.

"All the way to the top," he replied, never taking his eyes off the crowd in front of them. The rest of the team were filing in behind. When the four rhino-warriors emerged, frightened shouts erupted from the crowd of apelike people. More males with spears moved forward, while females, some quickly picking up small children, skirted off in the opposite direction. Jason watched as a spear pierced Traveler's thigh, blood spraying into the air; it seemed an artery was severed. Dira went quickly to his side and began working to stem the flow of blood.

Jason visually followed the contours of several switchbacks above until he found one that eventually egressed onto the cavern floor.

"This way. We need to keep going," he said, pulling Bristol along with him and hurrying off toward the path. Jason pushed Bristol forward. "Go. Don't stop till you get to the drone. Billy, take your team and stay with him."

Traveler had apparently lost too much blood to get back into the fight; Jason saw that he was alive, lying against the cavern wall by the cavern entrance. The two remaining rhinos stepped forward and created a defensive semicircle. No more spears were flying, but they seemed to have an ample amount of rocks to throw. Dira carefully moved in close to Jason and looked up at him.

"How's Traveler?" Jason asked.

"His internal nanites are working overtime but that cut artery makes me nervous," she responded. "He'll be okay once we get him into a MediPod."

"Good." He saw something in her expression. "What?"

"You have to admit, they're fascinating. The ape people. To think you're looking at the your own evolutionary beginnings." She smiled. "I have to say, I see a definite resemblance."

Jason didn't reply, giving her a brief smile. Turning his attention back to the ape people, several of the males had tentatively moved forward. They were becoming more vocal. One male, taller, maybe five and a half feet, stood in front of the rest. His face, albeit covered with hair, was humanlike and didn't have any of the Neanderthal characteristics Jason had seen numerous times depicted in books. His voice, sounding like a jumble of unconnected sounds, was now becoming intelligible as Jason's nano-devices started to translate his speech. Although the utterances were primitive, the ape-man was definitely talking. Jason held a hand up, signaling Dira to stay put. Slowly, he walked past the rhinos and stood several paces before the talking ape-man. Moving cautiously, he brought his hands up and unclasped his helmet and pulled it off his head. The prehistoric crowd hushed, then more excited murmurs rose around them. Jason, although he'd seldom used it, quickly configured his nano-device so he could speak directly with them.

"I am called Jason," he said.

Again, absolute quiet, then more murmurs. The ape-man spoke. "I am Pawn."

"We are not your enemy. We do not wish to fight."

"You must leave here. Now," Pawn replied, his face bunching into an angry snarl.

"Soon. Very soon. We need to find something." Jason used the muzzle of his multi-gun and drew a crude picture of the drone on the dirt floor. Pawn stepped forward, tilting his head from side to side, and looked back up at Jason. With eyes wide his face filled with fury. He jumped toward Jason with unexpected agility. Jason was bowled over and on the ground as clenched fists hammered at his face. He tasted blood in his mouth and his vision started to tunnel into blackness. Then, just as quickly, the ape-man was off him, suspended in the air—arms flailing and legs gyrating. Jason, catching his breath, sat up to see one of the large rhino-warriors outstretched arm—a hand clenched a fistful of Pawn's fur on his back.

The rhino watched the flailing ape-man, then looked down

toward Jason. *Was that a smile?* Jason got back to his feet and motioned for him to put the ape-man down.

"It's okay, just put him down."

The rhino released the smaller man, letting him fall to the ground. He quickly skittered backwards on all fours and then stood up. Once again Jason approached him. This time on guard for an attack.

"Why did you attack me?"

"We know you've come to take Ishima."

"Ishima?"

Pawn pointed a hairy finger toward the crude drawing in the dirt. "Ishima. God of land and sky." Other ape-men, over a hundred of them now, had moved in closer and stood behind Pawn. There was that same face; Pawn was turning furious again. Without thinking, Jason stepped in and delivered a roundhouse punch to the smaller caveman's jaw. He fell down to the ground and didn't move for several moments. The others behind him took several steps backwards. Pawn was slow to recover; first, getting to his knees, then standing with his balance wavering.

Jason hailed Billy.

"Go for Billy,"

With his eyes, Jason followed the switchback path up until he could no longer see it in the smoky haze above.

"Status?"

"It's here, Cap. Hovering at the top of this cavern. There must be fifty dead apes laying around on the path up ahead that, I'm guessing, got in too close to the drone. All of them have nasty-looking scorch marks to their upper torsos."

"Get the exact coordinates from Bristol and send them to me."

Dira was at his side and looking up at his face. She smirked and retrieved several items from her MediKit. He shook his head and placed a hand on her shoulder. "The nanites are already doing their thing. I'm fine."

"Let me at least wipe off some of the blood," she said, and proceeded to clean his cheek and then his forehead. She made a face marked with exasperation. "Seriously, you pick a fight with a prehistoric caveman?"

Billy, back on his NanoCom, said, "Here are the coordinates, Cap. Sending them now."

Jason retrieved the message packet and forwarded them on to Ricket. Then he hailed him.

"Go for Ricket."

"Got the coordinates?"

"Yes, Captain. I'm preparing to phase-shift the first paired drone now."

"We're inside of a rocky cavern. Will that make a difference?"

"It shouldn't. The *Minian* is less than a thousand miles away from your position."

Jason set his HUD to display Billy's helmet feed. He saw the drone and the bodies on the surrounding pathways ahead.

There was a white flash and a second identical drone appeared. It hovered ten feet below the other. Both drones came alive and spun one hundred and eighty degrees, while hidden panels opened and weapon muzzles secured into place with distinctive *clicks*. Jason waited—watching the standoff, both drones looking angry as if they would fire on the other any second. Then, in unison, they put away their weaponry, closed their panels, and quietly hovered there together.

Chapter 13

They left the cavern with two rhinos carrying Traveler, now in-and-out of consciousness. No more spears or rocks were thrown; apparently the ape-people were now appeased having two drones, *or Gods,* instead of just the one.

They made their way back to the shuttle late in the afternoon. Something was cooking on the open fire and Jason hoped it was antelope. Within minutes RCMs were unfolding and game, hunted by the rhinos on the return trip, was added to the fire. Dira was adamant that Traveler needed to be transported back to the *Minian* as soon as possible. Within minutes Ricket, on the *Minian,* had prepped one of the shuttles and remotely piloted it to their camp. Although smaller, it was virtually identical to the *Magnum*. The shuttle circled once overhead and then landed fifty yards from the other shuttle. With Traveler secured, and two others rhinos to accompany him, the shuttle was back in the air within five minutes.

Jason didn't like the fact that Traveler, his friend and now the rhino leader, would be out of commission for a while. Even though Ricket had insisted Traveler would be fine alone up on the *Minian*, Jason was convinced it was more prudent that he be protected, on the off chance something happened up there. Ricket assured him that the other two rhinos could be returned to the planet within minutes, if necessary.

More rocks were soon placed around the fire and everyone seemed to be in high spirits. Jason sat down next to Billy, who passed him a cigar. Rarely did he accept one of Billy's stink bombs, but he took it and leaned forward for a light. He stifled a cough, then drew in the rich, aromatic smoke.

"Not a bad day's work," Billy said, looking pleased with himself. "Hell, if the rest of the drones go that easy—"

Jason held up a hand and shook his head. "You know what you just did, don't you?"

"No, I didn't jinx anything. I'm just saying ..."

"We have four more of those suckers to pair up. I think we need to be ready for the worst," Jason answered, watching the glowing hot ember at the end of his cigar.

Rizzo was handing out platters of meat and some kind of roasted, locally harvested, potatoes. As Jason reached up for his, his eyes caught an image at the edge of the camp. Two gargantuan lionesses. Licking their chops, they watched as everyone ate. The rhino-warrior named Few Words walked up to the fire and tore off one of the large antelope legs. As he approached the female lions they rose up off their haunches, looking ready to bolt. But apparently the rhino's total lack of fear, and the aroma of the roasted meat, kept the lionesses put. They accepted the leg and wasted no time tearing and eating its flesh. But what surprised Jason the most was how they permitted Few Words to sit down on the ground next to them. At one point, the rhino gave the larger of the two cats a scratch behind her ears and left his arm resting along her back. Dira and Grimes, sitting together, both pointed to the sight with mouths ajar.

Jason tossed what remained of his cigar into the flames. He'd had enough of the acrid-tasting thing. Billy threw him a pained expression. Using one hand, Jason pulled his virtual notepad from a pouch on his belt and expanded it out in front of them.

"All right, let's take a look at where we're off to next." Rizzo and Orion got up and stood behind them. A map depicting

Europe hovered in the air. A pulsating icon came into view, then disappeared.

"Is that France?" Billy asked.

"Yes, northern area—a little place called Conches. I'd guess close to Paris," Jason replied.

Bristol, who had been thoroughly engrossed in his meal, stood up, threw several greasy bones into the fire and hovered behind Rizzo and Orion. "I may be able to find the next one somewhat easier."

Heads turned in his direction.

"I mean, what are the odds it will be in a cave, or underground, again?"

No one answered and Jason closed down his virtual notepad. Getting to his feet, he stretched. "Up at 0600. I need everyone rested—big day tomorrow." He nodded and smiled to Dira and Grimes, still deep in conversation, and headed off toward his RCM.

* * *

Jason was up at first light, well before 0600. The six remaining rhinos were clearing the campsite. As Few Words carried one of the fireside rocks and tossed it back out into the plains, one of the lionesses looked up, growled, then fell back into a bed of tall grass.

RCMs refolded into themselves as each of the SEALs and other teammates staggered out into the morning air. Jason had gotten coffee brewing first thing and offered up steaming mugs as they shuffled over to the shuttle. Orion, eyes half-closed, accepted the mug of coffee and smiled.

"Gunny, you'll want to reconfigure everyone's multi-gun default settings. I have a feeling stun levels won't cut it—not today," Jason said.

"Aye, Cap," she said, looking around. "Where's all the rocks?"

"Don't get comfortable; we're wheels up in ten," Jason said, staring at the one standing RCM. "Let me guess, Bristol?"

"Who else?" Billy said, shaking his head. "Want me to get him going?"

"Yeah, you better. Before you know it half the day will be shot."

* * *

As soon as Lieutenant Grimes flew the *Magnum* up into the air, the time-reference indicator on Jason's HUD started to change—slow at first, then changing every second or two. The total estimated distance between Johannesburg and Conches was 5,154 miles, and within four minutes, the shuttle was halfway there. Bristol, seated, was staring at the equipment on his lap. The rhinos, standing at the back of the shuttle, swayed and grabbed for handholds as the shuttle banked sharply to the left.

Jason sat in the cockpit next to Grimes. He watched her as she confidently handled the controls—always active, checking settings, making adjustments, and scoping out the terrain below. There was something edgy about her, which reminded him of Nan. His heart missed a beat at the thought of Nan, now gone; he would never see her or touch her again. He fought away the shroud of sadness that was rushing to overwhelm him, wanting to engulf him.

"Penny for your thoughts?" Grimes asked, quickly glancing in Jason's direction.

He smiled. "Huh, I haven't heard that expression in years."

"Midwest roots, there's a lot more where that came from,"

she said, smiling back.

Jason stared forward at the dense cloud-cover ahead.

"How about two pennies for your thoughts?"

Jason chucked. "I was just thinking that you reminded me of someone."

"Like how I look?"

"No, not so much look. More of a presence."

"Presence?"

"Yeah, I guess more like a state-of-beingness. Your confidence, edginess."

She nodded without looking in his direction, then said, "Well, I suppose a lot of that comes from being a female in a male-dominated environment. Ten years ago, I assure you, I was quite demure and ladylike."

"I never said you weren't ladylike."

With that said, Jason turned around to face the team, jam-packed in the hold behind him. "Two minutes. Billy, once on the ground, let's get out there and set up a defensive perimeter. Rhinos, give us a few moments to check out the surroundings before you vacate."

There were nods all around and expressions of anticipation, even excitement. The truth was, he was excited too. How often could one actually experience a form of time travel like theirs? And like the spin of a roulette wheel, they could easily fall into virtually any timeframe.

The *Magnum* descended as those on board looked out through the cockpit window or through the portholes on either side. Slowing now, breaks in the cloud cover reveal the terrain below; one that is covered in tall pines, an occasional winding road, and cleared farmland. Their vertical descent culminated with a gentle *thump thump* as the landing struts touched down.

Jason checked his HUD's time-reference date: June 2, 1944.

"Of course, why make it easy?" Jason asked aloud. He knew of this timeframe in military history. Four days before the invasion of Normandy—they'd landed in an inhospitable location in a most inhospitable year.

The back of the shuttle lowered and a gust of warm dusty air filled the cramped compartment.

"Hold on, everyone," Jason said, standing and scanning the terrain beyond. Definitely farmland but their were sounds ... distant sounds of motors, squeaky treads, and men's voices. His HUD showed too many life-sign icons to count, coming from all sides. In the distance a tall white clapboard barn stood solitary alone in a recently plowed field.

"There, Grimes. Get us over to that barn!"

The shuttle rose several feet and moved off in the direction of the barn. Heads were craning now to see out the rear window, or through portholes.

"There!" Rizzo pointed to the south, where plumes of dust filled the air. A distant convoy headed in their general direction.

Jason followed the sightline of the distant dirt road. Coming into view were hundreds of ground forces—the unmistakable outline of Panzer tanks and other armored personnel carriers. Grimes maneuvered the shuttle to the far side of the barn. Two closed barn doors stood before them.

"Go!" Jason barked.

Both Billy and Rizzo were out of the shuttle and running toward the big wooden doors. Within seconds they had them opened wide and pushed back against the outside of the barn.

"It'll be tight, Captain," Grimes said.

The shuttle was repositioned so its rear end was now pointed in, toward the open barn doors. Slowly, the shuttle began backing in.

Jason felt it in his ears, a compression followed by a release.

What followed next was loud: continuous booming thuds, one after another. Instinctively, everyone crouched down low. In the distance a line of tanks turned in their direction. One after another, white puffs of smoke appeared from multiple turrets.

"Incoming!" Billy yelled, as he and Rizzo ran back toward the rear of the shuttle. Two hundred yards out the ground exploded, shooting dirt and rocks high into the air. A moment later two more explosions came, each consecutively hitting closer to the barn. First Billy, then Rizzo, leapt and landed hard on the shuttle's back decking. Grimes wasted no time throttling fast forward, the sudden motion whipping everyone's head back. Two more explosions, the last one hitting dead center in the barn. Its sides and roof blew out with a massive concussive fireball. Wooden shards clattered against the shuttle's outer hull, several flying into the open rear hatch.

Jason watched as the barn exploded behind them and, a second or two later, saw a drone emerge from the burning embers. It flew past them at tremendous velocity. Then the shuttle's hatch closed and latched into place.

"That's our probe!" Jason yelled.

"I'm on it, Cap," Grimes replied.

The shuttle followed the drone over several open fields until it disappeared into the tree line.

"Shit!" Grimes spat. "Forest is too dense. I can't take us in there."

"Shoot the trees, do not lose that drone," Jason commanded, taking his seat next to her.

Grimes stole a quick glance at Jason. "Shoot the trees?"

"You heard me. Do it. Don't you dare lose that drone."

Grimes tapped several virtual keys in front of her and the light-blue holographic nav display reconfigured—adding another layer of red targeting components. Her thumbs tapped at small keys on the top of the control column. Energy bursts fired from the dual plasma cannons, positioned low at the shuttle's bow. Closing in on the tall tree line, Grimes continued to target the closest trees, cutting a swathe twenty feet wide.

Both Jason and Grimes saw the drone increase its lead on both the nav display and their HUDs.

"Stay with it, but let's keep our distance."

Grimes nodded. Trees continued to disintegrate before them but now at a slower rate. The drone's icon slowed and then came to a stop a quarter mile ahead. The shuttle emerged from the forest into a valley clearing below, where three sets of railroad tracks converged into what appeared to be some kind of railcar cemetery. Wooden shacks in disrepair dotted the landscape. Multiple rows of dark red and black boxcars were lined up and bunched together at the northern end of the desolate railcar scrapyard. At its center area, where once perhaps stood a bustling depot in years past, were row after row of ancient steam locomotives. From the shuttle's distance above, they looked like a child's discarded train set. One locomotive seemed precariously angled to one side, and almost obscured beneath it, in a slight hollow, sat the drone.

Jason glanced at his HUD's time-reference date: it was still June 2, 1944.

"Let's set down here, Grimes. Any closer and the drone might fly off again."

She brought the *Magnum* down close to the tree line and activated the opening of the rear hatch. The warm air from outside rushed in, along with the distant sounds of war. Far away rifle fire crackled, along with the *boom boom* of mortar exploding.

The rhino-warriors were the first out, followed by the SEALs, and Bristol. As before, Grimes and two SEALs stayed with the shuttle. Sounds of combat were closing in from two sides. As a second thought, Jason told Dira to stay behind, for Grimes to keep everyone else on board, and to keep the *Magnum*'s shields up. He locked eyes with Dira for a fleeting moment and then trotted off with the team.

Bristol quickly fell behind, spending as much time looking down at his equipment as he did looking forward. Stumbling, he said, "Shit!"

They'd reached the first set of train tracks. Beyond the depot, in both directions, the trees had been cleared ten feet into the forest.

"That's not good," Billy remarked.

From the east a column of tanks and dark grey uniformed men were following the tracks and heading in their direction. Jason had spied them on his HUD but hadn't expected them to be so close. He and his assault team quickly crossed the tracks and moved behind two adjoined wooden shacks.

"Wehrmacht," Rizzo said.

Both Jason and Billy looked back at him with blank expressions.

"German defense force. I'm betting this is the Panzer Group, led by General Leo Geyr."

"How do you know this stuff, Rizzo?" Billy asked.

"He went to Columbia; history major," Jason answered, urging the rhinos to move it along and get out of sight.

One of the larger, more portly rhinos, called Billowing Gust, Jason recalled, was the last one to cross over and took three rounds into his side and back. Blood flowed but he seemed to barely notice.

"So much for hiding until they pass," Jason commented. The last thing he wanted to do was take on the German Wehrmacht. "Let's hurry up and get to the drone."

An explosion stopped them in their tracks, taking out two

side-by-side boxcars up ahead. Jason turned away as wood and metal shrapnel cascaded onto him.

Rizzo was on his back and two Rhinos were obviously dead—one was decapitated, and the other had a wooden plank extending from his chest.

"Panzer's 75 mm howitzer. High-explosive shells," Rizzo said, slowly getting to his feet. The rhino called Few Words began to check over the dead rhinos while everyone else took cover.

Even with the knowledge that this wasn't their own relational time period, Jason was still reluctant to blatantly go up against the approaching convoy. But, in truth, his loyalties were with his own time, his own world. Taking out these tanks and men would be a simple task for the *Minian*, up in high orbit above the planet. He hailed Ricket and waited for over a minute.

"Captain," a hurried voice came back, out of breath.

Jason immediately knew something was wrong. "What is it, Ricket?"

"Can't speak for long ... we're being boarded, I'm evading—"

"Boarded? By whom?" Jason heard energy weapons firing over his NanoCom.

"I'm not actually sure," Ricket replied. Jason heard sounds of running footfalls and Ricket's heavy breathing over the line.

"Sorry, Captain. I'll contact you as soon as I'm able." The connection closed.

Billy, noticing Jason's alarmed expression, asked, "What is it?"

"*Minian*'s been boarded. Looks like we're on our own for a while," Jason replied.

Chapter 14

Ricket ran for the entrance to Medical with eight Caldurians in pursuit. They'd emerged onto the ship ten minutes earlier from multiple DeckPort locations. Ricket, alerted to their presence by the AI, watched them from behind a bulkhead. Armed with energy weapons and wearing hardened, dark brown environmental suits, the Caldurians quickly fanned out into multiple directions—as if they knew exactly where they needed to go.

Not wearing his own battle suit and unarmed, Ricket addressed the ship's AI. "AI, take defensive action against the intruders."

"That function has been deactivated."

"Who has deactivated that function, AI?"

"*Minian* command personnel prior to your boarding. It is for that reason your own access to the vessel has gone unchallenged."

"Can you at least keep me apprised of their location?"

"Yes," the pleasant AI's voice replied. "The insurgent forces are making their way toward the bridge, although they have been halted due to the fact the area has not been fully constructed. Within the last fifteen seconds another team has emerged at DeckPort L9."

Ricket tried to remember where that particular DeckPort was situated when he heard the sound of approaching feet. Coming down the corridor behind him were eight armed insurgents. Ricket ran as energy bolts flew by him, missing him by mere inches. He darted left, then right, then sprinted full out and dove into the closest DeckPort.

Ricket emerged out of a DeckPort two levels down, still

airborne, his arms extended. He tucked and rolled, using his own momentum to catapult him upright, and sprinted toward Medical. He called out to two rhinos, whom he'd learned were actually twins, First Reflection and Second Reflection. "Help! First Reflection!"

Sleepy-eyed, it was actually Second Reflection, the rhino with a chip on one side of his horn, who peered out from the entrance of Medical. Startled, seeing Ricket running towards him followed by eight close combatants, he quickly pulled his heavy hammer from the leather thong at his side, while drawing his plasma gun from its holster with his other hand. By the time Ricket skirted into Medical, First Reflection, the rhino's twin, was at his brother's side. Both fired at the approaching combatants. Ricket needed to get to his own battle suit, but that was three decks away.

The deck plates shook underfoot as one of the rhinos in the corridor went down hard. Ricket crouched low and took a quick look. It looked like Second Reflection was dead. But the brother rhinos had done well. Only two of the brown-clad combatants were still on their feet, now hiding behind the bulkhead of an intersecting corridor and firing at First Reflection. The rhino's hide was blackened with numerous scorch marks, and he was staggering.

"Take cover! Don't just stand in the middle of the corridor like that."

The rhino ignored Ricket and continued to fire his weapon. Ricket saw Second Reflection's plasma weapon lying on the deck, but it was not within easy reach. He took several steps backward, then rushed forward into the corridor. Staying low, Ricket reached the far side, snatched up the weapon, and darted back to safety. The handgun was huge in his small hands. There was no way he'd be able to use it single-handedly. Awkwardly, with one hand on the barrel and the other at the trigger, Ricket held the gun out in front of him. He took in a deep breath and edged around the corner, pulling the trigger. To his surprise, only one of the combatants was still on his feet, and between Ricket and First Reflection's combined fire, the last of them went down.

First Reflection staggered and rushed to his brother's side. Ricket joined him and felt for a pulse along the rhino's carotid artery. Ricket looked up at First Reflection, ready to give him the dire news, but the rhino had slumped forward, unconscious.

Ricket sat back, letting his back lean against the bulkhead. Only when he looked up did he see Traveler filling the entrance to Medical.

"What has happened here? Why are my warriors lying dead before me?"

Ricket felt a rush of relief that Traveler's time in the MediPod had completed. "Only one of them is dead. I'm sorry. Too much time has elapsed for him to be brought back. But First Reflection's still alive; help me get him into the MediPod."

Ricket moved aside as Traveler knelt down and scooped his hands under the unconscious rhino. Carrying him on his outstretched arms into Medical, he gently laid the rhino's body inside the largest pod's still-open clamshell.

Ricket made several setting adjustments and the clamshell began to close.

"You must tell me what has happened," Traveler asked, tension in his deep voice.

Ricket picked up the other weapon and handed it to Traveler. "You were injured on Earth—a spear to the leg. You were brought here by these two and placed into the large MediPod to recover."

Ricket continued to talk as he headed out of Medical and down the corridor toward the fallen enemy combatants. Traveler followed.

"A short while ago the *Minian* was boarded by these insurgents. Now they're all over the ship." Ricket knelt down and looked through the visor of the closest body. "Caldurian."

The AI was speaking again. "Another insurgency team of ten combatants has appeared through DeckPort L9; they are headed in your direction."

Ricket stood. Something didn't make sense to him. The Caldurians were wearing environmental suits—old fashioned, compared to the high-tech battle suits worn by the crew of *The Lilly*.

"AI, are these Caldurians returning *Minian* crew members?"

"No. These Caldurians are derived from that faction called the *originals*."

Ricket thought about that. He recalled Granger speaking of two distinct factions of Caldurians—the *progressives*, who embraced new multiverse technologies, and the *originals*, who'd put limits on the extent to which multiverse technology could be utilized.

"AI, is it because of the originals that the *Minian* crew is missing?"

"Partially."

"Are the originals and the progressives at war?"

"That is not an accurate statement."

"Explain."

The AI hesitated for a moment, then said, "In light of current events, there is a high degree of probability that the originals have aligned with another warring faction."

"I don't understand; who have the originals aligned with?"

"The Craing."

Ricket looked at Traveler. The news was an unexpected and dire development. Although the originals hadn't embraced multiverse technology, they were still hundreds, if not thousands of years more advanced than the Craing. Sharing their superior technology with the Craing would prove devastating to the Alliance. Ricket needed to contact the admiral.

They heard approaching sounds of running. With no place to run, Ricket stepped toward Traveler and grabbed his arm. "Let me access your phase-shift wristband." Using two hands, he opened its faceplate and quickly entered a new set of coordinates. Then, as an afterthought, he grabbed up the dead Caldurian's sidearm. Standing by Traveler's side, and holding on to his arm, he pressed the activate button. The Caldurians rounded the corner just as Ricket and Traveler phase-shifted three deck levels higher on the ship.

They were now standing in the room with the phase-synthesizer. If they were to have any chance of holding off the Caldurians, they'd need access to the phase-synthesizer's manufacturing capabilities. Ricket quickly moved to the console and started to scroll through its various drone options. He was more than a little familiar with Caldurian drone tech. He remembered seeing a smaller version of the transmitter drones that had been dispatched to Earth. *There it is.* What he needed to do was set the parameters for a drone to search and incapacitate only the Caldurians. With the help of the AI, he already had bio-reading references for Caldurian life forms. Within two minutes, the phase-synthesizer spewed out the first spherical black mini-hover drone. Ricket configured it for passive mode, not wanting to inadvertently risk shooting themselves. Both Traveler and Ricket took cover and remotely activated the drone. It quickly came alive; small panels opened on its surface and gun barrels appeared, poised to fire.

Sensing their own bio-readings, the drone quickly darted around the bulkhead they'd taken cover behind and hovered there, several feet off the ground. Then it was off, heading toward the room's exit.

"What will one drone accomplish?" Traveler asked, snorting indignantly. "Better to face the enemy with honor—not sending a machine to fight our battles."

Traveler turned to see that thirty more drones had already been dispensed from the phase-synthesizer and more were materializing every few seconds.

Ricket shrugged. "Do you want to stay here fighting the Caldurians, or to go help the captain on Earth?"

Traveler's frustration abated somewhat with the question. "I need to help the captain."

Ricket returned to the console, entering something. A halo-projection of the *Minian* displayed in the air before them. Colored icons, depicting both the Caldurians and the mini-drones, moved in respect to their onboard locations.

"AI, change the color of the unconscious Caldurians," Ricket said aloud.

Immediately, half the icons turned from yellow to pink. Nodding his head appreciatively, Ricket noticed something else and zoomed in on the *Minian*'s reconstructed bridge and its surrounding area. Traveler stepped forward.

"I hadn't realized the bridge reconstruction was completed," Ricket said.

One by one the yellow icons turned pink.

"How long will they be asleep?" Traveler asked.

"Until we wake them up," Ricket replied with a smile. "They've been tagged with small cerebral disrupters."

The single remaining yellow Caldurian life form icon turned pink. Ricket hesitated and looked up at Traveler. "We need to fortify the egresses onto the ship." He went back to the console and began to alter the drone's operation parameters.

"What are you doing now?" Traveler asked, seeming

impatient to leave.

"Changing the parameters. The drones will now, in addition, act as sentry guards, protecting DeckPorts, or any phase-shift access point within the ship."

"This space vessel has many such locations," Traveler said.

Ricket glanced over his shoulder toward the phase-synthesizer unit. Over one hundred more drones hovered, ready to be activated. "I think we'll be covered."

Several more taps at the console and the new drones came alive and headed out of the compartment.

Traveler said, "I need to return to the planet now."

Ricket nodded and was about to agree when the ship violently lurched to one side. A general quarters klaxon sounded.

"The *Minian* is under attack," the AI said.

Chapter 15

The German soldiers broke formation, spreading out on both sides of the train tracks that led into the forest. Jason felt multiple rounds ping off his protective battle suit. He hailed Grimes.

"Go for Grimes," she said.

"We're taking heavy fire; we need you to give them something else to shoot at for a while."

"Aye, Cap. I'm on it."

Within moments the *Magnum* was airborne and hovering at the east side of the depot. As expected, the Germans' attention was now drawn toward the shuttle. Heavy rifle fire erupted, none of it affecting the *Magnum*'s shields. The distant line of Panzers, still making steady progress alongside the tracks, had their big guns elevated. *Boom, boom, boom.*

Everything shook as the explosive rounds from ten tanks struck the *Magnum*'s shields. Again, there was zero effect on the shuttle.

"Let's move out before our German friends get bored and look for something else to shoot at," Jason said, taking up the lead and moving off toward the slanted locomotive ahead. From above, Grimes began to fire plasma bolts into the line of tanks. The first tank exploded in a ball of fire, but the other tanks didn't seem to exhibit any real damage. Jason figured Grimes had changed over to stun-level settings.

Once they'd reached the leaning locomotive, Jason signaled the SEALs and rhinos to keep a healthy distance away. Bristol checked his equipment and forwarded the drone's coordinates over to Jason.

Jason hailed Ricket.

"Go for Ricket."

"We're at the second drone. I'm forwarding the coordinates to you now."

"Captain, we're under attack. So far the shields are holding."

"Attacked by whom?" Jason asked, surprised by Ricket's calm reaction.

"Not sure. The bridge reconstruction has been completed. I'm on my way there now and will know more in the next few minutes. I'm dispatching drone pair number two—it should arrive shortly."

"Watch out yourselves; get back to me as soon as you're on the bridge."

Jason cut the connection.

Billy, at his side, asked, "What's going on?"

"The *Minian*'s under attack. Not sure by whom just yet. Ricket's sending the drone now."

The remaining rhinos formed a defensive perimeter around the locomotive. Each had been struck multiple times with rifle rounds, but their wounds seemed to be more of an annoyance to them than life-threatening medical conditions. Over the last few minutes, Jason watched on his HUD as more yellow icons appeared. They were slowly being surrounded by German infantry. Up to this point, the drone had remained perfectly still—almost hidden in the rusted train engine's shadow.

Rifle fire crackled nearby, followed by the familiar sound of *pings* ricocheting off the locomotive. Jason, Billy, and the SEAL team crouched low and turned toward the approaching Germans. The rhinos were returning fire with their own plasma weapons. It was then Jason noticed snipers had taken up positions on top of the boxcars. About to hail Grimes for some needed air support, he heard three more pings behind him and then the sound of the drone coming awake.

The drone's defenses activated as panels opened and multiple gun barrels protruded. It spun and changed direction with the close pinging of each new rifle round.

"It's going to flee," Billy said.

"We can't let that happen," Jason replied. Looking at the leaning locomotive, he was surprised it hadn't pitched over already. Carefully keeping low, Jason scurried around to its other side. The four remaining rhinos were taking cover behind the rusted remnants of an old steam-powered crane. By the sound of the increasing rifle fire, they were surrounded on that site as well. Above, but keeping adequate altitude, the *Magnum* appeared and began firing multiple plasma bursts. As the Germans ran for cover, Jason got the attention of the rhinos and signaled for them to come closer. One by one they positioned themselves around Jason. Momentarily struck by their colossal size, he spoke to them in a lowered voice. Once he was sure they understood, like a quarterback breaking a huddle, he clapped once and the rhinos moved off to their directed positions.

"Remember, we only have one chance at this and it has to be fast."

The rhino-warriors nodded their large heads and took up their assigned positions; poised, with knees bent, their huge hands firmly gripped around the upended side of the slanting engine's frame, its piston hardware and metal wheels. Then Jason noticed the *Magnum* had moved off and was firing at the tanks on the other end of the yard. Almost immediately, rifle fire returned. *Shit!* It was now or never.

"Push!" Jason yelled.

The four rhino-warriors stood up in unison, quickly bringing the train engine upward along with them. With a loud creak, bringing it past its tipping point, the locomotive flipped over onto its other side.

Jason and the four rhinos scurried around the engine to see if their efforts had succeeded. Billy crouched low and looked under the now toppled-over locomotive.

"Um ... I think I see it under there," Billy said, switching his helmet light on to get a better view into the darkness beneath. "Yep, there it is. Not looking too happy under there, do you think it'll stay put, Cap?"

"To be honest, I have no idea. We'll have to wait and see."

As if on cue, the drone's twin appeared overhead and slowly descended. Jason tugged on Billy's shoulder and they both stepped back. The drone spun one hundred and eighty degrees as it instigated its pairing configuration.

Jason said, "Billy, contact Grimes and work out a location to get us picked up."

He then hailed Ricket.

"Go for Ricket."

"What's your status?"

"We're on the bridge—"

"We?"

"Traveler is out of the MediPod, although another rhino is now in it. A third rhino is dead."

"Who exactly boarded the *Minian*?"

"Caldurians, but not its crew members. These raiders are from a faction called the originals."

"As in the originals from the Crystal City?"

"Exactly, and a similar vessel is now firing on the *Minian*."

"I'm totally confused, Ricket. Just tell me—what the hell's going on there?"

"The most important information you need to know is that this faction of the Caldurians have aligned themselves with the

Craing."

"What?! Why would they do that?"

"I cannot answer that, but it seems there was more to their dispute than differences over the use of multiverse technologies, as we were led to believe."

Jason watched as the *Magnum* landed in an open field in the near distance. Billy was reassembling the remaining team members, preparing to move out.

Jason brought his attention back to his conversation with Ricket. "What's happening with the *Minian*'s bridge?"

"From what the AI says, it is complete and operational again. Now that I have access to a working tactical station, I can see two Crystal City vessels are in local space and both are firing on the *Minian*. Our shields are holding at ninety percent. Do you wish me to return fire, Captain?"

"No, not yet," Jason said. "Until we know for sure what their beef is with the progressives, and if these originals have, in fact, aligned with the Craing, we'll stay passive. They don't seem to be posing any great danger to the *Minian* at present. Hail them—see what they want."

Ricket was talking but Jason's attention was pulled away toward the *Magnum*. The back hatch was open and the gangway extended. Two SEALs, who'd earlier been left behind to protect the shuttle, ran down the gangway and took up defensive positions. Grimes and Dira stood at the open hatch above. Both had removed their helmets and were talking; Dira laughed at something Grimes said.

Thirty feet from the *Magnum* the ground exploded—a fiery plume of dirt, and several small trees shot into the air. The two SEALs were gone and both Grimes and Dira were propelled back into the shuttle.

Jason ignored his connection with Ricket and ran flat out.

At two hundred feet and closing he saw two Nazi tanks appear, toppling several small oak trees in the process. *What am I doing?* Jason configured new phase-shift coordinates on his HUD and activated a phase-shift. Landing ten feet from the shuttle, Jason unexpectedly ran into two soldiers who crossed his path, colliding headlong into them. All three crashed to the ground in a tangle of arms and legs. German rifles and Jason's multi-gun were out of reach.

Two soldiers emerged from the shuttle's hatch, each holding on to a leg and dragging the unconscious bodies of Grimes and Dira—their heads bounced over the uneven surface.

Jason's hesitation cost him. The soldier lying on the ground nearest him had drawn a pistol and fired into Jason's upper body and visor. Although there was no damage to the protective armor he wore, the rounds repeatedly striking his body made it difficult for Jason to get back on his feet. With multiple flashes, Billy, the other SEALs, and the rhinos all began to appear in the clearing. Thanks to Rizzo, both German soldiers next to Jason went down with plasma bolts to their heads. In the distance, helmets appeared from the two tank turrets and within seconds machine gun rounds were tearing through the air. Again, Jason was pummeled and could not regain his footing. A rhino-warrior to Jason's left took an unrelenting barrage of fire to his exposed hide, killing him. An armored halftrack personnel carrier backed up beside one of the tanks. Like cords of wood, Grimes' and Dira's bodies were flung up into the back of the carrier, followed by several soldiers. What at first seemed like only a handful of Germans close-by could now be counted in the hundreds.

The personnel carrier closed up. The engine started and the truck slowly disappeared into the trees.

Chapter 16

Mollie awoke with a start. Sitting up in her bunk, she looked around the familiar surroundings of her cabin aboard *The Lilly*. There were noises coming from down the hall in the kitchenette. Then a raised voice.

"If you would get the hell out of my way, I'd be able to move. Stand over there. No, over there—just back up! Do you remember the words? Good. Okay, all of you, come on."

Her grandfather's deep baritone voice made Mollie sit up. *Who is he yelling at?* she wondered. Her grandfather moved down the hallway and entered her cabin; Uncle Brian followed, and close behind was Betty, with the green lizard alien bringing up the rear. Mollie beamed when she saw what her grandfather was holding in his outstretched hands—a large plate filled with a steaming stack of flapjacks, and nine flickering candles perched on top.

They all sang together: "Happy birthday to you, happy birthday to you, happy birthday, dear Mollie, happy birthday to you ..."

The admiral placed the plate on Mollie's lap and Brian handed her a fork and a napkin.

"What are you ... six now?" Brian asked with a wry smile.

"Ha ha," Mollie said, filling her mouth with syrupy pancakes. "I'm nine and you know that, Uncle Brian."

The hopper, still unnamed at this point, sat on his haunches and watched Mollie's plate with growing interest.

Betty, wearing a spacer's jumpsuit, her hair pulled back in a ponytail, sat down next to Mollie on the edge of her bed and asked, "What type of things do little girls do on their day of birth back home?"

Brian said, "It's called a birthday."

"Okay, what do little girls do on their birthday?"

The admiral picked up Mollie's napkin and wiped syrup from her chin.

"We go to amusement parks, like Disneyland, or we go to the beach, or have a party where all my friends bring me lots and lots of presents." Mollie smiled as she said this and raised her eyebrows expectantly.

The admiral made an exaggerated expression of alarm. "I'm so sorry, Mollie, but there's a rule in space. No gifts. No presents are allowed. Causes too much jealousy among the rest of the crew."

Mollie turned her head and squinted her eyes. "Grandpa, I'm not buying your act."

Betty and Brian laughed out loud and the admiral fought to keep a straight face. Teardrop then entered the room, holding a mountain of colorfully wrapped gift boxes. Mollie passed her empty plate to Betty and sat even further up in bed. One by one the gifts were placed on her lap. She sat back and looked at the horde of presents before her. They watched her smiling face change. Tears welled up in her eyes and her smile turned into a grimace of pain. The admiral sat next to her and pulled her small shoulders into his chest. Her body shook and her cries continued for some time. It was then that they noticed the tag on the top package.

To Mollie, Love Mom.

* * *

The admiral entered *The Lilly*'s bridge and took a seat in the command chair. On his display was Ricket, waiting patiently. The admiral still hadn't adjusted to Ricket's altered appearance. Gone were the old cyborg attributes: his once near-transparent skin covering moving mechanical parts on his face and body. Now, the younger-looking Craing, handsome in his own way, greeted the admiral with a quick nod.

"Admiral, we have a situation here."

"What is it? Is it something with the team on Earth?"

"No, sir. The *Minian* is under attack."

"By whom?"

"The Caldurians ... the originals faction, Admiral."

Ricket proceeded to tell the admiral what had transpired over the last few days, leading up to the *Minian*'s boarding by the original Caldurians, and the recent attack on the ship by two Crystal City-type vessels.

"Have you figured out what happened to Granger and the crew of the *Minian?*" the admiral asked.

"I have my suspicions. It may have something to do with Bristol's sudden appearance here, on the *Minian*—causing a multiverse time reference anomaly. I'm working on several ideas to bring them back."

"And you're sure the *Minian*'s not in any danger?"

"Our defenses are far more advanced. At least for the time being, we are not in any immediate danger. But Admiral, there is one more thing I've recently learned ... the originals may have aligned with the Craing."

The admiral stared back at Ricket's image with a furrowed brow. "Where did you get that information from? How sure are you about this?"

"It's not definite, but the *Minian*'s AI gives it a high probability."

"Well, if it's true, that could mean it's game over for the rest of us. Damn it! Caldurian technology, mixed with the Craing's ruthlessness, already spread throughout the universe."

"The originals do not possess the same level of technology as the progressives, but yes, still far more advanced than—"

The admiral cut Ricket off mid-sentence. "Listen to me. You need to figure out what happened to Granger and the *Minian*'s crew. Without help from the progressives, we're toast." The admiral seemed to be considering something, then added, "I'm bringing *The Lilly* back to Earth. Things are stable now in Allied space. With the addition of the Meganaught and hundreds of new warships added to our fleet, we're a formidable force here."

* * *

Ricket put out a general hail to the two colossal Crystal City vessels sitting three thousand miles off the *Minian*'s starboard beam. The two colossal-sized vessels, well over thirteen miles in length, continued to fire upon the *Minian*. If anything, they had increased their onslaught of plasma fire.

Traveler, standing beside the command chair where Ricket sat, huffed: "Why not return fire? Why do we simply sit here like a submissive cow, waiting to be mounted?"

"That's something for the admiral to decide when he returns. For the time being, our primary objective is to ensure that Captain Reynolds, and the away team, can pair up the remaining drones—without that, Earth will remain in flux."

"I look forward to the admiral's return then; perhaps he has sufficient-sized testicles to confront the enemy head on, like a true warrior."

Unfazed by the insult, Ricket climbed down from the command chair and headed out of the bridge. "Come on, let's check on First Reflection."

As on *The Lilly*, the *Minian*'s Medical was on the same deck level as the bridge. With the obvious exception of the *Minian* being far larger, closer in size to a Dreadnaught, the two ships had many similarities.

Entering Medical, Traveler and Ricket stopped when they saw the MediPod's clamshell open and First Reflection standing at the back of the room, in front of one of the tall glass containers. Standing before him in the clear liquid was an identical-looking rhino-warrior.

First Reflection turned and looked at Traveler. "What magic is this? My brother returns to the living. Why doesn't he speak? Is he in a trance?"

Ricket said, "That is not your brother, I'm sorry to say."

First Reflection turned back to the container and huffed, spraying a mist of snot onto the outside of the glass.

"I do not understand. He is my brother. His chest moves, he breathes; his eyes are open."

"That is a shape-shifting organism. They mimic the appearance of others."

"Then it mocks me. I shall destroy it."

First Reflection reached for his heavy hammer hanging from a leather thong at his side.

"No!" said Traveler. "It does not mock you; it honors you and your brother. Leave it be."

Ricket and Traveler exchanged glances ...Traveler said, in a lowered voice, "First Reflection was not the smarter of the two brothers."

Chapter 17

Jason, finally on his feet again, retrieved his weapon. He accessed his HUD multi-gun configurations menu and selected heat-seeking micro-missiles. He fired several times into both tanks. The resulting explosions knocked Jason and everyone else off their feet.

Playing nice was no longer an option. Jason communicated via his NanoCom for his crew to shoot to kill. Soon afterwards, the German soldiers were pushed back into the trees.

"Into the shuttle!" Jason barked as he ran up the gangway and into the *Magnum*. By the time he'd taken a seat at the controls, the last of the SEALs and the three remaining rhinos were also on board. Jason searched his nano-device database to see if he had the necessary updates to pilot the thing, but didn't find any reference to it.

"How hard can it be?" he asked out loud.

Billy, seated next to him, removed his helmet. Lighting up a fresh cigar, he urged, "Give it a try."

Based on what he'd seen Grimes do several times, and with his own knowledge from flying the *Pacesetter*, Jason got the shuttle powered up and its thrusters activated within seconds. Although the takeoff was a bit shaky, he soon had the *Magnum* elevated above the treetops and flying steady. Below, a crude dirt road cut through the trees. The halo navigation display showed multiple yellow icons, and two blue ones.

Billy leaned forward and pointed down. "There they are."

Slowly making its way through the trees was the personnel carrier. Jason switched on the targeting display overlay and fired multiple bursts—first, twenty feet in front of the vehicle, then twenty feet behind it. The truck came to a skidding stop. Two ten-foot-diameter craters, one ahead of them and one behind them, made it impossible for the vehicle to go anywhere.

The back gate of the truck opened and several soldiers emerged. Bringing their rifles up, they began shooting at the shuttle. Before Jason could return fire, another person climbed out of the open gate. It was Dira. The top of her battle suit had been removed and she wore a small tank top that highlighted the violet skin on her exposed arms. Preoccupied with firing on the *Magnum*, the two soldiers didn't notice Dira advancing from behind. She was holding a German rifle, trying to figure out how to work the bolt-action mechanism, when she gave up and swung the stock of the gun like a bat. One of the soldiers went down like a bag of rocks. As the second soldier spun around and pointed the muzzle of his rifle at Dira, Jason fired a plasma bolt. The German disintegrated. Dira looked up, shielded her eyes with one hand, and waved with the other.

"She's quite the little badass," Jason said appraisingly.

"Kicks ass and takes no prisoners," Billy added.

Jason landed the *Magnum* on the road directly behind the German personnel carrier. Men and rhinos piled out and made a defensive perimeter. Dira was attending to Grimes, who was still sprawled out on the bed of the truck. As Jason and Orion approached, Dira looked up.

"She's just now coming around."

Jason nodded and leaned in next to them. "That's quite a bump on her head. What did they hit her with?"

"A rifle."

Orion smiled. "So it's only fitting you returned the favor. You're a maniac—I'm going to start calling you *warrior* princess."

Dira lost her smile and glared back at Orion, not saying a

word. Jason wasn't sure what Orion meant when she said *princess*, and was about to ask when Grimes started to sit up.

"What happened? Where am I?"

Dira put a hand on her chest and gently pushed her back down. "Take it easy, Lieutenant. You've taken a bad hit to the forehead. Probably have a slight concussion."

Grimes brought a hand up to the lump on her head and moaned. "I take it you took care of the Germans?"

"Dira was a big part of that," Jason said with a smile.

Grimes looked out at the road behind them and saw the *Magnum*. "Who flew the shuttle?"

"I did. Piece of cake ..." Jason said.

"Next time you might want to lower the landing struts, Captain. Just a suggestion."

Jason didn't look. "Crap."

Dira helped Grimes sit up. Jason scooted out the back of the truck to the dirt road. He needed to find out what was happening on the *Minian*.

"Go for Ricket."

"Status?"

"Two Crystal City ships are firing on the *Minian*; no damage. We've been boarded several times and one rhino is dead. We now have all the phase-port accesses guarded by multiple hover drones."

"Have you returned fire?"

"No, Captain. We've just recently acquired access to the bridge."

"Any idea what they want, other than to destroy the *Minian*? Have you tried contacting them?"

"The boarding insurgents are definitely Caldurian, but they aren't the returning *Minian* crew. These are originals, coming from the Crystal City ships. As far as contacting them, my hails have not been acknowledged. And I don't believe they are trying to destroy the ship, more like disable her. We're getting hit with fairly light plasma fire."

"Ricket, we'll be moving after the next probe. I don't need to tell you the importance of you staying in one piece up there. The fate of the planet lies with our uniting the remaining drone pairs."

"Yes, sir. And also, Captain, I've spoken to Admiral Reynolds. As I mentioned to him, I think I know what happened to the *Minian*'s crew. It has something to do with Bristol's sudden appearance here on board the ship. It looks like he may have caused a multiverse time reference anomaly."

"So where's the crew now?"

"I believe they are here, but out-of-phase and residing on some other layer of the multiverse. One more thing, Captain: again, according to the AI, there is a high probability the originals have aligned themselves with the Craing."

Jason was quiet for several moments. If true, that could be catastrophic.

"You need to get this time reference thing figured out, Ricket. Find Granger. And talk to the admiral; request he bring *The Lilly* back to Earth."

"He's already made that decision, Captain. In fact, I'm seeing a wormhole spooled nearby as we speak."

"I'll check in later. Keep working on this time reference issue and find Granger."

* * *

Grimes, back in the cockpit, insisted she was fine and more than capable to pilot the shuttle. Jason sat shotgun and kept a close watch on her.

"I'm fine, Captain."

The shuttle rose into the air and Grimes throttled it up into the low-lying cloud cover above. "Next stop, South America," Jason said, turning to the passengers behind him.

Bristol was seated in the center seat closest to the cockpit, with Dira to his left and Orion on his right. Billy and his SEALs were seated in the rows behind them, with the remaining three rhinos standing in the aft cargo section. Dira stood up and Orion passed her the upper section of her battle suit. Jason's eyes flickered up to the curves of her body beneath her tight-fitting tank top. His mind flashed back to her identical naked shape-shifting organism on board the *Minian*. Catching himself, he brought his thoughts back to the present and turned his attention to Bristol. Like a small, snow-capped mountain range, a grouping of small pimples followed the contour of his chin.

"Bristol, Ricket believes when you arbitrarily phase-shifted onto the *Minian* it may have done something with the Caldurian crew, which is why they're missing. Perhaps some sort of out-of-phase anomaly."

Bristol looked up from the equipment satchel spread out on his lap. Seeming annoyed at the interruption, he looked over at Jason, shaking his head.

"No, not possible. Ricket's an idiot."

"Hardly."

Bristol shrugged. "Even if he's not an idiot, he's wrong."

"Explain."

Bristol pursed his lips and scratched at his chin with a bony finger. "Phase-shifting is extremely common, especially with a newer ship like the *Minian*. From taking a crap to moving between decks, phase-shifting matter is a constant occurrence."

He squirmed in his seat and scowled. "The only thing that could have such an effect is if the *Minian* was transitioning between multiverse layers when I showed up. The technology I used for my phase-shift device is somewhat different than the Caldurians'. My design may have lacked certain safeguards."

"So Ricket may be correct?"

"I don't know. Maybe."

"Can you work with Ricket and come up with a way to bring the crew of the *Minian* back?"

"Why bother? Seems like a pretty sweet ship. Keep it for yourselves."

"Just stay in contact with Ricket, okay? I want you to provide some constructive ideas ... work as a team."

Bristol shrugged. "Whatever."

"Captain, we're coming up on the continent," Grimes said.

Jason turned. Before clearing, the dense cloud cover had made it impossible to see anything. A blinking icon faded into view on the shuttle's holo-nav display. The contours of the landscape below changed from ocean to flatlands to mountains. Grimes brought the shuttle lower, decreasing speed. As the shuttle fell below the clouds a singular mountain peak reached up before them. Jason looked at his HUD's time-reference date: it was September 9. The year was 30,250,534, over thirty million years into the future.

Everything was black—nothing but scorched earth.

"No life forms," Bristol said, scanning his equipment. "No animals, no birds. Shit, not even an insect ... nothing. Welcome to the end of the world, everybody."

The interior of the shuttle went quiet as everyone looked out at the devastation beyond.

"There," Grimes said, pointing to a rocky outcropping ahead. "The drone's just sitting there out in the open."

As the *Magnum* approached the drone's position, Jason took in the surroundings. As if the Earth had been encased in a thick layer of molten black glass, the side of the mountain reflected the *Magnum*'s slow approach. The drone sat upon a plateau of sorts, its black housing blending in with the blackness of everything around it.

Sadness fell over Jason. Knowing that the world he knew would no longer exist millions of years into the future made him nostalgic for home. He thought of Mollie and then of Nan, and that she would never be a part of his world again.

"Captain, is there any reason we need to land?"

"No, I'll have Ricket dispatch the drone's pair. We'll be able to position it remotely from here."

Chapter 18

Gaddy finished winding a makeshift-bandage around her upper arm. Already soaked, it did little to stem the flow of blood. She leaned back against the large rock she'd been hiding behind to let her heart rate slow. She listened. Sweat dripped from her hair and into her eyes. She stood and peered around the smooth rock surface, back in the direction she'd come. Perhaps they'd found another prey to pursue.

Lightheaded, she leaned her face into the rock, absorbing the coolness leftover from the night's chill and thought back. At the start there had been four others. One had been a friend from childhood; the other three were fellow student dissidents. One by one, they'd succumbed to a violent end in this place Ricket called HAB 12. Two long weeks of running and hiding. The river of molten lava may have been the worst; Shakin lost his life there. But no, it was the relentless Serapins—they were definitely the worst. Pampel, Horsh, and, most recently, Stipp, were overcome and consumed by those ever-pursuing, remarkably hungry, giant blue Serapins. How she'd evaded them so far, she wasn't sure. The one energy weapon she'd brought with her was now completely drained of power.

In retrospect, Gaddy wondered if she shouldn't have pushed the others into joining her quite so hard. But the consequences of her not making the trek across this habitat would be far worse. The political climate had reached a critical stage; real progress was within reach. Breaking the bonds from a malicious dictatorship meant everything, not only to the youth of the Craing worlds, but to its mainstream populace, as well. What Ricket and Captain Reynolds had accomplished by killing Emperor Quorp and bringing down the Loop had started a chain reaction of unprecedented change within the Craing political system. For the first time, concepts such as freedom and democracy were more than just ideological abstractions. More and more of the Craing world citizenry were coming to understand that life could be different, perhaps even like some parts of planet Earth.

But that new hope changed in a matter of days. Seven massive, city-like vessels, crystal vessels, had entered Craing space. Advanced Caldurian technology was offered in exchange for the use of the Craing's far-reaching military strongholds sited throughout the universe. Together, they would be an unbeatable force. And the Caldurians would gain the numbers and might to stand up to their true enemies, the Caldurian progressives.

Looking back, Gaddy knew, even before Captain Reynolds and his team had reentered the portal, that she would someday need to reach out to them again. She had watched Ricket enter the ridiculously long code to open the portal. With her eidetic memory the numbers were still there for her to input two weeks ago, when her small team embarked on their mission into HAB 12. With luck, they'd be able to bring back help.

A distant screech broke the morning silence. She'd become very familiar with that sound and the dread it filled her with every time she heard it. The Serapins were coming, probably smelling fresh blood. Beyond fear now, she was almost resigned to the fact she would soon die, and join her friends.

As the sun climbed higher, so did the heat. She wiped her forehead and looked at the desert landscape before her. A flash. More like a reflection. Something metallic caught her eye. She estimated it was about a mile's distance away, but she'd already learned calculating distances here was tricky.

Two more screeches from behind, louder now. Without another thought, Gaddy took off toward the metallic reflection.

With a height of only three feet, average for an adult Craing female, Gaddy had a stride far shorter than those of her seven-foot-tall pursuers. Her only advantage was her head start. At a half mile, she heard them coming. *God, how many of them are there?* She ran on, not chancing a look behind, fearing it would slow her pace. With a quarter mile to go, she saw it. In fact, it was her own small utility ship, the same one she'd given to Captain Reynolds and his team to use so they could head back across HAB 12.

At fifty yards from the utility ship, the ground started to shake. There was a virtual stampede of hungry Serapins closing in on her from behind. She loosened the blood-soaked tourniquet on her arm and flung it over her shoulder. The thunderous noise stopped. Gaddy, so exhausted she wanted to retch, glanced back. There were six Serapins and two of them were fighting over the bloody cloth. As she reached the utility vehicle they were fast on her heels.

Outside the battered old vehicle, she entered the code on the well-worn keypad to open the mid-ship hatch. Nothing. The Serapins were running again, forty feet out, and picking up speed. Angered that she'd made it all this way to the finish line only to end up as breakfast for Serapins, she gritted her teeth and kicked at the small ship—once, twice, three times. Almost imperceptibly, she heard the internal actuators catch and the whirring sound of small motors. The hatch began to open. She squeezed through the opening and slapped at the red CLOSE button up on the bulkhead to her right. More whirling and the hatch began to slowly close. The Serapins reached the ship. Snapping jaws filled the narrow space, stopping the movement of the hatch. Saliva, long and stringy, whipped into the cargo hold and onto Gaddy's face. Angrily, she kicked out with every remaining ounce of strength she possessed. All six Serapins began to fight their way into the small opening. *No! No! No!* The hatch was opening, being pushed back in the wrong direction. Two Serapins got their large heads inside, only inches from Gaddy. Looking around frantically for something, anything, she could use as a weapon she spotted her old toolbox. Still kicking, she reached for the box and, one-handed, opened its small latch. They were pushing their way inside. Gaddy, without looking, clutched at the first thing she could wrap her fingers around. It was a wrench that had a sharp protruding angle to it. She swung it at the closest snout, ripping the flesh between its two flaring nostrils. Blood spurted, and the Serapin pulled its head back. This allowed the second Serapin to push in farther. She swung the wrench again, driving the pointed metal into its left eye. The beast pulled back screeching, taking the wrench along with it. Gaddy dove for the CLOSE button one more time—the hatch shut with a definitive *click* as it locked into place.

Gaddy fell back and fought to catch her breath. She stayed like that for a long time. Exhausted, she slept for three hours.

When Gaddy awoke, the utility vehicle was quiet. Midday light streamed in through dirty portholes and the cockpit window. Thirsty, she looked about the cargo hold for something to drink. Her arm sore, she moved into the cockpit and found a canteen. She shook it and heard the wonderful sound of sloshing water. With desperation, she removed the cap and drank deeply. It was warm and brackish tasting, but she drank it all and loved every swallow. Lowering the canteen, her eyes moved to the cockpit window. In the ship's far side shade, the ground was blue and alive. Easily a hundred Serapins were curled up next to one another, like sleeping dogs. Gaddy's heart momentarily skipped a beat—then began to pound faster in her chest. More Serapins were moving in from the direction she had come. Turning to the side window her expression turned from fear and frustration to one of hope. There stood the portal, glowing blue and wonderful, twenty feet from the ship.

There was no way she'd reach the portal before getting ripped apart by the Serapins. She moved over to the pilot's seat and contemplated her options. She had an idea.

"Come on, baby, start for me one more time."

Gaddy initiated the start function and waited. The vehicle shook as the thrusters tried to catch and ignite. They came alive and the dash controls came online. Smiling, Gaddy brought the small utility vehicle off the ground. Like a wave, the Serapins scurried to their feet outside. Angered and snapping at each other, they moved away from the heat of the thrusters.

Gaddy brought the ship around in a wide circle until the far side of the ship was butt-up against the portal opening. She brought the ship down to the ground and let out a long, slow, breath. Excited, she moved back into the cargo hold and peered out the hatch porthole. Sure enough, she was right up against the portal. She pressed the OPEN button and the hatch slowly slid open. Sunlight streamed in from the two- to three-inch gap between the ship and the portal. *Where was the keypad?* She looked from one side to the other and then remembered: the keypad had been moved several feet back, onto a pole. Disheartened, she let her own weight pull her back down in her seat. She sat there, looking into the portal, wondering how she'd be able to reach the pad safely.

Movement caught her eye. Something black, on the other side of the portal, rushed by—moving fast. There it was again, running in the opposite direction. Gaddy, back up on her knees, pressed her face up to the portal and peered through.

Chapter 19

Mollie couldn't stop laughing. Alice, her six-legged drog, was acting ridiculous. Uncle Brian and Betty stood at one end of the Zoo corridor, while Mollie stood at its other end. They threw Alice's favorite toy, a Frisbee. Full of teeth marks and barely able to fly, they'd been throwing the thing back and forth for twenty minutes. Alice never seemed to tire. Mollie was sure Alice smiled when she was happy.

"See? She's grinning."

From the far end of the corridor, Brian said, "You're crazy; animals can't smile. They're too stupid."

Mollie and Betty both laughed. "That's mean, Uncle Brian. Alice is smart."

Mollie's throw came up short and Alice leapt up and caught the Frisbee halfway between them. She lay down and began to tear and rip the plastic apart.

Mollie ran forward, shouting, "Stop that. Stop that right now, Alice!"

"Yeah, like I said. The animal's a real genius," Brian said, with a smirk.

"Be nice, Uncle—"

Mollie lost her train of thought. Standing before her on the other side of the HAB 12 portal window was a small woman. No, she was Craing. Dirty, sweaty and bloody. Mollie held out an arm and pointed.

Brian and Betty went to her side, both seeing what Mollie was pointing at.

"Gaddy?" Brian said. "I know her ..."

* * *

The Lilly emerged from the wormhole with her three rail cannons deployed. Ricket guessed she was already at general quarters and primed for battle. He watched as the sleek ship moved into position and fired onto both Crystal City ships. With her recent Caldurian defense upgrade, *The Lilly* was a formidable opponent. With the exception of the newer, more powerful *Minian*, few other ships would be able to best her in battle.

Admiral Reynolds' face appeared on a forward segment of the display.

"Ricket, what's your status?"

"No damage, Admiral. Multiple hails to the Crystal City vessels have gone unanswered."

"It's time to return fire; we need to get them away from Earth."

"Yes, sir."

Ricket targeted both ships and fired, continuously, with the *Minian*'s powerful plasma cannons. Within seconds, the two Caldurian vessels ceased firing and moved farther out into space. Moments later two wormholes had spooled and the vessels were gone.

"Ricket, I'm sending over a team to temporarily relieve you. There's something I need you to see. Make preparations to phase-shift to *The Lilly* immediately."

Ricket instructed Traveler and First Reflection to stay behind. He'd configured the two remaining drone pairs to be accessible remotely, allowing him to deploy them to Earth from *The Lilly*, if necessary.

He'd been directed to *The Lilly*'s Zoo, which was strange

in and of itself. Ricket phase-shifted to the Zoo's large, circular entrance area and spotted the admiral and several others halfway down the corridor. The admiral saw Ricket arrive and gestured for him to hurry it along.

Something was going on with the HAB 12 portal. It was darkened. Something was blocking the window on the outside. Ricket joined the group, composed of the admiral, Mollie, Betty, and Brian. He stepped in closer. Standing outside was Gaddy. She looked terrible. Bloodied, wearing ragged, torn clothes, she looked back at him with a curious expression.

"No one here knows how to open this thing," the admiral said.

"It has the highest-level security. Do you wish me to open it?" Ricket asked.

The admiral gave him an exasperated look. "Of course I want you to open it. Why else do you think you're here?"

Ricket moved over to the keypad and input the lengthy security code. *Beep, beep beep.* The portal window disappeared and Gaddy half crawled, half fell into *The Lilly*'s Zoo corridor. Ricket reached for her and helped her stay on her feet. She hugged him, pulling him into her arms. She held him close for several moments; Ricket was surprised at the amount of strength in her embrace.

Eventually, she stood back and looked up at Ricket. "Emperor Reechet?"

"Not Emperor. Not for a long time. But yes, it's me, Ricket. I've reversed the process commonly known as the transformation of life. Enough about me. What are you doing here? How did you get here?"

"For God's sake, give the poor girl a second to catch her breath, Ricket," the admiral admonished. "She needs time in a MediPod."

Gaddy shook her head. "Brian," she said, seeing him at the back of the group, "I need to speak to your brother. Where's Captain Reynolds?"

"He's on a mission. But whatever you need to tell him, I'm sure it can wait. Let's get that arm of yours fixed up first, okay?"

Gaddy swayed on her feet and Ricket moved in to hold her upright. "It's all right, lean on me." Together, Ricket and Gaddy walked toward the exit.

The admiral watched them leave, then looked down at Mollie. "What are you smiling at, birthday girl?"

"Oh, nothing. Just that it looks like Ricket has a new girlfriend," Mollie said.

The admiral grunted, "Perhaps. Seems like a lot of that is going around these days." He gave Brian and Betty a sideways glance before heading after Ricket and the young Craing female.

Betty, looking embarrassed, grabbed the Frisbee from Mollie's hand and threw it down the corridor. Alice took off after it.

Chapter 20

"Where to next, Cap?" Grimes asked. She pulled back on the controls and the *Magnum* rose up and away from the glassy-black mountainside. Two seemingly identical drone spheres sat side-by-side five hundred feet below them. Jason watched, still unable to shake his melancholy mood. Was it that the world he knew would no longer exist in thirty million years, or was it about death's seeming finality? Who was he kidding? What he really needed to do was come to terms with Nan's death. She was gone and there was nothing he could do to change that.

"Cap?" Grimes repeated.

"Sorry, Lieutenant. Guess my mind's somewhere else." Jason brought out his virtual notepad and projected the holographic image between them. He tapped at it and watched as the small representation of Earth slowly revolved on its axis. Five icons appeared; three of them were now light green. The remaining two icons, one in Asia and one in North America, still glowed a bright red.

The passengers in the rear compartment sat forward. "Looks like Montana ... maybe northern Wyoming," Rizzo said. "With luck, the next pairing will be as easy as the last."

Entering into thick cloud cover, the shuttle's interior darkened. Jason closed down his notepad and turned toward Bristol. A similar holo-representation hovered above the equipment on Bristol's lap. A red icon faded in and out several times.

"What's with the fading icon?"

Bristol didn't bother to look up. "The area here, what you

call North America, has nearly twice the number of fluctuating time realms. I wouldn't count on the next pairing being all that simple."

Jason sat back and watched the clouds outside. Bright white bolts of lightning branched across the sky, followed by three loud thunderclaps.

Dira screamed, "Did that hit us? Did we just get hit by lightening?"

Bristol's typically sour expression turned to a smile.

"What?" she asked, turning toward him. "That didn't scare the crap out of you?"

He shrugged, still smiling, and continued on with what he'd been doing.

Jason felt the shuttle's rapid descent in the pit of his stomach. As they broke free from the cloud cover, emerald green filled the landscape beneath them.

Jason turned again to Bristol. "We should be within a mile or two; can you pinpoint the drone's position?"

Bristol didn't answer right away. Jason watched him work. Somewhere along the line, he'd scratched at his now oozing chin.

"We have three time realms within a one mile circumference. I'm still waiting for more precise coordinates."

The shuttle, once landed, went quiet as everyone stared down at the holo-display on Bristol's lap. Two minutes elapsed and then it happened. For less than a second, the icon appeared and quickly flickered out. A moment later it blinked on at a slightly different location.

"It's either here or here ... not sure which one is a phantom reading," Bristol said, pointing.

"How close are we?" Jason asked.

"You got about, um ... maybe three or four miles in either direction. I guess this area is more unstable than the others. You found a good place to set down, Grimes," Bristol added, handing out a rare compliment.

"Pick one, Bristol," Jason said, starting to lose patience.

"I'd suggest we try this one to the west first."

"Then why not fly in closer—save some time?"

"Definitely not a bright idea. Drone's are already acting fidgety—better to sneak up on it. Increases our odds it won't bolt."

Jason continued to stare at Bristol for several beats. He slowly turned toward Grimes and nodded.

With the gangway extended, everyone grabbed their packs and equipment and moved into the warm daylight. Jason stood and turned to the pilot. "Grimes, again, you'll be staying with the shuttle. And Billy, we should have two SEALs, and one of the three rhinos to stay behind, as well. Set up camp with revolving sentries. Professor History, you're with us," he added to Rizzo.

"Cap, have you taken a look at the time-reference date?" Rizzo asked.

"Yeah, June 24, 1876. Is that significant?"

"Oh yeah. We're right dab in the middle of the western Sioux nation. My family visited the National Monument here when I was a kid. This is Montana. That water over there ... That's Little Bighorn River."

"As in Sitting Bull and Custer's last stand?"

"Yes, sir, as in the U.S. Cavalry versus the Cheyenne, Sioux, and Arapaho tribes."

Jason slowly turned three hundred and sixty degrees. In the distance were rolling hills with clusters of tall pines. The sky in all directions almost seemed charged, causing more of the wavering aurora borealis effect. "There's no one here."

"The battle's actually tomorrow. And I guarantee you there are eyes and arrows on us. We just don't see them."

"With luck, we'll be far away from here long before the fighting starts, and Custer gets his ass handed to him on a platter," Jason added.

Dira moved up to Jason's side. "Thought I'd see what the view was like at the front of the group."

Without warning, a maroon 1957 Chevy Belair station wagon appeared out of nowhere. Growing up in a scrapyard, Jason knew his cars. Traveling at close to sixty miles an hour, the car was several feet off the ground when it hit a nearby tree.

The sound of the crash echoed across the landscape. Startled, everyone crouched down low to the ground. Billy and his SEALs quickly moved forward and encircled the car. Steam rose from the crumpled hood. Two exposed bloodied heads were held fast, half-in and half-out of the smashed windshield.

Dira pushed through the SEALs and approached the car. "How do you get into this thing?"

"The door handle. Push the button and pull," a young SEAL, whom everyone called Scotty, said.

Dira tried to pull open the door, but with the car's body crunched, it only opened halfway. Scotty moved forward and with both hands pulled the door free.

Dira moved in and carefully felt for a pulse—first on the male sitting behind the wheel, and then on the female, who had been in the passenger seat.

Dira stood and shook her head. "They're both dead."

Bristol walked around the vehicle, still taking readings. "Now, this is cool."

"You think two people losing their lives is cool?" Jason asked, with a grimace.

"No, that's actually a bummer. But there's so many time realms around here, they're crossing into one another."

Jason turned, looking for Billy, and found him behind him

and to his left.

"Already on it, Cap. We'll dig some holes and put them to rest."

* * *

One hour later they were roughly heading in the direction of the fourth drone. Jason and Dira took point and had fallen into a fast-paced rhythm.

"Tell me about your family," Jason asked.

"Not much to tell. I have two sisters and a brother. My parents are still together. Everyone lives on Jhardon."

"Tell me about your dad. What's he like? What kind of work does he do?"

Dira's expression, behind her visor, changed. It was only for a second, but Jason caught it. Since Orion's earlier comment about Dira being a warrior princess, and catching Dira's reaction, he knew she was keeping something hidden.

"I don't know. He's just ... What does it matter what he does?"

"He's the ruling monarch," Jason said flatly.

Dira didn't answer right away, then looked over at him. "It's not something I want people to know about me. You'd be surprised how differently people treat you when they find out you are the daughter of a king."

"So that makes you, what? A princess?"

She shrugged. "This is embarrassing. I probably should have mentioned it somewhere along the line. But how do you start *that* conversation? Hi, my name is Dira Caparri; I'm from Jhardon; oh, and I'm a princess."

Jason laughed. "You are what you are. I wouldn't have treated you any different. At least I hope I wouldn't have."

Dira bit her bottom lip and then continued. “Before you ask, the reason I’m here and not playing princess back on my home planet is because of my mother. Three years ago I finished medical school. I was prepared to start my practice. My mother made it quite clear. It was one thing to get an education; it was quite another thing to embarrass the family doing that kind of work. A princess does not engage in something so pedestrian as doctoring. Before they could stop me, I ran away from home. I roamed around the Allied planets and several space stations, taking odd medical jobs here and there. But it was your father who helped me secure the Medical Officer position on *The Lilly*.”

“Have you been in touch with your family?”

“My father and I talk once a week. He’s working on my mother. On Jhardon, the queen is no less powerful than the king. The two are constantly at odds during the day, but somehow make it work—they love each other and, for the most part, are the epitome of the perfect married couple. My father thinks she’s coming around. He wants me to come home and make amends. He misses me and wants his family to be whole again.”

“Is that what you want? To go home ... perhaps be the princess they want you to be?”

“I definitely want to go home. But I’m not ready to play princess. I love what I do. I’ve built relationships on *The Lilly*. I’m not willing to give that up.”

Chapter 21

They trekked forward over several foothills and now looked down into a wide, expansive valley. What they saw seemed impossible. Like colorfully blurred curtains that reached into the sky, large areas seemed to be sectioned off, coming in and out of focus.

"There's 1957, Cap. Looks like part of a highway. That section to the far left must be from the future: there are some kind of weaponized droids moving about," Rizzo remarked, pointing, continuing his historical observations like a teacher on a field trip to the city's museum of natural history. "And there, all those tepees: that's a continuation of June 24, 1876."

"What's that fourth realm?" Jason asked, using his HUD's zoom to look at the furthest away time realm.

The others, using their zoom functions as well, didn't reply. Orion, standing at the back of the group next to the rhino-warriors, said, "No frigging way ..."

Bristol shuffled up to Dira's other side, on Jason's left. Finally looking up from his electronics, he said, "Um, maybe there's a way around that."

Jason continued to stare at the easily twenty-foot-tall beast. Unmistakably, it was a T-Rex. And there was another half-devoured dinosaur hanging from its massive jaws.

"It's eating a Stegosaurus," Rizzo chimed in. "See the large plates along its anterior spine?"

Everyone turned toward Bristol. Behind his visor, a sheen of perspiration was forming on his forehead. His fingers moved quickly over a small input device. After several expletives, some in a language Jason didn't know, Bristol glanced up, looking utterly defeated. "It's fucking right in the middle of that time realm. Wouldn't you know it? Right smack in the middle."

Billy had his visor up and was smoking a cigar. "No sense whining about it, Bristol. Hell, I'm sure it's no worse than fighting off a pack of Serapins. Right, Cap?" he asked Jason with a rueful grin.

Jason ignored the question and continued to look over the valley. "So, we need to make our way between cars on a 1957 highway; enter back into 1876 and go past Sitting Bull's campsite; then enter into some kind of futuristic land of droids; and, finally, go back in time sixty million-plus years to the Jurassic period."

Both Bristol and Rizzo nodded their heads in unison, neither taking his eyes off the scenes before them.

Bristol said, "From what I can tell so far the realms are staying fairly isolated from each other. But that won't last long."

"Let's head out," Jason said, taking the lead and walking down the rocky hillside. As he approached the bottom of the hill, he stopped and waited for the others to catch up. The rhinos were huffing; repeated bursts of steamy wet snot filled the air around them. Jason couldn't blame them. He felt trepidation himself. The first of the wavering aurora borealis-type curtains appeared a mere ten feet in front of them. Although somewhat obscured, every so often another automobile sped by. Jason stepped through the curtain and stood alongside a two-lane highway. Compared to modern highway traffic in the twenty-first century, this road was practically deserted. In the distance, a 1949 Buick approached. What looked like two full-grown elk were roped down onto its hood. Hunting season. As the rest of the team also stepped into the 1950s, the approaching Buick swerved and almost flipped. Obviously, seeing the battle suited assault team, not to mention two seven-foot-tall rhino-warriors, made an impression on the driver Jason was sure he'd never forget. As the car moved past, Jason saw inside a group of four young men, some maybe in their teens. Open-mouthed, their heads turned, looking back as they sped by.

Another car, an old forty-nine pickup, similar to the one that Jason's father was fixing up, meandered by. Oblivious to distractions, and obviously not aware of the fluctuating nearby time realms, the elderly driver never took his eyes off the road ahead. The team scurried across the road. They came upon a small parking lot and what looked like a diner. A well-worn, hand-painted sign reading *Grizzly Mo's* hung above the entrance. Apparently, this was a main attraction and the first stop into a small quaint town.

"Let's stay out of sight as much as possible," Jason said, continuing onto a smaller dirt road that ran parallel to the highway. Ten minutes later, cars approached them from two directions—both police cars. Jason noticed they were both 1957 Plymouth Belvederes. There was a similar '56 auto in his scrapyard back home.

"Don't shoot them," Jason said sternly. "I'm sure by now we have the locals a bit freaked out."

The shiny black squad car, a bright gold star on its door, skidded sideways to a stop. Its trailing cloud of dust hovered in the air, then slowly dissipated. The driver's side door flew open and a uniformed officer jumped out, pistol pointed in their direction. The cop was impeccably dressed; his creased uniform included a narrow black tie and a hat with a shiny shield emblem. Holding his weapon out in front of him with two hands, he yelled a commanding, "Halt!"

The second squad car arrived and another policeman, equally crisp and smart looking, jumped out and pointed his gun.

"Cap, I might be able to handle this," Rizzo said.

Jason turned to the young SEAL. "Are you sure? I want to avoid any trouble here."

"Let me try, sir. I have an idea."

Rizzo took a tentative step forward then stopped and looked back. "Dira, come with us."

Together, Jason, Rizzo and Dira slowly approached the nervous-looking cops. Rizzo held his hands up in a defenseless gesture, after first raising his visor, and smiled.

"Officers, my name is Timothy Sturges. I know this may look strange to you. Let me assure you, your town is not being infiltrated by aliens. Perhaps you've heard of my father, John Sturges? He directed *Gunfight at the O.K. Corral*."

One of the officers raised his head and looked appraisingly at Rizzo and the others in the group. "What, you're telling me this is some kind of movie thing?" he asked, not sounding at all convinced.

"That's exactly what this is. Your town's been selected to be the backdrop for the next big science-fiction blockbuster, *Asteroid Aliens*. Two months from now Kirk Douglas and Burt Lancaster will be wearing spacesuits, like these, instead of cowboy hats and six-shooters."

"So, um, these are what? Costumes?" the cop asked, lowering his gun several inches.

"In the movie business we call this a costumed walk-through. We're getting a feel for how these costumes will hold up on location. And, of course, our makeup, too. That's extremely important. You wouldn't want to see violet skin-toned paint dripping off a starlet's face, would you?" Rizzo asked. "Show him your makeup, Tammy."

Tentatively, Dira raised her visor and looked back at the officer. He holstered his weapon and took several steps forward.

Hands on hips he appraised Dira's face. She gave him one of her most-dazzling smiles and he smiled back. Her eyes flickered down to his name badge. "Hi, Deputy Sheriff Thom Duke. I'm Tammy Applegate."

"Impressive. Why, I'd believe she was an alien, all right. And a mighty pretty one at that!"

He gestured for the other police officer to put away his weapon and pointed to colorful curtain-like anomaly in the sky. "You have something to do with that, as well? Darndest thing we've ever seen around these parts."

"Nope. Nothing to do with that," Rizzo replied.

About to approach the rhinos, Rizzo held up a hand. "Please, I can't tell you how much trouble I'd be in if word got out about us being here in the middle of the day. The other studios are dying to get a glimpse of our special effects. If it's all right with you, we're going to head on back to our trailers and get out of this garb. My production supervisor will be in touch with your superiors shortly. But again, please, would it be possible to keep a lid on what you've seen today?"

With an expression somewhere between excitement and doubt, the officer eventually smiled. "This is going to be something, isn't it? I tell you, nothing like this has happened around these parts. Not since the Barnum & Bailey Circus rolled into town. Zowie! That was something; that sure was. Yeah, we'll keep this to ourselves. But when you come back to town, you look me up. You're going to need police support. I'll be your man."

"Deal," Rizzo said, extending his arm and shaking the officer's hand.

Both police officers returned to their cars. At the same time they did three-point turns and headed back in the directions they'd come.

Jason raised his visor and looked at Rizzo and Dira. "*Alien Asteroids*?"

Rizzo smiled. "Maybe I should have gone into acting, huh, Cap?"

Jason brought his attention to Dira. "Well, I know our own Tammy Applegate certainly has a new fan."

Jason continued to look down the highway and watched as one of the police cruisers disappeared into the distant horizon. Quiet now, but how long before the time realms start converging and ripping this quiet little town apart?

Chapter 22

Before leaving the realm of the 1950s, more and more cars turned down the dirt road. The cop's promise to keep things on the quiet side had been wishful thinking, but Jason couldn't really blame him. Hell, wasn't this even bigger than when the Barnum & Bailey Circus rolled into town? Hoots and hollers came from up ahead as an old woodie station wagon—packed tight with kids in the back—pulled up close.

An attractive woman behind the wheel, most likely one of the kids' mom, leaned out the window. "Is it true? You're making a movie? Here in town?"

No less than six small giggling faces appeared at the back window. Eyes wide, they watched the rhino-warriors as they huffed and puffed in their direction.

Jason raised his visor and stepped in close to her. "Well, that depends."

"On what?" one of the kids asked from the back seat.

"If we can keep this a secret." He held a finger up to his lips and smiled. The woman laughed and nodded. She stepped on the gas and they continued on down the road.

They left the little town and walked into the high desert terrain and endless clusters of dry chaparral. For close to an hour they walked before approaching the next time realm, indicated by another colorful curtain like anomaly. Startled, Jason stopped in his tracks as two galloping Appaloosas appeared before him. Barreling down, less than ten yards away, the two horses split up, veering around Jason and his team. Riding bareback were two red-skinned Native American warriors. Bare-chested and faces painted with white markings, they held bows in their outstretched arms, with arrows knocked and ready to fly.

The SEALs moved into a defensive formation with uncanny speed. Again and again, Jason had seen it, been a part of it. Whether facing an army of German soldiers, or two Indian warriors, SEALs were trained to the point where taking immediate action was almost instinctual—and more often than not, with lethal results. Jason pulled Dira down to the ground and, like the other SEALs, tracked the riders with his multi-gun. The warriors, both muscular and young, their long black hair flying in the wind behind them, shared the same bewildered, more like astonished, expression ... *men in space suits ... rhino-warriors*. Jason, preparing to relax, knowing bows and arrows would be ineffective against their battle suits, was suddenly surprised again.

Buffalo!

They poured through the wispy curtain in a thunderous blur. Jason watched as the men around him were bowled over like matchsticks. Then Dira, standing next to him, took a direct hit and was gone in an instant. When Jason saw the approaching herd before him, there was no time to move aside or take defensive action. Massive horns plowed into his chest area, propelling him up into the air, only for the same buffalo to hit him again as he landed ten yards away. After that it was just a matter of how long the trampling would continue. After several minutes, Jason realized he was going to live. He certainly felt uncomfortable, jarred for sure. But thanks to his battle suit, he'd be fine. Fewer and fewer buffalo legs were running past them, and Jason's thoughts went to the two rhinos. They didn't wear battle suits.

The buffalo were gone and only heavy dust and the distant sound of their running hooves remained. Slowly, Jason lifted himself off the ground. Getting to his feet, he wiped dust from his visor. Thankfully, it had closed automatically as the first buffalo approached him. Others were getting to their feet. *Where was Dira?*

"Everybody report," Jason said into his comms.

One by one, the SEALs checked in, but Jason stopped listening. He'd spotted Dira: her battle suit, smaller than the others, was unmistakable, and it wasn't moving. Rushing to her side, Jason fell to his knees and brought his head down to hers. Caked with mud and dust, she was almost indiscernible from the trodden dirt road around her. Carefully, he raised her visor.

Her eyes opened. "What ... the hell ... was that?"

Concerned, Jason stared back at her—then couldn't stop himself from laughing out loud, perhaps from sheer relief that she was alive. He started to laugh so hard he had a hard time catching his breath, and eventually he had to roll over on his back until the laughing subsided. He heard the others over his comms laughing as well.

Dira wearily sat up and looked around. Jason, remembering the rhinos, sat up and looked behind him. The two rhinos were standing, huddled together. Their voices were raised—they were speaking fast and obviously excited. Something about their behavior reminded Jason of teenagers. Yeah, excited teens after winning a football game. Four buffalo carcasses lay still around them. The rhinos, in the fray, had come out on top.

Billy stiffly came over to Jason and Dira. As he lit up a fresh cigar, Jason wondered if he had an endless supply of the stinky things.

"The funny thing is, Cap, we haven't completely made it out of a sleepy little town in the 1950s. Afraid to imagine what's coming next."

Jason nodded agreement at Billy and slowly got to his feet.

"Come on, Dira, we should probably look for Bristol." He held a hand out for her to grab. She took it and groaned as she got to her feet.

Chapter 23

Ricket stood beside the MediPod as the clamshell separated. Gaddy's eyes fluttered open and she turned her head toward Ricket.

"How do you feel?" he asked in the Craing native language of Terplin.

She thought about it for a bit, then said, "I've never felt better. Wow, I feel really good."

She sat up and looked around. "I don't remember coming in here. Is this a hospital?"

"Yes, it's our Medical department." Ricket held a hand out to her and she used it for balance as she crawled out of the MediPod.

"Are you hungry? Or would you like to sleep some more? There's a cabin ready for you."

"No, no more sleep, but I'd like to wash up. After two weeks in HAB 12 I feel totally disgusting."

"This way. I'll show you to your cabin."

Gaddy followed after Ricket. She still was amazed by his apparent physical transformation, from cyborg to an organic Craing being. He seemed a little stiff acting, but she guessed that should be expected. Plus, how old was he? Something like two hundred years. Ancient! But then again, he looked pretty good. *Really good,* actually. At twenty-two, Gaddy was used to getting attention from Craing men. She wondered if Ricket was attracted to her. *Why am I thinking about this?* She continued to watch him as they approached a cabin hatchway. He slowed, standing back, his hand gesturing for her to go ahead and enter first. Passing him, she smiled. *I don't think he looks that much older than me.*

After a quick tour of her cabin and how to work the shower and toilet, he showed her how to contact him, so they could later head down to the mess.

"I'll wait for you to contact me. Enjoy your shower." Ricket excused himself and left the cabin.

Enjoy your shower? Who talks like that? Gaddy smiled to herself and got undressed.

* * *

Feeling a thousand times better and dressed in a crisp white spacer's jumpsuit, Gaddy sat across from Ricket in the large mess hall. Starving, she'd piled her tray with as much food as it would hold. Ricket had confided he'd called ahead—spoken to the man behind the counter beforehand, someone named Plimpton. To her gleeful surprise, an assortment of popular Craing entrées had been prepared and were waiting for her to select from.

Without hesitation she dove into her meal. Too hungry to be self-conscious, she ate until she felt her stomach would burst. Dropping her fork to her plate and holding her belly, she looked across the table at Ricket.

"I'm sorry. That must have been unpleasant to watch. Disgusting, huh?"

Ricket smiled and shook his head. "No, not so bad." Smiling again he added, "Gaddy, the admiral would like to speak with you. He wanted you to get some food and rest—"

She stopped him: "Yes! Please."

Gaddy realized she'd lost all grip on reality. The whole purpose of rushing across HAB 12 ... Oh God, her friends had died to help her. Tears suddenly filled her eyes. "I'm sorry, I must seem like a childish twit. Believe me, there is nothing more important than bringing help back to the Craing worlds."

Ricket bussed Gaddy's tray over to a dispenser and they headed out of the mess hall. Walking at his side, Gaddy assessed him in her peripheral vision. She had many unasked questions: What does he remember, if anything, of his life as a former Craing emperor? What were his days like before that time? Wasn't he an inventor or a famous scientist? Where do his loyalties lie now—here with the Alliance or with the Craing?

They emerged through a DeckPort on Level Two and proceeded in silence. They turned left down an intersecting corridor and bumped headlong into Brian and the hopper.

Gaddy reacted out of instinct. She pulled Brian's sidearm from his holster and leveled the plasma weapon at the hopper's head. Eyes wide, her heart pounding, she tensed her trigger finger.

"Don't shoot!" Brian yelled, holding out his hands.

"What is that thing? What is it doing here?" she demanded.

Ricket moved between the two. "It's a hopper. He won't harm you, I promise."

The hopper stared back at Gaddy. His muscled legs tensed, his long claws protruded, looking ready to strike. His tongue slithered in and out in several rapid flicks.

"Hey, knock it off!" Brian barked, admonishing the green beast. "She's not here to hurt you."

Brian then looked back to Gaddy. "Lower that gun or he'll kill you where you stand. Do it now!"

"I've been chased by creatures like that for two weeks. They're monsters."

"This isn't a Serapin. Not even close. Put the gun down."

She lowered the gun and reluctantly placed it into Brian's outstretched hand.

"Sorry. I've lost some important people in my life over the last few days. I guess I overreacted."

The hopper seemed to relax and made a series of clicking noises. She watched as Brian faced the hopper, responding back in clicks and other sounds.

"You talk to it?"

"Yeah, I guess I do, kind of."

Gaddy looked at the hopper again but this time she made an effort to be calm. "I'm sorry. I overreacted."

The hopper turned his head, looking first at Brian, then back at Gaddy.

"Let's move it along here," came the baritone voice of Admiral Reynolds from the far end of the corridor. He gestured for Ricket and Gaddy to hurry up. Ricket waited and let Gaddy enter the captain's ready room first. She found the admiral sitting at the head of the table reviewing a virtual notepad. As they took their seats, the admiral looked up.

"Hello, Gaddy. How are you holding up after your HAB 12 ordeal?"

"The MediPod helped; in fact, I've never felt better."

She assessed the older man with the salt and pepper hair. He looked similar to Captain Reynolds, also handsome in a *human* kind of way. She had the feeling she could trust this man. She hoped so.

"That's good," the admiral said. "So let's get down to business. I want you to go over with me what is going on in the Craing worlds. You mentioned Caldurian vessels?"

"I have something for you, Admiral." She reached into her pocket and brought forth a small cube. "Many would consider me a traitor for handing this over to you ... the governmental regime, the military."

"What is it?" the admiral asked, looking at the object lying in the palm of her hand. The cube was small—no larger than a square inch per side, each of which was translucent and pulsated with intricate symbols and images, but nothing that made any sense to the admiral.

Excitedly she replied, "This is what—" Tears welled up in her eyes. Swallowing hard, she continued: "This is what so many people died acquiring, and then protecting. My friends Shakin, Pampel, Horsh and, most recently, Stipp all died in HAB 12 helping me bring this to you. It was Horsh who hacked the StratNET."

Ricket held up a hand. "Wait, what is that?"

"It's the empire's internal subnet. The only ones who had access to it are at the overlord level or higher, and high-ranking military officers. The StratNET's never been hacked; that is, before Horsh cracked it three weeks ago."

The admiral took the cube from her and continued to inspect it. He looked at Ricket. "We can read this?"

"Yes, sir, I'm familiar with the standardized Craing OS—their file structure is actually quite similar to that of the Alliance," Ricket replied.

"Gaddy, can you tell me what's on it?"

"You mean specifically?" She looked confused and shook her head. "I don't know ... exactly. Horsh repeated the phrase 'oh my God' about a thousand times when he saw it, though. At the minimum it will have military assets, Craing plans and strategies, information any of us would have been executed for if found in our possession."

The admiral raised his eyebrows, reassessing the importance of the small device.

"Were the Craing alerted that their network had been hacked? Do they know you have this thing?"

"Not at the time ... not when we first set off through HAB 12. I don't know about now. Perhaps."

The admiral looked at the small cube again and then back at

Gaddy. "First of all, you need to know that we—I—understand the sacrifice you and your friends have made to get this cube to us. Thank you. I also know you've done this in order to bring changes to the Craing worlds. Someday, you'll be remembered as a hero. Know that we'll do everything we possibly can to assist you."

He handed the cube to Ricket. "I need that converted as soon as possible. How long do you think it will take?"

"Two hours, sir," Ricket replied.

Gaddy watched the admiral's face. It seemed evident he was aware that what this small cube contained was extremely important. She watched Ricket place the cube in his pocket and wondered if she'd just handed over the fate of her people to the Alliance, just another empire, or truly opened the door to Craing independence—to freedom.

The admiral stood. "Let's meet back here in two hours."

Chapter 24

Apparently Bristol had been flung, kicked, or dragged fifty yards down the dirt road. His response to the buffalo stampede was similar to Dira's, although Bristol used somewhat more colorful language. Billy helped Bristol to his feet and retrieved the satchel, which contained the equipment Bristol used to hone in on the drones.

Jason, joining Bristol and Billy, said, "Best check it all over. Make sure it's still operational."

Bristol tore a clump of dirt from the top of his visor and turned in the direction the buffaloes had gone. "Not one of those furry fucking beasts missed the opportunity to step on me—and all you're worried about is the equipment?"

Jason kept his expression passive and didn't answer.

"Terrific. Just give it to me," Bristol said, ripping it out of Billy's hands. He went down on one knee, opened the satchel, and brought the familiar holo-display to life. It took several minutes, but the icon briefly appeared, flickered, and then was gone.

"Satisfied? The drone is still where it was before. Probably up one of those dino-gargantuous's ass. And that will be your problem."

Billy and Jason headed back toward the group. The SEALs had reassembled and the rhinos, who'd waited for them to head out first, were bringing up the rear. Still walking, Jason said over his shoulder, "Come on, front and center, Bristol."

Jason was the first to re-cross over into the 1876 time realm. The ground was trampled where the herd of buffalo had broken through into the time realm of the 1950s. A half-mile to their right was the Bighorn River. To their left, in the distance, was an Indian encampment. Dark smoke billowed up in the air above large teepees covered in animal hides.

"Let's try to stay out of sight," Jason said. "There's a line of trees by the river. Let's do our best to blend in."

Billy signaled for two SEALs, Rizzo and Scotty, to run ahead with him.

Dira asked Jason, "Where are they going?"

"Reconnaissance. Making sure there aren't any more surprises up ahead."

By the time Jason led the team to the trees, Bristol was lagging. Dira saw Jason's expression and pulled Bristol by the arm.

"Come on, grandpa, you have to keep up."

"Hey. Hands off, missy. My feet hurt."

Jason opened his visor and felt cool air on his face. He heard the sounds of the river rushing by and saw the largest rainbow trout he'd ever seen swimming near the shoreline. Jason was being hailed.

"Go for Cap. What's up, Billy?"

"You'll want to move ahead slow. We're, um ... There's a bear up ahead of you."

"Let me guess ... A grizzly?"

"That and a couple of Native American females."

"I don't understand."

"You'll see us in a few. Just ... take it slow. Don't want to startle the bears."

"So it's more than one bear?"

"Yes, I see you. Look to your left," Billy said.

Jason saw the three SEALs thirty yards ahead on his left. To his right, at the water's edge, were two Indian females ankle-deep in the river; one had her arm protectively placed around the smaller girl's shoulder. Between the SEALs and the young females was a family of grizzly bears—a mother bear, easily eight feet tall, stood upright next to her three medium-sized adolescent cubs.

Jason held up a hand to hold back the team behind him. The mother bear was already looking in their direction, undoubtedly curious about the rhinos. While everyone's eyes were on the mother bear, it was the largest of the cubs that sprang to the river's edge, tearing the smaller, younger girl away from the clutches of the older girl. Both cub and girl went into the river. The water turned red and in a blur the girl's flesh was ripped and torn. Her body went slack and submerged beneath the surface. Guns came up, poised to fire.

"Hold on!" Jason yelled.

The bears were now moving toward the other girl. She was sobbing and holding her arms snugly around her body.

"Cap, I can get to her," Rizzo said.

"Go ahead, Rizzo. Real careful like, though."

Two quick steps and Rizzo leapt, catching both the girl and bears off-guard. Rizzo and the girl went into the river, where the fast-moving current pulled them away from the others. But the too-strong current was quickly moving them along past Jason. Two rhinos, standing at the rear, rushed forward and waded into the water. They barely had sufficient time to grab them both and pull them to shore.

Up ahead, the family of bears quickly retreated into the trees. Dira was on the move toward the river's edge, where the mauled girl had gone under. She tried to pull the girl's body from the water, but the current kept a strong hold on her. Jason rushed to Dira's side and, getting a hand on the girl's arm, pulled. What was left of her arm came free in his grasp. Once released, the lifeless body proceeded to float down the river.

Jason let go of the mangled arm and watched it disappear beneath the surface. Dira was already running down the bank of the river toward the other girl. He heard her voice over his NanoCom.

"Jason, bring my bags!"

Jason looked around and saw two small medical packs at the river's edge. He retrieved the bags and headed downriver.

Dira crouched down to attend to the girl. Rizzo sat beside her. He had his visor up and was saying something. As Jason approached he realized the girl was actually older than he'd first thought, perhaps in her early twenties. She was watching Dira as she pulled several items from her bag and proceeded to clean and dress her wounds.

"How is she?" Jason asked.

"She's fine for the time being, but she'll need to spend some time in a MediPod."

Jason shook his head. "I don't think that's such a good idea."

The young woman was talking fast, as if pleading. Jason noticed she never let go of Rizzo's arm and had put all her attention on him. Rizzo nodded but eventually gently shushed her.

"Cap, her name is Chameli. She's obviously very scared."

"That's understandable, Rizzo."

"It's more than the bears, Cap. She's not of this tribe. She's not Lakota Sioux. She and the younger girl are both Cheyenne. Apparently they were left here. Meant to be taken. I don't really know the particulars."

Jason watched Dira finish up bandaging. The young woman was beautiful: her raven black hair fell to her waist, and her brown eyes were large and expressive. She started to talk fast again—trying to make some kind of point. Jason's nano-devices began to translate her words.

He held up a hand to her and nodded. "Everything will be all right. You are safe. Do you understand? You are safe."

Jason realized with the aid of his nano-devices, he'd just spoken Cheyenne. Understanding him, she nodded, and seemed to relax somewhat.

Jason stood up and looked past the trees toward the distant Indian encampment. A group of warriors on horseback were riding into the far side of the camp.

"Won't be long before we're discovered here," Billy said.

Dira stood and looked up at Jason. "I think we should bring her with us."

Jason shook his head, feeling unsure. "It could be several days before we're done with this mission. Too many dangers ahead—"

Rizzo smiled and interjected, "But don't forget, Cap, what tomorrow brings. Custer's Last Stand. Hundreds will die, many of them Native Americans. I don't think her odds are any better staying here. And remember, this isn't even her own tribe."

Jason knelt down again next to Chameli. "What do you want to do, Chameli? Before you answer, listen to me. We are not from your time. There will be things you don't understand. Things that you will think are magic ... unnatural. I believe you are better off here, but it is up to you."

"I come with you. With Rizzo."

Jason helped her to her feet. "Okay, here's how it's going to be. Rizzo, you'll phase-shift with Chameli back to the shuttle. She'll stay on board and Grimes can look after her. You report back here as soon as you can. You're relieved from watching over Bristol; I'll do that myself."

"Um, that's not such a great idea," Bristol chimed in.

"What's the problem?"

"Phase-shifting with so many time realms intersecting around here could be problematic. With the constant time fluctuations there's no guarantee you'll end up at the desired destination. It could be hit or miss. I wouldn't chance it unless it's an emergency or something. But you can do what you want."

Bristol was probably right. Jason thought about both alternatives and didn't like the idea of splitting up the team, sending Rizzo back to the shuttle. The time element was one thing, and it seemed there were too many risks.

Still watching the tribe in the distance, Jason said, "This isn't the best LZ to bring in another shuttle. Let's keep moving. When it's right, I'll have Ricket remotely fly in a shuttle to EVAC her back to the *Minian*. Rizzo, without a battle suit, she's extremely vulnerable. Watch over her."

Chapter 25

Jason turned as the last of the team entered 2214 A.D., a mere two hundred years into the future. The SEALs spread out, taking up a defensive perimeter position.

Before them were vast fields—endless crops reaching to the far horizon. Not wheat or corn, or any other crop recognizable to Jason. These were odd-looking: ten-foot-high purple stalks, with thick pink pods near their tops.

Wide swaths appeared in the fields as crops were cut down by hovering twenty-five-foot-diameter disks. Obviously drones, each disk was comprised of three razor-sharp, rounded, concentric segments. The segments, with a scissor-like action, were constantly spinning in opposite directions to one another. They were the cutting machines. Other drones, big and bulky, lumbered along on the ground, gathering and bundling the harvest.

Orion moved to Jason's side and raised her own visor. "Your planet looks a lot different in two hundred years. Organized harvesting. The air smells good ... the future's not such a bad place."

Jason didn't respond. Something seemed off-kilter here, but he wasn't sure what it was. In the distance a vehicle was approaching down a narrow road, some kind of long hovercraft. Jason signaled for everyone to move out of sight, get closer into the high stalks, and take cover.

"Everyone stay here," Jason said. "Billy, Rizzo, you're with me."

They headed off down one of the recently cleared swaths in the direction they'd spotted the hover vehicle. It took ten minutes for them to reach an intersecting clearing that led to the road. Jason had a problem getting a sightline; the purple stalks were too high to see over and trying to move between them was virtually impossible.

"Like a field of rebar. Can't believe we'll be eating this stuff in the future," Billy commented.

They reached the end of a cleared swath and Jason peered around the last of the strange stalk crop to the small road on the rise ahead. The hover vehicle was on the ground—it looked similar to a bus; probably used to transport day workers. He heard distant voices but couldn't make out the conversation. Crouching low, Jason signaled Billy and Rizzo to follow behind him. They scurried forward and, one at a time, ran up the rise, taking cover on the far side of the bus. Down the road, past the end of the vehicle, was another recently cut clearing. Still keeping low, they moved forward. Jason took a quick look down the swath.

"What did you see?" Billy asked

"Link to my helmet cam," Jason said.

He peered around the corner again, this time studying the scene a few seconds longer.

"Holy shit!" Billy said.

"Looks like eight of them," Rizzo said.

Jason didn't reply, trying to take in the implications of what he'd just seen. Yes, they were indeed day workers. But they weren't human, or even machines, for that matter. They were Craing. *Why would the Craing be tending fields on Earth?*

He had little time to contemplate further. He was being hailed by Orion.

"Go for Captain."

"Cap, we've got a problem," she said, sounding out of breath.

"What's up?"

"The disks, those hovering mowers. Well, there's a lot more of them now and there's no place to hide or get away from them. Hold on ..."

Jason started running back toward the team, with Billy and Rizzo close behind. In the distance, he saw the hover disks up in the air. At least ten of them. They didn't look to be harvesting. They were attacking.

"Orion, get to one of the cleared swaths where they've already harvested."

"That was the first thing we did! It seems they're coming for us."

Jason heard her rapid breathing over his comms.

Jason connected a comms channel to the entire team. "Shoot them, shoot them out of the air."

Plasma fire erupted from up ahead and two hover disks were instantly hit. Jason saw the closest of them falling, and it looked like it might land right on top of them. Not waiting, he brought up his multi-gun, quickly changed his HUD setting to tracking mini missiles, and fired. Billy and Rizzo, apparently having the same idea, also began firing mini missiles at the targets. Three hover disks exploded and were vaporized. The remaining disks, evading the same fate, had descended back down into the fields.

Led by Orion, Jason saw the rest of the team entering the clearing and running toward them. One of the rhinos was in the middle of the pack, carrying the young Cheyenne female, Chameli. Her face was taut with fear. Jason did a quick head count: Orion, Dira, eight SEALs, Chameli, and two rhino-warriors. *Where the hell was Bristol?*

Checking his HUD, Jason saw Bristol's life-icon located a hundred yards away. He was still alive, but definitely not moving.

The noise around them, like a thousand buzz saws, filled the air. The first of the hover disks to enter the opened swath was flying low to the ground and heading directly for Orion's team. Before Jason could raise his multi-gun, she fired and destroyed it.

Almost at once, four disks appeared from multiple directions, cutting new twenty-five-foot-wide swaths in the surrounding fields. As the disks broke into opened areas and sped toward them, the SEAL team reacted appropriately. Too close for missiles, they used rail munitions and shredded the disk mowers into burning slag. Still, half a football field distance away from them, Jason felt a sense of pride in how Orion, the SEALs, and the rhinos had again handled themselves in battle.

Jason watched as four new mowers appeared in the open area. Then two more mowers surprised the distant team by moving down on them from above. By the time Jason raised his weapon and took out one of the high-flying disks, the second one had descended on top of three SEALs. They were shredded to their knees, leaving only boots and leg stubs behind. As the disk rose up, Orion screamed something unintelligible and shot the disk into oblivion. The remaining SEALs and rhinos continued to fire until the last of the disks was destroyed.

By the time Jason, Billy, and Rizzo reached the others, Dira was attending to the injured. Orion, obviously angry, strode directly toward Jason.

"What the hell is wrong with our HUDs?"

It hadn't even occurred to him that those disks hadn't shown up on their HUDs. If they had, the three dead SEALs might have had a fighting chance.

"I don't know, Orion. The truth is, you know more about our battle suits than any one of us. At least any of those here."

She stared back at Jason, her anger dissipating. "This was a clusterfuck, Cap. Those boys didn't have to die."

"No, Orion they didn't."

Jason heard the now familiar buzzing sound in the distance. "Incoming!" he yelled.

Everyone crouched low, quieted down, and raised their weapons at the ready. Then Jason noticed the young Cheyenne woman. She lay shielded alongside the bulk of a protecting rhino-warrior. Her eyes were wide, not comprehending the horror she'd witnessed. Jason bet she regretted her decision to come along with them.

This was madness ... They'd only made it halfway to the drone. And they hadn't yet reached what would probably be the most dangerous realm of all, the Jurassic period. Jason thought about the two remaining advanced technology, nearly impossible to detect, drones. Was there another way, other than trudging along on foot like this? The shuttle instrumentation had proven to be far too inaccurate to be effective from the air. The best he could do was keep at it with Bristol's equipment and keep the shuttle close.

He hailed Grimes.

"Go for Grimes."

"Pack up. We need your help."

"Aye, Cap. Um, I'm actually at the controls now. The drone's position is not showing up at all. I've been trying to track your movements. With all the shifting time realms, I'm not getting a definitive lock on your position."

"Then we'll have to do it the old-fashioned way. I'll give you visual directions. But you'll need to move it we're under attack."

"Aye, Cap. Where do I head first?"

Chapter 26

It took less than five minutes for the shuttle to arrive—and not a second too soon, as more mowing disks were attacking. Although they hadn't suffered any more fatalities, exhaustion was setting in. As the *Magnum* came into view from the south, its dual plasma cannons easily eradicated the remaining disk mowers.

The shuttle hovered overhead and soon descended onto the open swath where Jason's team waited. Once on the ground, the shuttle's gangway lowered and the team quickly moved inside to safety.

"You ready to get out of here, Cap?" Grimes yelled over her shoulder.

"Not yet. Bristol's still out there somewhere," Jason answered, as he joined her, taking the passenger seat. He pointed to a blinking life-icon on her nav display.

"I see him." Grimes brought the shuttle up and turned her around one hundred and eighty degrees, and slowly moved her forward across the fields.

"There!" Jason said, pointing to a cleared section of the field. Toppled stalks covered the ground. "I think I see a leg."

Grimes brought the shuttle down nearby and lowered the gangway.

"Dira, you're with me," Jason said, moving through the cabin. She grabbed up her MediKits and followed.

Walking over the toppled stalks was tricky. Both Jason and Dira fell several times before reaching Bristol's location. They quickly started to pull stalks away from his body. Both hesitated.

Bristol wasn't moving. Face down, the back of his battle suit was sheared in several spots, as were his helmet, pack and rear end.

Dira leaned in and cleared more debris from around Bristol's helmet. Jason could tell he was still alive; his life-icon on his HUD still indicated strong life signs.

"How you doing in there?" Dira asked, peering into his visor.

"Oh, let's see. I've had spears flung at me; arrows shot at me; been trampled by too many buffalo to count; and now, nearly shredded to death by maniac flying saucers. I couldn't be better."

"Well, then, why don't you try to get up? You seem to be in one piece."

Bristol slowly moved. First one arm, then the other. Then his legs. Sitting up, he looked at Jason. "I quit. No more. I don't fucking care if you find those drones or not."

Dira stood. "He seems to be okay. At least physically."

"Thank you, Dira. Go ahead and head back. I'll join you in a few minutes."

She nodded, picked up her MediKit satchels and moved off in the direction of the *Magnum*.

"You're right. You've been through a lot."

Bristol shakily got to his feet and looked at Jason. "Damn right. Enough is enough. Get me back to the *Minian*."

"Well ... the truth is, I have no more need for your services. Now that you've quit."

"What's that supposed to mean?"

"It means you're free to go. Make a life for yourself. Good luck, Bristol. You'll need it."

Jason turned and walked several paces away.

"Wait, what the hell are you doing? You can't just leave me here."

"I most certainly can. Remember, Bristol, I have zero compassion for you. If it weren't for you and your brother, Nan would still be alive. You're lucky I haven't snapped your neck. Truth is, there was only one reason I didn't. You were useful."

"I'm still useful. For God's sakes, I'm the most useful person around. And how will you get close enough to the next drone? No, you absolutely do need me!"

"Look, I don't like you. I don't like your sniveling. I don't like that I just lost three good men—men who gave their lives for this mission, while you constantly dribble complaints. You're a self-serving little boy. And the truth is I don't trust you."

Jason continued toward the shuttle.

"Wait! Wait! Will you just wait one second?"

"What?" Jason barked back.

"Let me prove myself. Okay? I mean, I can't promise to be perfect or anything, but let me try. Come on, for shit's sake, I'm going to die out here!"

Jason continued several more paces, then, without turning back, said, "Find your equipment; hurry up, before I change my mind."

* * *

The mood on board was somber.

"Billy, I'm sorry. Those three were the real deal. The best of the best ... everything that being a Navy SEAL meant. McMillian, Brown, and Scotty were nothing short of stellar."

"Aye, Cap, that they were. So we owe it to them. We need to complete this mission."

Jason scrutinized those who were left. They looked like they'd been through hell and back. SEAL battle suits were gouged. Faces behind visors looked tired. The rhinos were showing the effect perhaps more than the others. Their hides were streaked with blood from deep lacerations—far too many to count. Rizzo sat in the back row of seats with Chameli sitting next to him, her arms wrapped around his arm. Meeting Jason's eyes, Rizzo smiled and looked confident. Gazing at Chameli, Jason was surprised to see she wore a similar smile. Perhaps she was tougher than he'd first thought. Off to their right Bristol was working away at equipment that looked as battered as his battle suit, with sections of the case sheared away.

"Equipment still work?"

Bristol looked ready to give him a flippant answer but seemed to catch himself. "It's not one hundred percent, but it's operational. I'll make it work, Captain."

Jason nodded, then caught Billy's eye. He shrugged and gave a look of surprise at Bristol's proper use of the title Captain.

"Cap, shall I lift off?" Grimes asked.

"Yeah, but I don't want to leave this realm quite yet. Let's take a look around here first. There's something we need to verify."

"You mean like this planet now being part of the Craing empire?" Billy asked.

All heads turned toward Billy.

The SEAL next to Billy, Petty Officer Chris Myers, glared. "That's not funny. Don't even joke about that."

"Unfortunately, it's no joke, Myers," Jason responded. "Let's just see what we see, all right?"

Grimes lifted off and kicked in the thrusters. Staying low, the *Magnum* moved across the fields and banked left over the rise, flying over the bus and the Craing day workers. Cresting a hilltop, a deep valley came into view where a modern, strikingly white city encompassed much of the valley floor. Towering spires reached into the sky where flying vehicles were circling like bees around a hive. Midway into the city, another great aurora borealis-type curtain rose into the sky. Like the others, this one too marked a separation between time realms.

"Stay on the outskirts and circle the city," Jason told her.

More city detail came into view. Jason felt a sinking feeling in his stomach. He'd seen this type of architecture before. But not on Earth. He'd seen it on Halimar. Halimar of the Craing worlds.

"Over there, Cap," Billy said, leaning forward and pointing a finger toward the far side of the city. "Looks like an airfield."

Jason gestured for Grimes to head in that direction. As they approached, familiar shapes came into view. Hundreds of spacecraft. They were, perhaps, of a more modern, sleeker design, but they were definitely Craing heavy cruisers. Jason used his HUD optics to zoom in on a group of people standing on the airfield. Sure enough, they were all Craing.

"Let's get out of here," Jason commanded. "Take us back, Grimes, on course to find the drone."

"Captain, over there—toward the curtain. That's the direction we need to go," Bristol said, looking up from his equipment.

A flash caught Jason's eye and he turned to see a ball of flame burst through the curtain. Two small crafts followed, one of them trailing smoke. Seconds later five large birds flew inside the curtain.

"Those are Pteranodons, Cap," Rizzo said, smiling from ear to ear. "They lived during the late Cretaceous geological period in *North America*. Look at their wingspan, it must be thirty feet."

"Looks like Craing City will be having some visitors," Orion interjected.

Jason nodded, watching the massive birds head for the circling aircrafts above. "Take us in, Grimes. Bristol, once we're clear of the curtain, get us the drone's rough coordinates as soon as possible."

Chapter 27

Quickening his pace, the admiral knew he was already late getting back to the conference room to meet with Ricket and Gaddy. More pressing business had needed attending to: business that was four feet and one inch tall; far more opinionated than any nine-year-old should typically be; and the most adorable, the most important thing, in his life. Mollie had been insistent. She wanted to continue with her self-defense classes, and with Orion away, that meant finding an adequate substitute. Apparently among the remaining SEAL security team personnel on board *The Lilly*, there was a close quarters combat instructor. Supposedly, he was a real badass. The admiral finally tracked him down in the gym, where he was going through his own unique form of calisthenics.

The admiral did his best to stand up taller and hold in his belly while he watched the SEAL complete the hundredth of his alternating leg squats.

Recognizing he wasn't alone, Chief Petty Officer Woodrow came to attention and saluted.

"Sorry, Admiral, I didn't see you there."

"As you were, Woodrow. Look, I'm late for a meeting. I need to know if you're up to providing a little combat training for one of the crew."

"Close quarters combat, sir?" Woodrow asked, already nodding.

The admiral assessed the tall petty officer. He wore a black tank top, and his arms looked thick and muscular, with prominent protruding veins running along the inside of his forearms. His broad shoulders made his waist seem ridiculously thin. The man was obviously a maniac when it came to physically conditioning his body.

"Yes, close quarters and weapons training. The gunny's already started her training, but, as you know, she's on a mission right now."

"You're not talking about the kid, are you?" Woodrow seemed to regret the tone of his question as soon as it left his lips.

"That kid happens to be my granddaughter, Mister."

"Sorry, sir. No disrespect intended. It's just that, well, I might not be the best person to help her."

"And why is that?"

Woodrow took an extra few seconds to answer. "I'm tough, sir. Hell, my training makes grown men cry."

"So you're saying you're too tough to train her?"

"Well, no, sir. Of course I'll train her. It's just—"

"For God's sakes, spit it out, man. What is it?"

"I don't train people to merely defend themselves. Not that alone. My training is nothing like she'd undergo at neighborhood Taekwondo classes. I train people to kill. As quickly and efficiently as humanly possible. My students learn to kill their opponent by any means necessary, including fighting dirty, if that's what's called for. Falling dead lasts a long time—I make sure that won't happen due to ill-preparedness."

"I can live with that. Expect to have classes every day. She'll be here in thirty minutes."

Woodrow saluted. "Yes, sir."

* * *

The admiral entered the conference room ten minutes late. Both Ricket and Gaddy were seated, as well as the XO. Perkins had been a last minute invite.

"First off, Ricket, who's minding the *Minian*?"

"Two rhino-warriors: Traveler and Second Reflection. Additionally, Admiral, there's an armed security force of thirty SEALs, and all portals are secured by armed mini-hover drones."

"Fine," the admiral said, taking his seat. Before he could utter another word, he was being hailed.

"Go for Admiral Reynolds."

"Sir, we've got new contacts in Earth space. There's an incoming hail for Captain Reynolds," Ensign McBride said.

"What are the contacts?"

"Those same two Crystal City ships."

"And who is it I'll be talking to, Ensign?"

"It's Granger, sir. I don't understand what he's—"

"Just hang tight, I'm en route to the bridge."

The admiral stood up. "We'll need to move this meeting to the bridge. You too, Gaddy."

As the admiral entered *The Lilly*'s bridge, he was greeted with the image of Granger's smiling face on the forward two sections of the wrap-around display.

The admiral nodded for McBride to enable the audio link.

"Hello, Admiral. You're looking a bit distressed. I hope I haven't caught you at a bad time."

"Drop the small talk, Granger. I need to know what's going on. Why are you contacting us from a Crystal City ship? Originals and progressives, from what I understand, don't play well together. Truth is, we thought you'd been taken with the rest of the *Minian*'s crew."

"Let me do my best to explain things, Admiral. It's far simpler than you may think. First of all, I like this particular thread of existence I'm on within the multiverse. This is my home. But my brethren progressive Caldurians? Not so much. Truth is, they haven't set foot here for hundreds of years."

"How can you say that? The *Minian* showed up in Allied space, fired on an Allied vessel, and is now sitting in Earth space."

"First of all, as far as the progressives are concerned, the *Minian* no longer exists. She was destroyed by a phase-shift anomaly, in a time and dimension far removed from this one."

"In other words, you've pirated the damn vessel to take as your own."

Granger simply stared back at the admiral.

"What the hell happened to her crew?"

"That's a bit more tricky to explain. To be honest, I'm not really sure. Many of the crew were accomplices, eager to start a new life here. The others, the progressives, who still prided themselves on being adverse to violence, well, obviously, they needed to be dealt with."

"You killed them? Killed your own damn crew!"

"No, not killed. Let's just say a few crewmembers will live out the balance of their lives on another plane of existence."

"And the others, your fellow pirates? Tell me what you've done with the *Minian*'s crew."

"There was a spatial time phase-shift anomaly. I know that's a mouthful. Basically, someone, or something, phase-shifted into the *Minian* at an inopportune time. Perhaps while the vessel was entering a wormhole, or when the ship was phase-shifting itself. There are redundant safeguards built into Caldurian technology, so I'm more than mystified."

The admiral knew in an instant. It was Bristol. Somehow, when he phase-shifted off that passenger liner ship of his brother's, he had adversely crossed paths with the *Minian*.

"So why are you still here? Why didn't you disappear with the rest of the *Minian*'s crew?"

"I wasn't on the *Minian*. Truth is, I was right there, on *The*

Lilly. Doing a little reconnaissance work."

"You were spying?"

Again no answer came from Granger.

"What is it you want?"

"I want the *Minian* back, isn't that obvious?"

"That's not going to happen. It's the consequence you pay for firing on an Allied vessel. Why don't you tell me about the agreement you've made with the Craing empire?"

"So you know about that? I'm impressed. Then you know you don't want me for an enemy."

"Seems that decision was already made when you fired on the *Independence* and befriended the Craing. You are an enemy, Granger."

The smile was gone and Granger sat up taller in his seat. "Think about the repercussions, Admiral. Where before the Craing needed days, often weeks or months to travel the universe, with Caldurian wormhole technology any number of their fleet, which I assure you are many, can now show up on Earth's doorstep in a matter of minutes. By this time tomorrow, Earth could be nothing more than space dust."

The admiral glanced around at Ricket and Gaddy, standing at the back of the bridge.

"I'm wondering, Granger. What would interest the Craing enough to make such a unilateral deal with someone like you? Perhaps turning over the *Minian?* All her advanced technology? The problem is ... You don't have possession of that ship—I do."

Granger's expression now turned to a blatant glare.

The admiral continued, "Now it's clear why you used minimal force when firing on the *Minian.* She wouldn't be much of a bargaining tool if she was shot to hell, would she?"

Granger's smile returned. "I've already passed on enough technical information for the Craing to be in my debt for years to come. Sure, the *Minian* is a marvel of technology, but she can't go up against five or ten thousand Craing warships. If you want Earth space to become that battlefield, then so be it. You need to ask yourself: is keeping the *Minian* more important to you than the welfare of Earth itself? We'll leave ... for the time being. You have twenty-four hours to decide."

Chapter 28

Mollie arrived in the gym wearing her new martial arts outfit. Orion had given detailed instructions, including Mollie's small-size specifics, to a garment replicator for processing. She was excited to see whom her grandfather had chosen to fill in for Orion. Excited and nervous.

Woodrow sat on the large, wall-to-wall padded mat and snickered as Mollie approached.

"It's not polite to do that. It's rude."

"Who's that?" Woodrow asked, looking at the drone.

"That's Teardrop. He goes everywhere with me."

"Why do you want this training so bad, little girl?"

"My name is Mollie."

"Tell me why, Mollie."

"I just do."

"That's not nearly good enough."

Woodrow got up and headed for the exit.

"Wait. Just wait. Okay!"

"Well?" he asked, slowly walking back to the mat and sitting down again.

"I don't want to feel helpless like that ever again."

"This because of what happened to your mom?"

Mollie didn't say anything, then tears welled up in her eyes. She quickly brushed them away and put on a fake smile.

"There's a price. There's something you'd be giving up; you know that, don't you?"

"Give up? What do you mean? Why do I have to give something up?"

"You go down this road, there won't be room for two of you. Not with what I'll be teaching you."

"Two of me? Okay, now I'm totally lost."

"I teach people to kill, Mollie. Not defend themselves. Not just fight. I teach people to kill before they themselves are killed. Look at you! You're too small, too young to defend yourself against an adult. So you'll have to be sly, have to be cunning, have to be totally ruthless and, most important, be unpredictable."

"I can do all that."

"You do that and you'll be giving up something in return."

Mollie thought about that for a while, met the big SEAL's eyes. "What?"

"Being a kid."

"Being a kid?" she repeated.

"Yep. Listen ... why don't you take some time to think about it? Maybe this isn't such a good idea. You should talk to your dad—"

"No! I don't need to think about it. And I don't want to talk to my dad, so why don't you get up on your feet and start teaching me?"

"All right. First, go back to your cabin and put on your street clothes. In the real world you won't have time to put on a special costume like that one. And you can leave your robot out in the corridor."

Mollie nodded and gestured for Teardrop to come along.

Before she got to the door Woodrow said, "When you enter the door again, you'll have eight seconds to try to kill me. Try to remember what is in this compartment that could be of use to you."

Without turning around, Mollie left the gym.

* * *

The admiral watched Earth from a large porthole in the captain's suite. He'd been staying there, watching over Mollie while Jason was on mission. His eyes moved to the *Minian*, a mere five miles away. He'd moved *The Lilly* closer to her after his conversation with Granger. *Anything happens to that ship and Earth wouldn't return to the twenty-first century*, he thought. There was no way Granger or the Craing could be allowed to get the *Minian* in their clutches. But sitting here, doing nothing, was only prolonging the inevitable. Bold action was required.

The admiral got to his feet. He walked down the hall and made himself a cup of coffee in the kitchenette. His mind was racing. An idea was brewing: *Could it be done?*

When the admiral entered the captain's ready/conference room area, he sat at the head of the table. Perkins, Ricket, and Gaddy were already seated.

"Let's start with the cube. Break down for me what you've discovered, what we can use."

Ricket glanced quickly at Gaddy and said, "The Craing do, in fact, have new technological information. Caldurian inspired, without a doubt. Everything from spooling wormholes, to nano-device technology, to more powerful weaponry, to broader MediPod specifications."

The admiral was about to say something when Ricket continued: "Upon closer examination, I've discovered that each technology offering was deficient in some way or form. Key information, information necessary to make the technologies viable, was missing."

"Smart, on Granger's part. Tease them with just enough data to hook their interest, but not sufficient to implement actual employment of the technology," the admiral said.

"There's something else," Gaddy interjected. "There seems

to be a layer of hidden code associated with the Caldurian's technical information. But with the proper software key, the missing information could become accessible."

"So both sides need to uphold some kind of agreement. The Craing want the rest of the missing technology, as well as the *Minian,* but what is it the Caldurians want?" the admiral asked.

"That's easy," Gaddy said. "They don't need riches, and they already have the highest level of technology. What they don't have is the one thing the Craing has more of than anyone else."

The admiral nodded. "Power."

"They're angling to take a big portion of the Craing Empire for themselves, would be my bet," Gaddy said.

"And what section of the vast Craing Empire has shown to be the most problematic for them in recent months?" Ricket asked.

"You're thinking of Allied space," the admiral answered. "But that's not part of the Craing Empire."

"The way the Craing view the universe, it is. There's *undiscovered* space and there's Craing Empire space. That's it; nothing in between," Ricket replied.

"Their never-ending grasp for complete control of space and power over the universe are what we and other dissidents want to change," Gaddy said. "They mustn't be allowed to continue."

The admiral nodded and thought about what his next move should be.

"Ricket, Granger seems able to come and go with relative ease. I need to ensure that he can no longer access *The Lilly*. Can you make that happen?"

"It's already been done. *The Lilly*'s AI monitors all port accesses—doesn't control it, but monitors it. I've set up a subroutine that watches for any non-typical phase-shift activity, as well as duplicate, or questionable, DNA attributes. As done on the *Minian*, we'll also need to instigate mini-hover drones at each portal access."

"Do it, at least until Granger is no longer a factor."

Ricket entered several keystrokes onto his virtual notepad. "Done."

"How secure is this room? Could Granger or some snooping-type devices be present?"

"No. This room is secure, Admiral."

"So then here's our situation as I see it." The admiral paused as if to collect his thoughts. "One, it is essential that the *Minian* stays in our control. Captain Reynolds' mission and the very survival of our planet depend on that. Two, Allied space is about to become the ward of a band of rogue Caldurian progressives. We need to stop that from happening. Three, the Craing Empire is very close to possessing additional technological capabilities that would make them virtually unbeatable. Advances the Allied forces gained over the last few months would quickly be stripped away."

Perkins squirmed in his seat and then held up a hand.

"No need to raise your hand, Perkins, what is it you want to say?"

"Won't the Craing hedge their bets? I mean, once they have all that tech, won't they take back Allied space anyway?"

"Of course they will," the admiral affirmed. "But Granger isn't dumb. I'm sure he's stacked the deck somehow. We'll just have to figure that one out as we go along."

Perkins, Ricket and Gaddy looked to the admiral.

"What's the best defense?" the admiral asked.

They all answered at the same time, "A good offense."

"We need to attack," the admiral said with conviction. "We need to attack the Craing worlds."

Gaddy sat up straighter in her seat, her expression showing concern.

The admiral shook his head, "We're not looking for conquests, Gaddy, we're looking to defend billions of lives."

Chapter 29

Jason tried twice to reach Ricket but couldn't make a connection either time. He turned his attention to the view outside the *Magnum*'s side window and studied the lush, tropical world below. The abundance of life was incredible. Grimes was flying low and waiting for directions from Bristol seated in the rear passenger compartment.

"Anything, Bristol?"

"I thought I saw something but it was gone too fast. I'm not sure if it's the equipment or the location, but everything's whanky."

"Would it help if we landed?" Grimes asked.

"Maybe. I don't know—this works a lot better on the ground. Wait! There it is! Found the drone. Change course to a northeast heading; continue on for one point four miles."

Jason turned toward Grimes. "You know the real trick will be finding a safe LZ. One misstep with a Brontosaurus and this shuttle is toe jam."

"No such thing, Cap," Rizzo said from behind him.

Jason turned around. "Why?"

"Turns out the dinosaur Brontosaurus was a case of mistaken identity in the early nineteen hundreds. The dinosaur you're referring to is actually called Apatosaurus. And that species died out millions of years before this time period," Rizzo added.

Jason glanced at his HUD's time-reference date: it showed September 28, 69.3 million years B.C.

"So what predators will we be dealing with?"

"T-Rex. Definitely T-Rex. Maybe velociraptors, but they

lived in a somewhat earlier period, the Cretaceous period."

"What period is this?"

"The Maastrichtian age of the Upper Cretaceous period."

Billy turned around and looked at Rizzo. "You didn't get out much as a kid, did you? I bet you had a killer rock collection, too, huh?"

"Actually, I did," Rizzo replied with a grin.

Bristol interrupted, "This is just about where the drone should be. We need to be on foot to get more precise readings."

Grimes said, "Well, there's no clear place to set down. But a mile to the north there's a rock formation. Maybe there." Grimes brought the shuttle lower, positioning it between several monstrous-sized sequoia trees. Hovering thirty feet above the ground, they slowly edged forward.

Jason, along with everyone else, was transfixed by what he saw outside. Colors seemed unusually bright, although a mist hung in the air. Condensation quickly formed on the large side porthole windows and front windshield. Grimes tapped a virtual key and the condensation evaporated.

Jason noticed Dira was smiling, her face pressed to the glass. Looking over to Jason, she said, "This is what my home, Jhardon, looks like."

As if on cue, a large bird struck the shuttle's side, causing the *Magnum* to drop several feet in elevation.

"But without the dinosaur birds; no dinosaurs on Jhardon," she added, and laughed nervously.

Jason's eyes lingered on Dira's profile for several moments longer. The smile was back, along with her almost child-like enthusiasm. She must have felt his stare because she slightly turned her head and gave him a quick wink. Jason smiled and wondered if people winked on Jhardon or if it was something she'd picked up from *The Lilly*'s crew. In any event, the effect went straight to his heart. *She's truly magnificent.*

Breaking through Jason's trance, Grimes said, "Trees are just too dense to land anywhere around here. And if this drone is like the others, it's found a secluded place to hide in."

"All right, let's find that rock formation. We'll just have to hoof it back here and hopefully go unnoticed."

That evoked chuckles around the passenger compartment. The shuttle rose above the treetops and headed in the direction of a rocky outcropping ahead. The trees thinned below and more indigenous life came into view, including a herd of Triceratops lumbering along a wide clearing. The shuttle's holo-display was alive with moving life-icons.

The approaching rock-faced cliffs weren't dissimilar to those they'd seen in HAB 12. Now, if they could only find similar, unscalable ledges or outcroppings to settle down on.

"Maybe that one," Grimes said, pointing to the right. She brought the shuttle in closer and hovered there.

"Don't think it's big enough. Plus, there's a ... what is that?" Jason asked.

"It's a nest," Dira said. "Oh, look, babies."

Something large blocked the sun and cast a shadow on the rocks ahead.

"Get us out of here!" Jason barked, but Grimes was already maneuvering the *Magnum* down and away. An agitated mamma Pterodactyl flapped protectively over her nest.

"Let's keep looking."

For close to an hour they moved along the rocky cliffs in search of a protected, open ledge to set down on. Spotting a likely few, they found the ledges either inhabited by Pterodactyl, or too small, or too accessible for other lurking creatures.

"Does it have to be on the cliffs?" Orion asked, looking out the opposite porthole from everyone else.

"What are you thinking, Gunny?" Jason asked.

"There's a medium-sized lake. See it?" she asked, pointing. "I don't know if this thing will float or not, but it may be something to consider."

Jason looked over to Grimes and raised his eyebrows.

It was Bristol who piped in: "Pretty simple physics: the shuttle is light, so as long as we don't take on water and we don't flip over, she should be pretty buoyant."

Jason thought about it. "Opening the back hatch will flood the compartment."

Grimes pointed to a rectangular seam at the top of the cabin. "Top hatch. Works like a sunroof."

"Let's give it a try. But be on the ready to quickly take us back up."

The shuttle moved away from the cliffs, crossed over a half-mile of sequoias, and hovered above a lake that was blue and remarkably clear. Jason kept his eyes on the holo-display. There certainly was abundant life below the surface, but nothing of ginormous size. Once Grimes navigated the *Magnum* to the middle of the approximately mile-and-a-half-diameter lake, she throttled back, hovering several feet above the surface. She gave Jason a questioning look.

"Go for it, Lieutenant."

Ever so slowly, she settled the shuttle onto the lake's surface. Jason sat up straighter in his seat so he could check out their watery landing from a higher vantage point. He looked out the porthole.

"We're definitely going below the waterline. Keep it going."

A moment later Grimes laid off the controls. "She's floating on her own, Cap."

Jason took another look. "We're sitting about two feet submerged. This might actually work."

Grimes spent a few seconds working on the holo-display. Eventually, the top hatch panel was unsealed and slid backwards, providing a five-foot square opening. Jason, his visor open, immediately felt the moist humidity in the air.

Orion was the first one up. "Let me, Cap," she said, already moving down the narrow aisle between the seats and scurrying toward the hatch. Using the back of the pilot's seat as a step-ladder, she climbed up and onto the shuttle's roof. A moment later she poked her head back in from outside. "Lots of room up here—seems safe."

One by one, they climbed up and onto the shuttle's fifteen-by thirty-five-foot roof. The three rhinos went last and it took them a little longer. The back of the pilot's seat couldn't support their weight, but eventually they muscled their way up and out using their own upper body strength. Jason went back below and brought up his and Dira's packs.

Bristol stood and faced in the general direction of the next drone's location. Without looking up, he asked Jason, "If you're having so much trouble with your communications to Ricket, how are you going to tell him where to send the drone's pair and give him the specific coordinates?"

"I've been thinking about that, too. What if I sent a NanoText message?"

Bristol furrowed his brow and finally looked up. "You know, that actually might work. If the message doesn't go through directly, it will buffer the data and keep trying until it times out. Why don't you try it?"

Jason didn't answer Bristol but brought up the hovering ocular keypad for NanoTexting, wrote a short message, and sent if off to Ricket.

Less than thirty seconds later Jason received a message in return.

Receive inbound NanoText: Science Officer Ricket:

Received message, Captain. This may be our best method for communicating while you are in that particular time realm. I will stand by for drone coordinates. Also, Traveler is requesting to rejoin your group.

Capt. Jason Reynolds:

That is fine, we could use his help. I'll send coordinates once I'm on solid ground.

Receive inbound NanoText: Science Officer Ricket:

Also, Captain. As soon as you have a free moment I'd like to bring you up to speed on developments here. *The Lilly* is back in Earth orbit. We've located Granger.

Disconnect NanoText Command: Science Officer Ricket.

Jason was about to inquire about *The Lilly*, as well as Granger. Two subjects that were, of late, constantly on his mind. But they would have to wait.

"Bristol, take a break and help the rhinos with their phase-shift coordinates. But first, see that wide beach area?" Jason asked, pointing across the lake. "Would that put us in a good position for moving toward the drone?"

"That'll work. They don't know how to set their own coordinates?"

"They might. I want you to double-check their settings. Matter of fact, set up the coordinates for all of us, link our belts, and we'll phase-shift together."

Bristol shrugged and went to work on the settings. Billy was at Jason's shoulder. "So much for having an improved attitude."

"As long as he does his job, I'm willing to put up with it."

Bristol was soon back and looked bored. "Done."

Jason caught Orion's eye.

"Aye, Cap?"

"I want everyone's weapons set to their most lethal rail-gun settings."

Although Gunny gave the appearance of staring into space, Jason knew she was accessing each of the team's weapons configurations, via her HUD, and making the necessary adjustments. "We're all set, Captain."

Jason gave a quick nod to Grimes, Petty Officer Chris Myers, and the young Indian woman, Chameli. All three were staying behind with the *Magnu*m. Chameli looked at Rizzo pleadingly, not seeming to understand why she was being separated from the young SEAL.

"Bristol, phase-shift us onto that beach," Jason said.

Chapter 30

Mollie had changed her clothes and was halfway to the gym when she stopped. *Did he mean my spacer's jumpsuit or my regular everyday clothes?* She looked down at her jumpsuit and shrugged. *Probably, this is fine ... this is what I usually wear.*

Teardrop quietly hovered along at her side. As they approached the gym entrance, she turned to the drone. "Stay right here, Teardrop. If I need you, I'll contact you with my NanoCom."

"I've been instructed to stay with you, Mollie."

"You don't go into the bathroom with me, do you?"

"No."

"You don't go into the mess hall with me, do you?"

"No."

"I'm only going to be a few feet away from you. Stay here."

Mollie hesitated before entering. Although it felt somewhat like a game, and she loved games, trying to kill someone was serious. *How serious was he?* She'd been racking her brain which items in the gym could be used as a weapon. There was a jump rope hanging on the back wall. There was also a set of dumbbells closer to the entrance—maybe the smaller one could be used to conk him on the head. But her mind was going somewhere else. She thought back to Chief Petty Officer Woodrow's exact words: "When you enter the door again, you'll have eight seconds to try to kill me. Try to remember what is in this compartment that could be of use to you."

He never actually said I'd have to use the items in the gym, only to remember what was there that I could *use, and that I'd only have eight seconds.* She thought about that some more and smiled. She entered the gym.

Woodrow was right where he'd been when she left, sitting on the mat with his back against the far wall.

"Eight seconds and counting," he yelled, getting to his feet.

Mollie stood perfectly still, as if paralyzed.

He continued the countdown, "Six, five, four ..."

Mollie moved to her left and Teardrop entered the gym. With less than a second to spare, a small panel on the drone's torso slid open, its weapon instantly deployed, shooting Woodrow where he stood.

It took him several minutes to come around. Mollie was sitting cross-legged in front of his prone body and waiting for his eyes to open.

He groaned and leveled one unfocused eye on her. "You wretched little scoundrel."

Mollie smiled. "Did I do OK?"

Woodrow slowly sat up and rubbed his temples. "Fine. You did just fine. I can see I'll need to be very explicit giving you instructions in the future."

"What is emlicit?"

"Explicit. I'll need to be more exact with what I mean."

Woodrow got to his feet and walked to another door. "Come on, we're going to work on your ability to throw things."

"I've got mad skills throwing a Frisbee," Mollie said, jumping to her feet and following him into the adjacent compartment.

She'd been there before, with Orion and her mother. This was the shooting range.

There were four long lanes. At the far end of each lane was a full-sized target holding the outlined diagram of a man tacked to it. The second lane's target was moved in closer, perhaps ten feet away, and its shooting barricade moved off to the side. A counter held a collection of five different items. Mollie stepped over and looked at each one carefully.

First was a regular knife, like a steak knife; second, an old fountain pen; third, a long piece of broken glass; fourth, a long screwdriver; and fifth, a scraggly piece of sharpened metal.

"What the heck are these for?"

"As I said before, you won't be able to fend off an adult attacker in hand-to-hand combat. At least, not until you've learned to fight dirty. You'll need to take advantage of the things around you." Woodrow stepped over to the group of five items and picked up the screwdriver. Without even looking at the target, he flicked the screwdriver underhand down the lane. Mollie looked around Woodrow to check the target. Dead center in the heart! She let her jaw drop and her eyes widen to show him she was impressed.

"I want to learn to do that!"

In a blur, Woodrow snatched up the remaining items and again, without looking at the target, in rapid order flicked the knife, fountain pen, glass shard, and sharpened piece of metal. Where the original screwdriver was seated dead center in the heart, the other four items landed in a perfect circle around the screwdriver.

Mollie simply stared at the target without saying a word.

"Okay, pay attention. This looks a whole lot more impressive than it really is. Practice is all it takes. Once you come to understand certain fundamentals, like an object's center of gravity; gauging an object's weight and the necessary force needed to throw it; and, most importantly, visualizing a target in your mind when you're not actually facing it, like you're in a room that's pitch dark, then tricks like these can save your life."

Woodrow pointed to the target. "Fetch."

Mollie retrieved the five sharp objects and brought them back to the counter. Woodrow picked up the screwdriver and flipped it around, end over end, several times in his fingers.

"Let's start with this. We'll begin with basic overhand throws, nothing fancy." Woodrow moved over to a cabinet and returned with twenty identical-appearing screwdrivers. The tips on them were slightly sharpened.

"Do you always hold the object by the blade?"

"Good question. No. You'll discover much of this over time, but it's all about rotation. Depending on your distance from the target, you may want to hold the object by the blade, or its heavier end, the handle if there is one. You'll come to instinctively know, based on how far you are from your enemy, and some other factors we'll get into later. For now, we'll keep things consistent. I want you to watch me throw these screwdrivers. Watch my hands, watch the position of my feet, and how I turn my body each time I throw—take it all in."

Woodrow positioned himself in a straightforward manner, one foot back, and one forward, at a line on the deck. He held the first screwdriver by its tip, brought it back over one shoulder and let it fly. Again, a dead center heart shot. Keeping the same slow methodical pace, Woodrow threw the rest of the screwdrivers. The target showed tight groupings in head, heart, and stomach.

"All right, you ready to try?"

"Yes!"

"Fetch."

Mollie removed the screwdrivers from the target and returned. She handed them to Woodrow and took his position on the line. He handed her the first screwdriver.

"Remember what I said. Nice and easy now."

Mollie threw the screwdriver. It hit the target handle first and bounced onto the deck.

He handed her the next one. "Remember, the weapon needs to rotate. I've found there's a full rotation per three meters."

She threw again and this time the tip of the screwdriver stuck in the target's upper thigh area.

"Oops, I missed."

"What you did is incapacitate a potential enemy. Good job. Again."

Three hours later Mollie was hitting the target consistently. Headshots went to the head; heart and lower torso shots too found their mark. Her groupings weren't as tight as Woodrow's, but she was feeling more and more confident.

Then he moved the target further back another ten feet and she started throwing once again. Nothing stuck and her aim was completely off. Frustrated, Mollie screamed at the target, "I hate you!"

Woodrow seemed to find that funny, so Mollie laughed with him. In time, she nailed the target with even more precision than when it was sited closer. By the end of the day, Mollie had practiced throwing all the items, some with better results than others. She'd come to a basic understanding of the principles involved. The steak knife was by far the simplest to throw and enabled her to hone her targeting skills.

"That's enough for today, Mollie. You did very well. Much better than my first attempts were at throwing sharpened objects. You'll come here every day and practice throwing these objects at multiple distances. Over time, you'll learn how to throw a variety of knives. Some you'll throw from the handle, others from the blade. As you've learned, it depends on where a weapon's center of gravity is. You understand?"

"I understand. And I'll be here, I promise," she answered, feeling a sense of accomplishment. She only wished, with sadness, that her mother could see how well she had done.

"I have a gift for you, in addition to the other objects you will practice with."

Woodrow went to the cabinet and brought back an item. It was a small knife in a dark brown leather sheath. "This knife is designed for throwing. It's very old, impeccably balanced, and forged of the finest steel. It's small enough to fit around your wrist or be kept in your pack, whatever. It's not a toy. It cuts through flesh like butter. Treat it with respect and it will last you a lifetime." Woodrow held out the knife and Mollie took it. Holding it up, she pulled the small blade from its sheath.

"The blade is light blue. Kinda pretty."

"Careful with that."

"I'll take good care of it. Thank you. Can I practice with it now?"

"Sure, for a few more minutes."

Chapter 31

*Adm*iral Reynolds was on the horn for the better part of three hours. Over the past sixteen years, he'd made friends and strong alliances with many of the Allied planets' ruling officials and military leaders. Above and beyond his command position with the Earth Outpost for the United Planetary Alliance—EOUPA—the admiral had retained his position as commanding officer for all Allied forces. With the latest Allied space victory against the invading Craing fleet, the admiral was heralded as nothing short of a hero. The reali*ty was the wa*r was far from over. In fact, they'd inflicted little damage to the Craing's overall defenses. Sure, they'd struck a surprise offensive jab to the Craing's military machine, but not enough to bring them to their knees.

Recent *estim*ates ran as high as one hundred thousand to one hundred and fifty thousand Craing warships in fleets spread across the universe. Every day, new Craing warships embarked from orbital shipyards situated far out in deep space, ensuring them of no single location of vulnerability.

But, as the admiral had quickly realized, Allied complacency had already set in. It was taking more time than he'd planned on, but slowly he was getting the Allied forces to awaken to the chilling reality of their situation. Added to that, the prospect of the Craing acquiring the latest Caldurian technology, as the admiral warned them would assuredly happen, sparked new fear in *those* in power of the Allied planets. What he'd been driving into their heads was that their new reality demanded quick action. It demanded they go quickly on the offensive. From their latest reactions, they were ready.

The ball was in the admiral's court. But before any kind of preemptive attack could be instigated, he needed more intelligence. Specifically, he needed to know what Granger, and the Craing leadership, was planning. And he needed to know if the Craing and Caldurians had vulnerabilities, and what those were ... if any.

A familiar melodic chime indicated there was someone at the captain's ready room door.

Without getting up, the admiral instructed the AI to allow entrance.

"Admiral, we have a situation," Ricket said, entering the ready room.

"Have a seat. What's going on?"

"I've been getting acquainted with the Minian's bridge, her functionality and capabilities. There's still much to learn. But while I was reviewing the various sensor settings, specifically the short range scans, let me tell you, the levels of sensitivity are really quite—"

"Ricket, for God's sake you need to get to the point."

"Yes, sir. I found something."

"Here, in local Earth space?"

"Closer to Mars, actually. It's a ship, drifting, and she's cloaked."

The admiral stared at Ricket for a moment and then nodded. "I bet I know which ship that is. It's the, um, Her Majesty. That ridiculous luxury liner turned warship. We were wondering what happened to the late Captain Stalls' ship. We knew it was cloaked and out there ... somewhere."

"Truth is," Ricket continued, "I found it by accident. Even the Minian had a hard time detecting her."

The admiral was only half listening to Ricket. His mind was

already contemplating the possibilities. The ship could be just the thing he was looking for. A way to get close-in to the Craing undetected.

"Ricket. Here's what I want you to do and with all haste. Put together a boarding party and bring back that vessel."

"The cloaking device would need to be deactivated, sir. Difficult, on a near-invisible ship."

"But possible? You could do it?"

"Admiral, I'm needed here to deploy the last two paired drones down to Captain Reynolds. As automated as I've tried to make things, I'd feel nervous getting too far away from the Minian."

"No, you're absolutely right. Earth's very survival is at stake. Who else could do this—get on board that ship and reconfigure her cloaking device?"

Ricket looked at the admiral and made a sour expression. "Well, there's really only one person. That would be Bristol."

The admiral's expression turned equally sour. "That pimply kid? I thought he was one of the pirates?"

"He is, was ... He's currently down on Earth assisting with navigating through the various time realms. As unpleasant as he is, he's quite intelligent and he already knows the configuration and operation of Her Majesty."

"Okay, here's what we'll do. You'll take Bristol's place on Earth. Send back Bristol, and maybe Billy or Orion; either of them could lead a team of the available SEALs still here on board The Lilly. We'll intersect with Her Majesty, and deploy Bristol and the team."

Ricket nodded and seemed to be contemplating the logistics of it all. "That still takes me away from the Minian. Although we have concluded, it seems, that data transmissions do work effectively, such as NanoTexting; I can pre-program the automated systems and control them remotely."

"Whatever, Ricket. I don't need to know how to split an atom here. If you feel it can be done with relative certainty, then we need to move ahead," the admiral urged him.

"Yes, sir. I'll get on it right away."

"Wait. Before you go, I want to ask you something."

"Yes, Admiral?"

"Undoubtedly, the plan would be dangerous. My thoughts are this: acquire that cloaked vessel, make her space-worthy, and equip her for wormhole travel. If all that is possible, I want a small team to take her to the Craing worlds. Since *Her Majesty* will be cloaked, she'll go undetected."

"I understand, Admiral," Ricket replied.

"That's not the difficult part, Ricket. Once you get back from the mission on Earth, I want you and Gaddy on that team. You'll infiltrate whatever meetings, discussions, taking place. As Craing yourselves, you shouldn't stand out. I need intel and I need it fast."

"I am somewhat recognizable, Admiral."

The admiral chuckled. "The way you are remembered by the Craing populace is someone who has undergone the transformation of eternity. You look twenty years younger now, and you also have a head full of hair, which you'll have to shave off. I think your true identity is relatively safe."

Ricket looked unsure. The admiral knew he'd loaded a lot onto his longtime friend. But Ricket needed to become more than solely a science officer; he needed to become a leader.

"Look, you'll have support. I'm going to talk to Brian. He's actually a fine officer, when he puts his mind to it. He can captain that ship, if you can lead the team."

Ricket nodded, his mind obviously spinning.

"That's all, Ricket. Get down to the planet, bring Bristol up to speed, and let's make all this happen."

"Yes, sir."

Chapter 32

Jason and his team phase-shifted to the middle of the beach. SEALs and rhinos moved into a defensive formation keeping Dira and Bristol in the middle of the pack. Undefined things were moving, scurrying about, up ahead deeper into the trees. A chorus of strange animal sounds filled the air. Jason felt as if a thousand eyes were watching their every movement.

Bristol, without looking up, held out an outstretched arm, with his index finger pointed toward the trees. "Drones in that direction. There's also another shuttle close by."

"Here? What do you mean—"

Jason cut his question short. His HUD now registered what Bristol's equipment had already detected. It was the sister shuttle to the Magnum, the Perilous. It did an overhead pass and landed a little farther down the beach.

Jason arrived as the rear gangway extended and settled onto the sand. Ricket and Traveler moved quickly down the ramp and hurried over to meet him. Standing at the top of the gangway, Lieutenant Wilson, the commander of The Lilly's Top Gun pilots, gave a quick wave.

"Good to have you back with us, Traveler," Jason said. "Ricket? What the hell are you doing here?"

"Yes, sorry, sir. Apparently even NanoTexting is hit or miss. I tried to contact you repeatedly and failed to receive a response."

"So how are we going to deploy the two remaining drone pairs with you down here?"

Ricket pointed to the Perilous. "The two drones ... They're locked down in the rear of the shuttle, Captain. Even if there need to be modifications to their code, I should be able to manage things from here."

"We'll want to move that shuttle out to the lake, next to the *Magnum*. Nothing's safe on the beach."

"Yes, Captain. Also, there have been other developments we were unable to communicate to you." Ricket looked over to Bristol, who had wandered over to the gangway and was peering into the stern of the shuttle. "We've discovered the vessel *Her Majesty* abandoned and adrift in space."

"Stalls' ship?"

"Yes. She's cloaked ... nearly impossible to detect. The admiral wants to board her and make use of her for a mission to the Craing worlds."

Ricket proceeded to update Jason with everything that had happened over the last twenty-four hours, including the arrival of Gaddy from HAB 12, and *The Lilly* being contacted by Granger, and his threats of bringing the might of the Craing Empire to Earth if the *Minian* was not returned to him within twenty-four hours.

Jason, musing over Ricket's information, felt his temper rise. He knew Granger was two-faced—he shouldn't have trusted him. Now, it seemed pretty obvious he'd been working some kind of self-serving angle all along.

"I agree with the admiral's logic," Jason said. "It's time we take the battle to the Craing, break the Alliance's constant cycle of playing defense and start playing offense. Okay, so we send Bristol back to *The Lilly*. Wilson can shuttle him back there in the *Magnum*; we'll use the *Perilous* to complete our mission."

Jason didn't want to lose either Billy or Orion, knowing what he and his crew might be going up against shortly. In the end, he selected Orion to head back with Bristol, and for her to later lead the mission onto *Her Majesty*. Bristol, all too happy to get away from planet Earth and the fluctuating time realms, handed over his equipment to Ricket. Orion gave Billy a quick hug and together she, Wilson, and Bristol phase-shifted over to the *Magnum* on the lake. Jason watched them appear on the shuttle's roof and then separately crawl inside through its top hatch. Next, Grimes and Petty Officer Chris Myers climbed onto the roof and phase-shifted over to the beach. Less than a minute later, the *Magnum* was airborne and heading toward the horizon.

Traveler joined the three rhino-warriors on the beach. They gathered together, excitedly relaying the events of the previous day. Jason headed out, taking up the lead, with Billy and Rizzo on either side. The other five SEALs took up perimeter positions, while Traveler and the other three rhinos moved into place, bringing up the rear. Ricket, several paces behind Jason, hurried to keep up as he balanced the awkward drone detection equipment that was strapped around his neck and hung down to his hips. Jason slowed and looked back over his shoulder, and caught Dira's eye. She smiled back at him, but then became serious. Her eyes had left his and were focusing on something in the distance.

Billy began yelling into his comms, "Multiple contacts approaching straight ahead!"

The ground came alive with what looked like small rodent-sized lizards—thousands of them running toward the beach. Their sound, like screeching, was near deafening, and Jason found himself feeling small bodies scrunch beneath his boots as he stepped along.

Trees whipped and jostled fifty yards up ahead, and according to what Jason's HUD readings were telling him, there were seven large contacts approaching.

"Take cover, we've got company!" Jason yelled over his

comms.

The rhinos quickly moved to the front of their formation, which was their standard practice, and held a line. Jason stayed low and watched Traveler race past him. With his heavy hammer tightly gripped in one hand, Traveler strode forward with amazing agility for a being his size. And something else: Jason had come to know Traveler's expressions and, beyond a doubt, he was smiling. This is where the big rhino most loved to be, in battle alongside his compatriots, who now surged forward after him. It was then Jason noticed Billy and Rizzo wearing similar expressions. And so did he, probably, for that matter. Feeling his adrenalin kick in, Jason straightened up and raised his multi-gun. The ground began to shake and the first of the fearsome beasts came into view.

"Holy shit," Billy yelled. "What is that? That's a T-Rex, isn't it?"

"Not even close," Rizzo yelled back. "I think that's a Nanuqsaurus. Distant cousin to the T-Rex. No, these guys are much smaller. Probably only a thousand pounds."

The three rhino warriors continued moving forward. None of them had drawn their plasma weapons, preferring to hold their ground with heavy hammers. Jason almost felt guilty anticipating which beast would best the other in battle. Especially since Traveler was a friend. There wouldn't be long to wait. Two of the seven dinosaurs, both walking on thick back legs, their heads bobbing up and down, tentatively approached Traveler—seeming almost like two large birds. But the analogy stopped there. Similar to their bigger T-Rex cousin, their heads were large, with ridiculously oversized jaws. When Jason got a glimpse of their huge upper and lower canines, the seriousness of their situation came to roost.

The two dinosaurs split up and approached Traveler from

both sides. Traveler wasn't going to play their game. He attacked. Spinning around backwards a full one hundred and eighty degrees, he let his heavy hammer build-up momentum—only extending his arm out straight at the last moment. The Nanuqsaurus to his right never had a chance. The business end of the heavy hammer blew through the creature's upper and lower jaws shattering both bone and teeth along its unyielding trajectory. Surprisingly, the dinosaur didn't die straight away. With much of its head torn away, it flailed its tiny upper arms, arms far too short to be of use for much of anything.

The second Nanuqsaurus attacked, its jaws opened wide and mere inches from Traveler's back when Jason aimed his multi-gun and took the shot. Not wanting to miss, or hit Traveler, two quick bursts of rail munitions tore into the dinosaur's hindquarters. The dinosaur's dead weight continued forward and plummeted into Traveler. Both fell to the ground—only one got back up.

The other rhinos charged. In less than a minute, the other five Nanuqsaurus were plummeted by heavy hammers and lay still on the ground. A new wave of screeching started up as the tiny lizards returned. Like a school of hungry piranha they quickly engulfed the two dinosaurs Traveler had killed. Soon, all that remained of both carcasses were bones. Angered, the rhino-warriors were quick to lift their own quarries off the ground, kicking out at the small predators who snapped at their feet.

In the end, only two Nanuqsaurus carcasses were saved. Jason wondered if eating dinosaur meat was such a good idea, but then remembered his internal nanites would protect him from any parasitic organisms. He also recalled that the feast served up by the rhinos after their battle with the Serapins was one of the best fireside meals he'd ever eaten.

Jason checked on Dira and Ricket. Both were fine—by this

point, almost immune to the sheer violence residing here. Long shadows stretched out along each tree trunk. Soon, evening would be upon them.

Ricket looked up from his equipment. "There is a clearing fifty feet from here, Captain."

"Lead the way, Ricket," Jason said, turning toward Billy.

"I want perimeter fires set up all around camp tonight. Keep them stoked. Two rhinos and two men together, on rotating watches. The last thing we want is a surprise visit by a T-Rex in the middle of the night."

Rizzo chimed in: "Cap, the latest archeological and scientific findings reveal it's the raptors that hunt at night—not T-Rexes. They're the ones we need to keep an eye out for."

They reached the clearing. A pair of rhinos moved into the open space carrying a Nanuqsaurus carcass as if they were handling a sofa. They dropped it, waiting for the second carcass to be similarly unloaded, while staying close by to fend off the small lizards.

Darkness was quickly setting in. Jason looked out at the surrounding forest.

"We'll need firewood. Lots and lots of firewood."

Chapter 33

Separate fires didn't work. The small lizards still entered. After some trial and error, the team simply encircled the camp with a continuous ring of burning fire. Although there was not an actual opening going in and out of the campsite, several areas had low enough burning fire barriers for them to easily jump over. In addition to their patrolling duties, sentry teams were constantly foraging close by for more wood.

Jason hadn't thought it possible, but the night sounds were louder than those of daytime. The campsite was filled with smoke, making it a necessity for them to keep their helmet visors closed. RCMs, Retractable Camp Modules, were clustered close together in the middle of the clearing. A central, larger campfire was now roaring and billowing smoke high into the air. Their seating consisted of a six-foot-long log, several boulders, and a large dinosaur skull. Ricket and Rizzo began talking animatedly between themselves, and Billy left to scout for more firewood.

Jason, standing to the side, watched the rhinos as they handled the meat. Like a ritual, the preparation of the meal was as important to them as the kill itself. The four rhinos talked, probably telling old stories, or recounting today's events. Although Jason couldn't hear what they were saying, their deep voices, more like murmurs, carried nicely across the campsite. It was relaxing and gave Jason time to let his mind wonder. He missed Mollie more than ever before. He wondered what she was doing this very minute and then remembered she had just celebrated her ninth birthday. With a heavy heart and a feeling of some guilt, Jason vowed to himself he'd someday make his absence up to her. But clear sudden insight told him Mollie wouldn't trade her life with anyone. The adventures she'd lived through the past year were one of a kind. Like her father, and her grandfather before him, she would probably find herself seeking out adrenalin-pumping situations the rest of her life.

Jason got up—he needed to move around and their encircling campfire would need refueling throughout the night. He strode off in the opposite direction and leapt over the fire's border into the darkness beyond. He reached down and picked up a thick branch, then gathered up two similar ones. Soon, both arms were filled. His stack rose to eye level.

Making the jump back over the fire was trickier with his arms full. He doled out his fresh stack of wood every twenty feet or so around the perimeter of the camp.

Jason returned to the same boulder he'd sat on before. Two rhinos were seated across from him, and two SEALs sat to his left. Platters of meat were handed out, and Jason accepted one from Traveler.

"Enjoy, my friend. The meat is tender and full of the rich taste of this wild place."

Jason accepted the platter of thickly sliced meat and placed it on his lap. Using his HUD controls, he raised his helmet's visor and took in the meat's rich aroma. No one used forks, or any other kind of utensil; for some reason, using one was an insult to the rhinos, who'd prepared the meal. Jason picked up one of the smaller cuts of meat, smelled its unique gaminess, and took a bite. Indeed, it was tender and had a strong woodsy flavor—which may have come from the smoke of the burning sequoias.

"Hey, Cap," Rizzo queried, taking the boulder to Jason's right and pointing to his plate, "How's the Nanuqsaurus?"

"Um, I'm not sure. The word *strong* comes to mind. Like venison, it's probably an acquired taste. So tell me, Rizzo: how on earth do you know so much about dinosaurs?"

"I've always loved anything to do with history, archeology, dinosaurs. I wanted to be a paleontologist ... you know, study dinosaur artifacts for a living. I come from a pretty poor family; I joined the Navy as soon as I turned eighteen. After my stint I went to college for four years."

"How old are you, Rizzo?"

"Twenty-eight."

"And what brought you back into full service, in becoming a SEAL?"

Rizzo held up a hand while he finished chewing a large bite. "You're right, this meat tastes kinda funny. I actually went back in the Navy when my brother got killed in Afghanistan. I don't know—guess I felt I needed to go one more round."

Billy sat down with a fresh cigar occupying a corner of his mouth. A platter of meat was placed on his lap by the rhino called Few Words. Billy nodded at the rhino and placed his cigar on a small rock next to his foot. After tearing off a chunk of meat with his teeth and chewing on it for several seconds, he spit the wad into the fire.

"This shit tastes like ass. Dinosaur ass."

Several of the rhinos glanced over at Billy, but apparently used to his peculiar sense of humor, they ignored him. Jason and Rizzo, on the other hand, thought his comment funny and had a hard time stifling their laughter.

Jason didn't immediately notice Dira and Petty Officer Myers had taken seats on the other side of the fire. Both had their visors up and were talking normally.

"Can you believe that sky, Cap?" Rizzo asked, looking up to the star-filled heavens.

Jason, and those sitting around the fire—including the rhinos—looked up. The stars were as bright as he'd ever seen them. Spectacular.

"Don't move. Nobody make any quick movements." The voice was Ricket's, and it was coming from behind Jason.

Taking his warning seriously, Jason lowered his visor. "What do you have, Ricket?"

"They look like birds, Captain. Carnivorous birds," Ricket replied.

Slowly, Jason turned around and faced Ricket, and the smallish creatures behind him.

"Acheroraptors," Rizzo said quietly.

"What the hell are they?" Billy asked, eyes wide and unblinking.

"Yeah, definitely, no one move," Rizzo said. "This species has only recently been discovered. Not Velociraptors; they died out long before this time period. These are Acheroraptors. Definitely not birds. They're highly intelligent little killers that hunt in packs. Probably think strategically, too."

Dozens of three-foot-tall, feathered birdlike lizards were moving in around Ricket; their snouts were long and snapping jaws revealed sharp, pointed teeth. There was a growling clattering noise as they surrounded Ricket.

"I don't know … those things really give me the creeps," Billy muttered.

Jason saw movement out of the corner of his eye and moved his hand closer to the butt of his sidearm. It was Few Words. The big rhino held fists-full of meat in his hands. Fearlessly, he strode into the throng of small carnivores and began flinging pieces of meat onto the ground. The raptors quickly went into a feeding frenzy. As Few Words continued to walk to the edge of the campsite, the raptors followed.

Few Words turned toward the stunned onlookers. "This would be a good time to stoke the smoldering fires." With several pieces of meat left in his large hands, he continued walking out into the darkness.

Jason was the first to his feet and running toward the dying fires. The others joined him and began throwing more wood on the fire that had been reduced to glowing embers. The ground shook as Few Words leapt back over the fire, landing into safety. Astonished, no one said anything for several beats.

"I can't believe you just did that," Jason said.

Few Words did his own version of a shrug. "Animals in nature can detect fear, also benevolence. I was not in any danger."

"Just the same, you may want to have our medic take a look at that leg," Jason noted.

Few Words looked at the back of his left calf and saw a stream of blood coming from a small bite. "They were just excited. It wasn't intentional."

Dira moved to his side and looked at the bite. "Let me at least clean and disinfect it. I'll get my kit."

As Dira jogged by Jason, her eyes met his for a fleeting moment and she smiled. Then she was gone.

Chapter 34

Mollie ran directly at Woodrow and then, at the last moment, let her body fall to the deck where she slid the rest of the way. Tightly gripped in one small fist was what Woodrow referred to as a nutcracker. Nothing more than a solid piece of rounded heavy steel, it delivered more than a little extra punch—especially when the punch targeted vulnerable areas: nose, solar plexus, throat, and testicles.

Mollie wasn't holding anything back. Punches needed to be thrown with everything she had, and for that reason Woodrow was wearing a padded helmet and a cup. As she slid and came to a stop between his feet, she maneuvered onto her side like Woodrow had taught her—perfectly positioned to fire off a strategic blow to Woodrow's most vulnerable area. She punched with everything her nine-year-old body had to offer. Purposely missing the obvious target, Mollie nailed Woodrow in the solar plexus.

He immediately doubled over, reaching for his gut. Through clenched teeth he spat, "You tricky little—"

Mollie wasn't done. Woodrow had spent a good hour showing her how to throw an effective uppercut. With Woodrow's head lowered, she just had to take the shot. She connected a solid blow to the side of his head, and saw it whip upwards and back.

"Damn it! Will you wait a flippin' minute?"

Smiling, she shook her head. "You told me not to show mercy. You told me to stop fighting like a little girl and go for the kill."

Woodrow, finally able to stand upright, nodded his head.

His grimace turned to a wary smile. "All right, let's move on. I think you've got that maneuver pretty well mastered."

Mollie's confidence level was bolstered up with every new trick and sly move Woodrow instructed her on. At first she'd felt guilty, as if she was doing something wrong; now she embraced what Woodrow called her *inner Wonder Woman side.* She'd been skeptical she would be able to inflict pain on an adult, but no longer. If she *used* her brain—didn't panic—she definitely could deliver ... what did he call it? Oh yeah, *a world of hurt.*

"What am I learning tomorrow?"

"I'm going to show you how to escape from various bonds."

"What do you mean bonds?"

"Like ropes, duct tape, plastic zip ties; anything that makes you a prisoner and unable to fight back. By the end of the day, you'll be a little Houdini."

"I don't know what that is, but it sounds like fun." Mollie handed over the nutcracker to Woodrow, who placed it back on a shelf in the cabinet.

"We're also going to spend more time at the firing range. You need to be a crack shot. Sometimes all you get is one chance. I want to make sure, even under pressure, you don't miss what you're shooting at."

* * *

Bristol watched Orion check her multi-gun, then move on from one SEAL to the next checking theirs as well. She acted different when she was in charge, away from the captain. Domineering. Not attracted to women in the slightest—never had been—Bristol found himself strangely bemused by the tall, highly muscular female. There was something primal about the way she moved. She made Bristol uncomfortable when she was close, but he wasn't totally adverse to it, either.

"Did you hear me, Bristol?"

"No. What did I miss?"

Bristol returned her stare and then realized he was the only one with his visor open. He closed it and looked around the shuttle's hold. Five SEALs stood at the ready, each looking back at him with an expression of contempt. *So what, they don't like me. I don't care.*

"I need to know you're paying attention. We're at *Her Majesty*'s forward starboard hull. You're clear on where we should phase-shift to, right?"

"Probably."

Two of the SEALs' facial expressions turned from contempt to out-and-out anger.

"Why don't you show some respect?" the larger of the two men asked.

Bristol glanced down at the soldier's name tag, *Carl Gibson*, and took his time answering. "I'm not part of your little army here, Carl. So why don't you back off; give me some room to think. Can you do that?"

Carl looked as though he was ready to throw a punch.

"Relax, Gibson, you'll get used to Bristol. It's just the way he is," Orion said flatly.

"Where should we go first? Once we're inside?" Orion asked Bristol.

Bristol glanced out the porthole to where the mammoth vessel supposedly sat. The brainchild of his brother, the late Captain Stalls, it had been a colossal job acquiring the toric-cloaking device. A large unwieldy thing, they'd pulled it from a wrecked destroyer drifting dead in space. Once the destroyer had been scavenged from stem to stern, *Her Majesty*, a converted luxury liner, was enveloped in a highly-conductive type of mesh netting, which was then tied to a phenomenal piece of technology called a toric-device. A device using black zodium crystals that could no longer be found anywhere in the universe, and couldn't be synthesized in a lab. Its only source came from a planet the Craing destroyed over a century earlier. Now, from off the ship, she was totally invisible. Bristol thought about his dead brother, who was unquestionably ruthless, a totally unscrupulous pirate, but still—he missed him.

"Bristol!" the gunny yelled.

"Yes, first the promenade deck. It's wide open; ample room for us to phase-shift into, without the possibility of landing on a bulkhead, or something equally dense," Bristol said, looking directly at Gibson. "From there we'll head for the bridge. Once we're there I can find the control for the toric-cloaking device and shut it off."

"If your coordinates are accurate we should be phase-shifting into the center of the compartment, several feet above the deck, just in case you're off."

"Whatever."

Gibson gave Bristol another sideways glance and shook his head. Orion relayed all of their phase-shift controls over to her HUD.

"On three, two, one ..."

Orion's team phase-shifted two feet above *Her Majesty*'s promenade deck. Everyone bent their legs anticipating the drop, but hadn't needed to.

"Looks like *grav* is offline," Orion said.

Bristol took back control of his own phase-shift capability and set its coordinates for the far side of the promenade deck. In a flash he was across the compartment.

"Come on, Bristol, we need to stay together," Orion admonished.

He waited for them to phase-shift next to him and then reached up to the bulkhead where there was an access keypad. A doublewide hatch slid open and Bristol pulled himself through it. Overhead lighting flickered, and between strobes of bright light, Bristol saw two bodies floating along the corridor. He thought he recognized them—at least, what was left of them. Decomposition had run its course. Their bloated, rotting faces looked more like wet, shriveled prunes than the tough guys he once knew.

Bristol held back, letting Orion and Gibson move ahead of him down the corridor, then jumped ahead of the four SEALs. As Bristol moved closer to the first body, he tried not to look at it; it was one of his brother's pirates. Like most of them, he'd worn a long ponytail, which now floated close to his distorted face. Bristol cautiously edged by the body and pulled himself forward in close pursuit of Orion and Gibson. But as Gibson moved past the second corpse, without a backward look, he gave the dead body a glancing shove, putting it on a direct trajectory toward Bristol.

It was too late by the time Bristol reacted. The dead pirate's body veered backward, spun around and floated headfirst toward him. Bristol grimaced as cloudy, vacant eyes bore down on him. Frantically, reaching for the bulkhead, anything to push off against, Bristol saw first the corpse's swollen face first, then its body, as it careened into his helmet. A wet, pinkish smudge splattered his visor. Disgusted, Bristol kicked out at the body, sending it rotating down the corridor in the opposite direction. Curses erupted from the SEALs behind him.

It took another thirty minutes for the team to reach the bridge. Bristol positioned himself in front of the nearest console and went to work running the ship's diagnostics. Apparently, the AI was only minimally operational, and there was substantial damage on multiple decks, many of them now open to space. *Her Majesty* was in worse shape than he had figured.

Within an hour, gravity had been restored and Bristol determined the massive drives would, in all likelihood, be operational soon, as well.

With the toric-cloaking device deactivated, more personnel were arriving from *The Lilly*. The bridge was filling up; crewmembers began situating themselves at consoles. Something inside Bristol found this more than a little irritating. The truth was, with his brother dead, the ship was rightfully his.

Three more entered the bridge: Brian Reynolds, the woman Betty something or other, and the hopper.

"How you coming along getting my ship operational, Bristol?" Brian asked, taking a seat in the command chair.

Chapter 35

No one got much sleep through the night. Even with their encircling fire barricade, the sheer size, the scale, of the indigenous animal life here necessitated that the fire be kept equally large. Apparently, the nocturnal predators were proportionate to, if not more abundant than, those of the day. As it turned out, anyone not on sentry duty was needed to add kindling to the fire and help keep it stoked.

The rhinos, without having protective battle suits, were showing the most wear. Monster mosquitoes the size of golf balls zeroed in on their exposed hides, resulting in painful stings as if from large hypodermic needles. Dira was in constant demand. The bites were bad enough, but the intense itching that followed was debilitating.

By 0600 all the wood gathered the previous evening had been burned.

"What time is sunup?" Jason asked Ricket.

"0640, Captain. The swarms of mosquitoes are already starting to dissipate."

Jason looked over to Traveler who, like the rest of the crew, was periodically firing stun-level plasma bolts into the surrounding trees. His hide was covered in swollen, oozing boils. Dira, having just finished treating Few Words, moved in to attend to Traveler.

Jason saw movement in the trees and fired off several plasma bolts in the same general direction.

"How am I supposed to light up with those damn things hovering around?" Billy asked, joining Jason and Ricket.

"Maybe this is a good time to quit," Ricket answered, looking up at the tall Cuban SEAL.

Billy ignored the comment. Noticing Jason's preoccupation with Dira and Petty Officer Myers, he said, "Look, a woman who looks like she does, who can even make a battle suit look sexy, is going to attract attention. Especially on a ship where the male to female ratio is so off-kilter."

"Are you getting to a point anytime soon?" Jason asked.

"Cap, it's no secret that you and Dira have something going on. Okay? Your own daughter sees it."

Jason's eyes turned toward Billy and glared.

"Hey, I'm just telling you how it is here, my friend. Anyway, um ... looking the way she does, she's had to turn men away on a daily basis. I know all this because she and Orion are friends, they talk."

"So what are you saying? Petty Officer Myers hasn't taken no for an answer?" Jason asked.

Billy shrugged and said, "She's a big girl, Cap. She'll speak up if she needs help."

A low-flying mosquito hovered in close to Ricket's visor, causing him to bat it away with an audible thump.

Dira was finished with Traveler, having applied ointments and salve over much of his exposed hide. As she headed off toward her RTM, sure enough, Myers followed not far behind.

Jason turned toward the petty officer. "Myers, we're breaking camp. I want you on task."

Turning to Billy, Jason said, "I want to get the next drone paired off and get us the hell out of Jurassic Hell."

Both Ricket and Billy answered at the same time, "Aye, Cap."

The two moved off in separate directions while Jason continued to watch Myers, who lingered outside Dira's RTM for a moment, then jogged off toward the others.

* * *

With the evacuated campsite now twenty minutes behind them, Ricket's best-guess estimate was the drone was about a half mile away. He and Jason continued to stare at the holo-display, waiting for the drone's icon to reappear. What came into view was a slow moving herd.

Jason leaned forward, using his HUD optics to zoom into the distant landscape. Sure enough, they were dinosaurs.

"What are those things, Rizzo?"

"Triceratops, Captain. There must be thirty or forty of them."

They approached single file, in a long line. Soon they'd be upon them and Jason nervously took in their girth—huge, almost beyond belief. Sure, he'd seen their pictures in books, their skeletons propped up in museums, but here, in real time, they were truly frightening.

"Perhaps we should get out of their path."

"Although they are believed to be fierce fighters, they're herbivores. I don't think they'll pay us much attention, unless we directly confront them or make a surprise movement," Rizzo said.

As the lumbering dinosaurs moved by, Jason and the rest of the team stepped several paces back into the trees to let the long procession pass. Each one had a large boney frill protruding upward behind its head, and three horns, not dissimilar to those on the rhino-warriors. As Rizzo suggested, they didn't seem to have an interest in them. Thick stubby legs trod forward, kicking up layers of dust. To Jason, their behavior reminded him of huge cows. Even their repetitive jaw movements were like cows chewing their cuds.

Few Words made a sudden shoulder jerk that turned into

an almost flailing motion. He quickly reached an arm behind himself to scratch one of his oozing mosquito bites. That was all it took to startle the closest of the Triceratops. It charged. Head low and horns pointed forward, it came directly for Few Words. Holding his ground, the rhino-warrior brought up his heavy hammer instead of drawing his plasma weapon. Jason brought up his own multi-gun but before he could get off a shot, Petty Officer Myers stepped in next to Few Words, blocking Jason's clear shot angle. Myers fired continuously but the massive beast kept coming. Spouts of blood erupted from its head and forward torso as mini-rail munitions peppered the Triceratops's hide. No more than ten yards out, Traveler and the two other rhino-warriors rushed in from the dinosaur's left flank. With one swing of its massive head, the Triceratops's forward horn took one of the rhino-warriors's head clear off at the shoulders.

Two more Triceratops charged. Jason pivoted and fired. Changing from rail to mini-missiles, the closest Triceratops's eye exploded in a plume of smoke. Its steps faltered and it came to a stop. Shaking its head violently, it turned and ran off in the direction of the other fleeing dinosaurs. Two crazed dinosaurs remained and both were out for blood, but heavy hammers swung and multi-guns fired until both triceratops lay still on the ground.

The four rhino-warriors went down to three in number: Traveler, Few Words, and the one called Born Late. Another SEAL was lost, as well—John Parker—leaving Jason, Billy, Rizzo, Myers, Chang, Goldstein, and Mead as the remaining Navy combatants. Dira and Ricket both survived and were attending to the injured.

This mission was taking a bloody toll. As the casualties added up, Jason was becoming more and more convinced that how they dealt with their enemies, the Craing and now this faction of the Caldurians called the Originals, needed to change. No longer could he and his father afford to hold back advanced technologies from their own government, fearing they would be misused or cause an imbalance of power among the rivaling nations on Earth. It was only from strength that Earth and the Alliance would survive. But first he and his team needed to be successful here—because in this realm of time, the Earth that was home didn't exist.

Both the SEAL's and rhino-warrior's remains were phase-shifted deep below ground. There was little time for any kind of memorial service in such a perilous environment.

The injured, attended to by Dira, included Myers. Apparently he'd been stepped on by a triceratops; his battle suit saved his life. But even battle suits had protective limits, and Myers had one, maybe two, broken ribs. Myers' internal nanites would repair the damage in hours, so it mystified Jason why he needed so much attention. The upper portion of his suit was off and Dira was wrapping his chest with a bandage.

"In ten minutes you'll be completely healed. It's just not necessary," Dira explained, sounding more impatient than she probably had intended. She finished up. She looked at Myers and didn't return his smile. "You're all set. Thank you for wasting needed medical supplies." She collected her supplies, stood, and strode off without acknowledging Jason's presence.

Jason watched as the petty officer's eyes leveled on her, tracking her as she walked away. He brought his attention back to matters at hand. With their latest round of casualties, everyone was quiet, introspective. Jason and Ricket took point, following in the rough direction of the last sighting of the drone icon. Jason took a quick look behind; everyone was on edge—heightened senses coincided with the violence of the land. Jason saw Billy in the process of lighting up.

"Not now, Billy. We don't need to announce our approach any more than we already have."

Billy withdrew the cigar from his lips and lowered his visor. Behind him Dira and Myers walked silently together.

Chapter 36

The following two hours were uneventful. Rizzo continued to share his knowledge about the late Cretaceous period as they passed by several small dinosaurs, a few odd-looking mammals, and various plant genomes and how they differed from today's varieties. Ricket was the most interested and never short on questions.

Ricket slowed as he accessed his locator equipment. "What do you know ... the icon appeared on the first try," he said.

Jason looked at the holo-display and saw the now-bright and steady icon. "Where is it? Maybe only a hundred yards out?"

"Yes, Captain, no more than that," Ricket replied, nodding; he continued to look at the display as if waiting for something to happen.

"If we're this close we should move on and get it over with," Jason said, turning away.

Ricket stayed still. "It's just that ..."

"What is it, Ricket?" Jason asked over his shoulder, now several paces ahead.

"If you look at the surrounding terrain, the drone appears to be close to another lake and some large life forms."

"Dinosaurs *are* large. We've certainly determined that," Jason shot back.

"No, these animals are of a whole different magnitude. And from what Rizzo has described, we're not looking at your everyday T-Rex, either."

Jason and Rizzo both fell back, rejoining Ricket.

Rizzo bent over and took a closer look at the display. "Well,

I don't know what we're looking at here, but during this period, the late Cretaceous, T-Rex was the biggest badass around."

"Why don't we just keep walking and see for ourselves?" Dira remarked from behind them, looking mystified.

"I agree, let's just go. Close that up, Ricket. We're almost there," Jason said, heading off into the trees.

As Jason led the team forward, the surrounding forest seemed to thin out. In the distance, he could make out the shimmering surface of the lake Ricket had mentioned. It certainly looked to be as large as the one the *Perilous* was currently floating on. *It might be a good idea to bring her here; closer to us, more accessible,* he thought.

Approaching the lake, only a few trees grew close to the shore. Jason stood and took in the picturesque view. The lake was large and blue, with distant snow-capped mountains off in the distance. Numerous streams and tributaries fed into the lake; one such stream was directly to their left.

"Now this is making me homesick," Dira said, smiling as she took in the postcard perfect view.

"I have a small cabin, probably not far from here," Myers said, leaning in close to Dira.

"Maybe in sixty-five million years you can show it to me," she replied, sarcastically.

Ricket assessed his equipment, nodded, and pointed to a clearing farther down the beach. "There, and inland just a bit, we'll find the drone."

"And those life forms you were talking about?" Jason asked.

"Also there. Although I'm getting readings from—"

Ricket's words were cut short by a disturbance in the water. It took Jason's brain several moments to wrap around what he was seeing. First, a long slender snout broke the surface, like that of a crocodile, although this one was of a massive scale. As the dinosaur continued to rise out of the water, it became apparent it was not a T-Rex. Dragon-like, the beast had a curved dorsal ridge of long spines along its back and was easily a third bigger than a T-Rex. The size of the thing seemed nearly incomprehensible.

"That's not possible," Rizzo said, astonishment in his voice. "What you're looking at is a Spinosaurus. There simply was no bigger dinosaur ... ever."

"And I take it that it, too, is carnivorous?" Jason asked him.

"I honestly don't know that much about the species, other than they lived both on land and water, and were supposed to have died out millions of years before this time period. It shouldn't be existing here!"

"No one make any abrupt movements. Let's let him go wherever he's going."

Standing like statues, the team had learned well from their previous encounter with the Triceratops. Jason took in the massive beast as it stepped out of the water and onto the beach. With every step, the ground shook. With casual glances downward and to the left, the Spinosaurus turned its long snout toward the team, standing still in the shadows of a few trees. As it disappeared into the tree line, only its moving head was visible.

Jason let out a sigh of relief and nodded toward Rizzo. "Let's hope we never have to see that thing again."

"Captain," Ricket said, "we may have to. Indicators show the probe is situated in that general direction."

"Yeah, of course it is."

Jason moved out in front and followed the large footprints into the tree line. He'd learned from experience it wasn't a good thing when the forest was this quiet. Bringing sudden attention to yourself when in the proximity of large predators was a good way to get yourself dead. The team moved with more speed than usual, and stayed close together. About to tell everyone to spread out, Jason came to an abrupt stop. He held up a clenched fist, and those behind him held their positions and crouched down low.

Jason spoke quietly over his comms. "Slow it down ... Tread quietly, everyone." The team moved further into the trees toward the commotion Jason had heard. Although the trees obscured much of what was going on ahead, something was happening on a gargantuan scale. As they crept closer, it became clear there was more than one Spinosaurus. Jason next witnessed something he wished he hadn't.

"Wow. There's been speculation for hundreds of years," Rizzo whispered. "I now have to admit, it makes perfect sense."

Dira, smiling, brought her hand up to cover her mouth and exchanged a quick glance with Jason. The ground shook and trees swayed. The team took in the violent scene before them. Obviously, it was the female of the two dinosaurs that was on her side, almost on her back—her long, sharp, fin-like spikes pushed off at an angle into the ground and away from the towering male above her. Her jaws were agape and tightly clenched around the male's thick neck. As he drove his seven-foot-long member into her, she tightened her jaws with each frenzied thrust. Blood flowed freely from his torn neck. It ended quickly and the male was off her and running deep into the forest before she had a chance to gain her feet. It was only then that the nest came into view.

Ricket pointed, but no words were necessary. Not substantially different from a typical bird's nest, other than its enormous size, the nest was circular and made from an accumulation of tree trunks, branches, foliage, and, surprisingly, other dinosaur bones. The six eggs seemed proportionally small, considering the size of the female Spinosaurus, now up and standing nearby. But what the team's eyes were transfixed on was the six-foot-diameter sphere sitting in the middle of the nest, as if trying to pass itself off as one of the much smaller eggs around it.

Dira was the first to start laughing. Her helmet obscured the sound from the outside environment and, fortunately, from the mother-to-be Spinosaurus. Soon Jason and Rizzo, followed by Ricket, saw the humor in the unlikely placement and started to laugh too. As if sensing their presence in the trees, the dinosaur abruptly looked down from her towering height to their low position. Already agitated, she took quick steps forward. Blood continued to fall from her mouth, and several large drops splashed at their feet. The seriousness of the situation brought Jason back to the mission at hand.

"We're going to need a diversion to get her away from that nest," Jason said. Both Ricket and Rizzo stared back at Jason with blank expressions. "Ricket, get that other probe prepped and ready to land here. I'm going back to talk to Traveler ... you hang tight here."

Jason waited for the agitated dinosaur to move toward her nest before scurrying back toward his waiting team. He saw Traveler's life icon position on his HUD and changed direction. He found him standing tall at the side of a large tree trunk.

"Captain Reynolds. You have witnessed a great thing."

"You saw the ... um ... situation with the dinosaurs, I take it?"

"Yes, Captain. It was unmistakable, of course."

"There's a dinosaur nest and an agitated mother who's ill-disposed to move more than a few feet away. Unfortunately, our sphere's right there, in the nest along with her eggs."

Traveler was nodding his head; Jason did not need to explain further. "We will distract this great beast. When she comes after us, you must act fast, Captain. We have never faced an adversary such as her. One so huge!"

Jason had seen this look in Traveler's eyes before. It was a look of eager anticipation. Challenges such as this one were what the rhino-warrior lived for.

Chapter 37

Brian was well aware what the new crew of *Her Majesty* was saying behind his back. Truth was, he didn't particularly care. He'd been walking the corridors of the converted luxury space liner for the better part of the afternoon. Bristol, shuffling along at his side, he guessed was harboring resentful feelings of some sort. Perhaps he felt the massive ship was still his brother's vessel, or Bristol felt *he* should be captaining the vessel for this next mission. *Ludicrous.*

Betty and the hopper walked several paces behind them. And that was another thing. Betty was getting more and more impatient to return to her own people, to go home. Well, that would just have to wait. Actually, he didn't mind having her around. She was different from the women he typically associated with. There was a quiet intelligence about her and she didn't make airs—didn't try to impress him, or anyone else, for that matter.

"So here's the toric-cloaking section of the vessel," Bristol instructed them. "Anything happens to this part of the ship, you're screwed. No replacement parts anywhere. This is one area where keeping the shields up will be imperative. You got that?"

"Yeah, we'll keep the shields up. Got it. What else do you have to show me?" Brian replied, sounding bored.

They passed three drones that were moving in unison, making repairs to a breached inside hull bulkhead. As Brian passed an expansive window, he saw that the admiral had brought over another few hundred warships from Allied space. *The Lilly* and the *Minian* occupied the center of the growing fleet's presence. Viewing all the vessels maneuvering here and there, Brian wondered why his father wanted him to lead this next mission. He certainly hadn't done anything to garner that kind of responsibility, in fact, just the opposite. Brian knew he'd always placed himself and his own needs well above those of others. Hell, he'd been working hand-in-hand with the Craing up until a few weeks ago. The money was great, over-the-top ridiculous. But it was having the freedom to be his own agent that had been the most compelling. So what had changed? Not only in the admiral's unfounded faith in his abilities, but in himself. Why had he agreed to take on the mission—a mission that held a strong possibility he'd get himself killed?

"Brian, he asked you a question," Betty said.

"Yeah, weapons. What about them?"

Bristol stood with his hands on his narrow hips and glared back at Brian. "What my brother intended to accomplish was to outfit a warship that could go up against anything in space. This ship was his ticket toward building an undefeatable fleet of pirate ships. What he didn't take into account was that much of the weaponry he'd pilfered from other ships was far from state of the art. With the admiral's help, we're now in the process of correcting my brother's mistakes and short-sightedness. Shields are being updated; new, more powerful rail and plasma cannons are being retrofitted. Added to that, with the toric cloaking device, *Her Majesty* should be able to hold its own against several Craing heavy cruisers. That is, if the *captain* is up to the task."

Brian let the dig go. He couldn't care less what the geeky kid said or thought.

Betty moved to Brian's side and spoke in a hushed voice. "What am I supposed to be doing while I wait for passage home?"

"What do you want to do?"

"I'm pretty good on comms or nav. Anything but tactical."

"Comms it is, then." They continued to follow Bristol down one of the ship's many long passageways. Betty nodded, looking down.

"Or Navigation. Whatever you want," Brian said, realizing she probably wasn't thrilled with either option.

"It's just that I feel out of place here. Not really sure what I'm—"

"You're here because you're my best friend ... Other than the hopper behind you, I've pretty much alienated everyone I've come into contact with. Listen, if you really want it, I can get you home."

She looked up at him and held his eyes. "That's the nicest thing I've heard come out of your mouth since I've met you. Why don't you ask me to stay? Not because you need the help, but because you want me to ... and I will?"

Brian wasn't used to this level of emotional communication, especially when it came to women. Women in the past who'd attracted his attention had always been paid for their time spent together. Again, someone was showing trust in him, and he didn't really know why.

"And as far as the hopper goes, you might want to consider asking him if he wants to be here."

Brian stole a quick glance over his shoulder toward the hopper. He wasn't there. Then, looking farther back down the passage, he saw the hopper squatting. *For God's sakes, what's it going to take to housebreak that thing?*

"I'll do that, Betty. And thank you."

She simply smiled and looked down the passageway. Bristol had stopped and was waiting for them to catch up.

"We're back at the bridge soon; it's only a little farther down the corridor. As the new captain, your suite is here," Bristol said, gesturing toward a double hatchway, with gold scrollwork painted above and on the side bulkhead. “It was my brother’s—”

“Hey, if you want your brother’s old quarters, have at it,” Brian snapped.

“No. The round bed and mirrored ceiling tend to make me want to puke. It’s all yours, Captain.” Bristol said the last word with enough disdain to show he clearly didn’t consider Brian captain material.

* * *

Admiral Reynolds chose to hold the Allied Forces officer’s conference on the *Minian*. Not only did the spaceship have an adequate-sized conference room, the commanders who were attending had been chafing at the bit to see the advanced Caldurian ship ever since they’d joined him in Earth space. Each of the major planetary system commanders was here. Not all were on board with the admiral’s decision to take a more offensive approach— first in dealing with the Craing, and also with the Caldurians. And that’s where Gaddy would come in. Young, and still full of piss and vinegar, she held the right kind of passion to get these old farts off their collective fat asses. If anyone could convey the seriousness of their current situation, he was hoping she could.

The conference tables were set up in a large U-shape. No one was placed in a position of importance over another. The admiral sat at the farthest end of the U and scanned the room. Those assembled were both male and female, representing the military might of their respective governments. It was a strange collection of aliens. Eighty-four beings in all had made the decision to attend: the Blues, the tall aquatic beings, in cocoon-looking environment suits; the moss-covered, earthy-smelling Knogs; even the Carz-Mau were represented. He recognized Ti, with her frightening open-mouthed grimace. Happy to see that she'd been elevated to the rank equivalency of admiral level, he nodded at her and smiled. He had no idea if she returned the smile, but she did nod her head back in his direction.

The admiral stood and walked over to the pedestal at the center of the room. As the room fell silent, the admiral was surprised when a general from the Gorthow system stood and steadily began to clap his hands. Soon, all were on their feet, applauding the admiral. Touched, the admiral raised a hand in a gesture of thanks. At the back of the room he saw Brian and the pretty young woman from the freighter enter and lean against a bulkhead.

"Thank you. Thank you very much. There's no one in this room who hasn't sacrificed a tremendous amount over the last few decades. Mere months ago, we were at the brink of defeat at the hands of the Craing. The Alliance was crushed in a matter of minutes by their fleet of two thousand without losing many casualties themselves. Those of us who survived limped home to lick our wounds, and we were left to wonder what the future fate of our home worlds would be. Would we see our wives and children forced into slavery to serve the Craing Empire, or would our worlds simply be obliterated, like so many others had, across the universe? But then something unexpected happened—"

A robust, spidery-looking being positioned next to Ti interrupted. "Yes, Captain Reynolds is what happened!"

The assembly clapped again and the admiral was all too pleased to let them show their appreciation. "Less than a year ago," he continued, "Captain Reynolds indeed did save the day at the very edge of this solar system by taking out close to five hundred Craing warships. And just weeks ago, he again was instrumental in bringing down the remaining fifteen hundred ships of that same fleet. The truth is, Captain Jason Reynolds is quite the innovative thinker. Obviously a risk taker, but also someone who rarely follows the orders he's been given."

That produced more chuckles and side conversations. The admiral held up both hands to quiet them down. "What we've all accomplished is remarkable. But we need to be realistic, as well. The Craing Empire is vast. Much of the known universe has, in some way, been affected by their aggression. Thousands of worlds have been subjugated into slavery. Those that are too difficult to control are simply blasted into space dust. The Craing Empire has shipyards in every major system, working night and day, building more and more ships. Our estimate, and it's only a rough one, is that there are now well over one hundred and fifty thousand Craing warships throughout known space."

The admiral let that sink in. The room went quiet at the sobering numbers. "We've been fortunate and had a bit of good luck. But let's not kid ourselves for one moment that we can match those numbers, in either ships or military forces—forces often composed of the inhabitants of the worlds they conquer. So, my question to you, what I have brought you here today to ask, is this: are we *finally* ready to begin warring aggressively, offensively? Take the battle to their worlds, before they visit ours?"

More side chatter erupted among the military leaders. This was obviously a heated subject among them. The admiral took this time to motion toward the side of the large room. Gaddy appeared through a door and slowly made her way toward the pedestal. Wearing all white and with her hair tied back, she looked nothing like the scraggly young Craing who had recently traversed, and survived, the perils of HAB 12. The assembly went quiet as the admiral stood aside. Gaddy stepped onto a small footstool, enabling her to be seen, and nervously returned their hostile stares.

"I am Craing. Until recently, I have always lived among the Craing worlds, specifically a world called Halimar. I am proud of my heritage and I love my people."

"Then why don't you go back there!" retorted a dignitary, dressed in a long gold robe.

Unfazed, Gaddy continued: "I certainly do not love their political system, nor the blatant disregard the Craing Empire has for other life forms. I am ashamed and I'm sorry. Please know we were not always this way. Several hundred years ago, our civilization was not so different from your own. We were a culture that loved the arts, sciences, and exploration; we were even good neighbors."

Gaddy paused for a moment, then continued: "I am young—a student at university. But my opinions are shared by many, and not just by the young. Our people, millions of them, are ready for change but are too frightened to act. We are a people ready to coexist with the other planetary systems. I am here to help ... but not destroy, the Craing people. Please don't think that. A political change is needed. In secret, I am a dissident and an underground leader. But I am also the niece of High Priest Overlord Lom, who is now the interim-emperor of the Craing Empire."

Her last remark got everyone's full attention, including the admiral's.

"It's true. What's more, I have unfettered access to both my uncle and the Emperor's Palace. You are planning an attack. I am aware of that. But first you will need information. I can get that for you. All I ask in return is that you join me in overthrowing a corrupt, misguided government, but do not destroy all peace-loving Craing people in the process."

Chapter 38

A brief nano-text message appeared from Mollie. She missed Jason and was wondering when he would be coming back to *The Lilly*. She mentioned something about continuing her self-defense classes but the message abruptly cut off in mid-sentence. Again, Jason's thoughts returned to home at the scrapyard, having Mollie around, and even enduring his father's cursing as he tinkered with the old '49 Ford pickup truck. As Jason finished chewing on an energy bar and watched distant movements beyond the trees where the mother dinosaur had her nest, he knew returning home wouldn't be an option until all the drone spheres were fully disabled.

Jason had the *Perilous* shuttle moved over from the other lake and was now sitting on its extended gangway. Having seen the type of life that lurked beneath this lake's surface, Jason opted to have the shuttle powered up and situated, instead, on the sandy beach. Grimes was instructed to stay at the controls while the next phase of the operation began.

Chameli, the young Cheyenne woman, was back at Rizzo's side and looked relieved to be free of the shuttle's cramped confinement. As he let the team take a final few minutes to relax, Jason thought about Mollie and wondered whether he could, realistically, expect to survive the day. If not, what would happen to her? Would his father, or perhaps Brian, step forward and be the father she would need in her young life?

His attention moved to Dira. She had her helmet off and was crouching down at the shoreline. Wetting her hands, she ran her fingers over her face and then through her short black hair. It was times like this, seeing her violet skin and her long eyelashes, that he recognized how different, non-Earthlike-human, she actually was. Yet, she was the most beautiful creature he had ever encountered. More than the sum of her physical parts, she was captivating and spontaneous, intelligent and magnificent. Jason wondered if she knew how important she really was to him. How he hated having put her in harm's way. He realized he would make it a priority to visit her home planet of Jhardon and meet her father—do whatever it was he was supposed to do when courting a Jhardian woman. *What the hell was he waiting for?*

Back in the present, Jason realized she was looking back over her shoulder at him, smiling. Yeah, she did know.

Traveler and the two other rhinos emerged from the tree line and headed toward Jason. He glanced again in Dira's direction, but she had moved further away down the beach.

"We are prepared, Captain," Traveler said, coming to a halt as he reached the shuttle.

"And you think it will be enough to get her away from that nest of hers?"

"Yes, there is no doubt about it."

Ricket appeared at the top of the gangway and hurried down to join in the conversation. "Captain, the next probe is ready. With that said, the time realms here are becoming more and more unstable. We have far less time to pair the two drones than calculated."

"In what way unstable and how much time are we talking about?" Jason asked.

"Perhaps unstable isn't the correct terminology. What seems to be happening is the opposite of that—more of a process of stabilization? The five probes have begun *talking* to one another again. They're synchronizing, as they were originally programmed to do."

"Setting the timeframe to one hundred years earlier?" Jason asked back.

"It could be that, or it could be any other past or future timeframe. Its priority is to lock down a unified time period—no matter the era."

Jason's mind flashed to the Earth's desolate, glassy landscape that they'd witnessed when paring the third probe, some thirty million years into the future.

"Hell, the chance that a human is even present when the probes lock down a timeframe could be astronomically low."

"That is correct, Captain," Ricket said. "I estimate we have no more than two days to pair up these probes, as well as pair the last remaining probe in Asia, before we lose the option to change the timeframe back to our own."

"Then we need to move it along. You're ready, Traveler?"

"Yes, we are ready."

"You've been practicing phase-shifting. You won't have time to fiddle about setting new coordinates. You'll need to have that aspect nailed."

Traveler made no attempt to justify himself any further.

"The drone is sited within the far side of the nest. Well away from the eggs. You get too close to the drone and its proximity sensors will activate. It'll bolt and we'll have to start all over."

"We understand, Captain."

"One more thing. She'll be defending her young, or what are her future young-to-be. We're not here to indiscriminately kill that dinosaur unless absolutely necessary."

* * *

They'd taken up their positions in the forest around the

mother Spinosaurus' nest. She began acting restless, agitated, seeming to sense the strange activity that was going on around her in the forest.

Jason split his forces into three teams. The first team consisted of the three rhino-warriors: Traveler, Few Words, and Born Late. They would be the egg handlers. Ricket along with Navy combatants Billy, Rizzo and Myers comprised the second group; their duty entailed encircling and guarding the nest once the mother dinosaur was on the run. Chang, Goldstein, Mead, and Jason comprised the third team. Their task was to lure the beast away from the nest for as long as possible. Dira and Chameli would remain with Grimes, airborne and hovering close by, in the shuttle.

The teams' objective was a simple one: get the dinosaur up and away from her nest—allowing Ricket sufficient time to bring in the other probe and pair them up—before any of them become the Spinosaurus' lunch.

Jason's plan was to get her to move all the way back to the lake where he and his team waited. Two hundred feet above him he saw the *Perilous*; her rear hatch was open and the second-to-last probe, although barely visible, was poised and ready to be deployed.

Jason used his NanoCom and hailed Traveler.

"We're in position, Captain, and waiting for her to move away from the nest."

Jason had tied his HUD to Billy's helmet-cam and he could see Traveler and the other two rhinos in the distance, standing to the left of a large tree. The display on Traveler's phase-shift wrist panel was open and he held a thick finger there, poised to initiate his phase-shift.

The giant dinosaur seemed perfectly content to sit on the eggs in her nest.

Jason hailed Billy.

"Go for Billy, Cap."

"You're going to have to motivate her to move off that nest."

"How am I supposed to do that?"

"I don't know ... try approaching her. Phase-shift away if she gets too close."

Billy didn't respond but Jason saw him on the move through his helmet-cam feed. Billy ran into the clearing, then ran back to his position behind a large boulder. The dinosaur stayed put.

"You're going to have to get in closer. Don't be such a baby. Try to act threatening," Jason suggested.

"You do realize I'm the size of a rodent to that thing, don't you?" Billy replied, sounding out of breath.

"Do it one more time. This time, try shooting her with a few stun bursts."

Billy was on the move again. The female Spinosaurus turned her massive head in Billy's direction. At thirty yards out, Billy moved closer than Jason would have risked, but then again, they needed to get things moving along. Billy brought up his multi-gun and fired off several quick plasma bursts into the beast's posterior.

Her reaction was near instantaneous and totally unexpected. A ball of fire, the size of a Volkswagen, blew from her gaping mouth and enveloped Billy. By the time the flash of fire cleared from Billy's video feed, Jason was about to phase-shift over to help him.

"I'm okay," came back Billy's startled voice. "Battle suit held up fine." Billy looked down at the grassy brush smoldering at his feet. When he looked back up, the colossal snout of the Spinosaurus was mere inches away.

He screamed. "Holy mother of—"

The dinosaur ate Billy.

Paralyzed, Jason's heart stopped. Billy's video feed showed nothing but blackness. Again, Jason was ready to phase-shift over when there was another flash from Billy's feed. It was coming from deeper in the trees.

"Billy?" Jason asked tentatively.

"How about next time *you* shoot that dinosaur in the ass. And by the way, this battle suit is completely shot."

"I take it you phase-shifted out of her mouth?"

"Oh no, not her mouth. Do you have any idea what it's like to be swallowed whole by a fucking dinosaur?"

Jason couldn't help laughing out loud from relief. "Well, at least she's off her nest." He opened another channel. "Traveler … time for you and your team to get busy."

Billy's video feed was acting flakey, so Jason tied into Rizzo's helmet-cam. Rizzo's visual perspective was from the opposite side of the dinosaur's nest. She was loudly pacing back and forth about seventy-five yards from her nest; her massive head swung up and down, similar to a bird pecking for food. Traveler, Few Words and Born Late flashed into view behind the nest. They wasted no time climbing the ten-foot-tall collection of wood and bones. Traveler lost his footing and fell onto his back on the ground. The noisy impact was enough to catch the dinosaur's attention. Surprised, or simply stunned, she didn't move right away. Traveler was back on his feet and quickly climbed the nest wall before she could swing her massive girth around and storm back. Few Words and Born Late disappeared into the nest and then both stood up tall, holding bowling ball-sized eggs high over their heads. Moments later, Traveler stood next to them, holding up a third egg.

Exactly what Jason didn't want to happen — happened. Its proximity sensors must have triggered and the spherical drone shot up into the air, hovering there twenty feet up. "Stay, stay,

stay … no, don't go …" Jason said aloud, as if the drone could hear him. It hovered like that for a moment before settling back on the ground in a secluded area several hundred feet away between the thick trunks of two large sequoias.

Incensed, the Spinosaurus charged. The rhinos waited, transferring the pilfered eggs to the crooks of their elbows and, at the very last moment, they accessed their phase-shift wrist panels. In a flash, they vanished. The momentum behind the dinosaur's rush was such that she careened into the nest. Of her three remaining eggs, only one remained unbroken. The roar of anguish and pain that erupted from the dinosaur was mournful and deafening. She pointed her long snout into the air and let loose a fountain of gaseous flames that spread across the sky. Then she noticed the three rhino-warriors standing at the edge of the trees, each holding high one of her beloved eggs.

The chase was on. Never appearing so far ahead of the dinosaur that she would give up pursuit and return back to her nest and the one unbroken egg, the rhinos let her come close—then, at the last moment, phase-shifted another thirty yards farther away.

Jason felt the earth tremble and shake as the chase moved closer. Now was the time for Ricket to deploy the paired drone. As if on cue, he saw it speeding away from the rear of the shuttle above. Between the heavy earth pounding by the approaching dinosaur and the phase-shifting rhinos, Jason had a hard time staying on his feet.

Jason opened a channel to Chang, Goldstein, and Mead. "We need to give them more room. Let's give them a wider berth."

As soon as they'd phase-shifted deeper into the forest, the rhinos flashed back into view. Again, they held up the stolen eggs—taunting the frenzied dinosaur. Jason noticed that Few Words was looking a little worse for wear. One arm, and part of his chest, had been scorched and smoke was rising into the air off his hide.

Another fireball-burst preceded her as the dinosaur thundered forward. The rhinos disappeared, with hardly a second to spare, only to reappear another hundred yards away by the edge of the lake. Again, in the distance, more taunting—the dinosaur's eggs held up high. As soon as the Spinosaurus rushed past their position, Jason and the other combatants fell in behind her.

She abruptly slowed and looked backwards. Jason brought up his multi-gun. It was clear she was weighing what to do: return to the nest and defend a single egg, or continue pursuing the rhinos, who held three of her eggs.

Jason was being hailed.

"Go for Cap. What's up, Billy?"

"We've got a problem here, Cap. Papa Dino is back and he's not looking too happy about the mess we've made."

Jason heard repeated multi-gun fire in the background. Eyeing his HUD, life icons were spread out and moving here and there erratically.

"Our current attack plan, using stun-level bursts, simply doesn't work," Billy reported.

"Well, keep evading him as long as possible. Bring him down only if absolutely necessary. Sorry, but we've got our own crazed dinosaur to deal with." Jason cut the connection as the female Spinosaurus seemed to have come to a decision and was charging back in the direction of her nest. Jason, standing directly in her path, fired his multi-gun, as did Chang, Goldstein, and Mead, at the approaching dinosaur. She stopped and brought her head down low, spitting fire in the process. Jason felt his battle suit's temperature-control compensators kick into full gear. Everything around him, except for his teammates, had turned into charcoal.

Jason hailed Ricket.

"Go for Ricket."

"What's going on with the drone pair?"

"It's here. Hovering fifty feet up, but it hasn't paired yet. The male Spinosaurus must be making it nervous," Ricket replied.

Jason had to cut the connection short. Again, the female was poising to charge. Jason phase-shifted twenty yards to his right—Chang, the same distance to his left. Both Goldstein and Mead hesitated too long.

"Get the hell out of there!" Jason barked over an open channel.

While Mead miraculously made a successful dash through the dinosaur's legs, and phase-shifted away once he was clear, Goldstein wasn't so lucky. First he was sprayed with an up-close fireball, then snatched between the dinosaur's forward teeth. With an audible crunch, the lower portion of Goldstein's torso and legs fell to the ground.

The female Spinosaurus rushed toward her nest, and it was apparent nothing was going to stop her. Jason, his two surviving team members, and the three rhino-warriors, followed behind her, phase-shifting in leaps.

"Captain," Ricket's voice blared into Jason's NanoCom. "She's paired! The male Spinosaurus heard, apparently recognized, the female's familiar snorts and left the area long enough for our probe to settle close to the other one in the trees. They've paired! We're done here."

Jason phase-shifted once more, along with the others. The three rhinos, each still holding an egg, phase-shifted somewhat farther back into the trees.

Jason watched as the two goliath dinosaurs frantically paced near the nest and its one lone egg. "Traveler, we need to get those eggs back into their nest."

Traveler set the phase-shift coordinates on his wrist panel, then took ahold of the other two eggs from the two rhinos. Nearly dropping all three eggs, he precariously cradled them in his arms while carefully extending a thick finger to press the *activate* key. Without further conversation, Traveler flashed away.

In that very instant, Traveler reappeared, now in the middle of the damaged nest. Still unnoticed by the two pacing dinosaurs, he gingerly placed the eggs down next to the other one. Jason, Billy, Rizzo, and Ricket yelled simultaneously: "Get out of there, Traveler!"

Both dinosaurs emerged from the far side of the clearing. Startled, Traveler looked up. He hesitated momentarily and by the time he opened his wrist panel they were practically upon him. He froze.

As if seeing everything happen in slow motion, Jason was sure his friend had just lived his last few seconds on Earth. Jason was paralyzed by Traveler's inevitable outcome.

So when four galloping steeds carrying blue-clad, U.S. 7th Cavalry riders broke into the clearing, Jason's jaw dropped. Behind them, and in close pursuit, were more horses and more riders: Indian warriors. But it was the soldier in the lead who first drew and held Jason's attention. It was none other than a terrified-looking General George Armstrong Custer—his eyes wide open and long blond hair flowing in the wind behind him. His wide-brimmed hat flew into the air, just as he was snatched up by his head and plopped into the mouth of the closest dinosaur, the mother Spinosaurus.

So stunned was everyone by the sudden co-mingling of the two disparate time realms that no one noticed Traveler. He had completed his phase-shift maneuver and was safely back with the rest of the team.

Chapter 39

Jason had Grimes take the *Perilous* above Earth's atmosphere into low orbit where the drones no longer affected time and, more importantly, their communications. The admiral was on comms within minutes and clearly eager to hear how their progress was coming along.

"Four down, one to go," Jason explained. "But Ricket tells me the drones are now communicating and trying to sync, so our timeframe has been pushed forward. We need to get the last one paired by this time tomorrow."

"What happens if you don't?" the admiral asked.

"They'll go ahead and sync to some unified time realm. One that would be, in all likelihood, different than our own."

The admiral grunted, then proceeded to give Jason an update on the repairs being made to *Her Majesty* and his work with Gaddy—developing a strategy for her to gather information when she entered the Emperor's Palace.

"I'm just surprised that little bug, Overlord Lom, is her uncle."

"Interim emperor. He's about as powerful a Craing dignitary as you can get."

"And you're sure he has no idea his niece is associated with the dissident underground?"

"She says she's been careful. She sees no way he could know. It's a risk she's willing to take," the admiral replied.

"And she realizes that we'll be using her subterfuge and information-gathering to ultimately hold the advantage when we attack the Craing?"

"Definitely, but she's made it clear this is not about the

Alliance attacking the populace of the Craing worlds. That's off limits. She's looking for the overthrow of Craing governmental and political factions. She understands we are confronting the Craing leadership strictly on a military level."

"So talk to me about *Her Majesty*."

"We're still retrofitting her and making repairs. Her cloaking device is operational and her weaponry formidable. But in the end, she's still a converted luxury liner. Nothing nimble about that ship," the admiral added.

"Why did you select Brian to captain her?"

"Your brother knows Craing space better than any human alive. He also is a master at weaseling himself out of tight situations. *Her Majesty* is not an Allied vessel and has no ties to the Alliance, thus providing us a layer of separation. If you think about it, Brian is the perfect choice to enter Craing space."

Jason let that comment hang in the air, not needing to ask him the unspoken question.

"Yes, Jason, I do trust him. I've seen changes in him over the last few weeks. Everyone deserves a second chance, so I expect you to support your brother on this. Can you do that?"

"Sure. What else do you need from me?"

"We need Ricket back here as soon as you're done with him. He'll be instrumental for our plan to come together. He'll be accompanying Gaddy, posing as a prospective boyfriend she wants to introduce to her uncle."

"Seriously? Ricket's over two hundred years old! They'll recognize him—hell, he was the Craing emperor, for God's sake!"

"Calm down. We'll alter his looks. As for his age, he doesn't look that much older than Gaddy. Have you really looked at him lately?" the admiral asked, defiantly.

Jason let his eyes fall on Ricket seated in the shuttle's cockpit, next to Grimes. Truth was, since he'd gone through the process of becoming fully organic, he did look much younger. But Gaddy's boyfriend? And Brian captaining a ship for the Alliance? It seemed to him the admiral's plan was a deck of precariously stacked cards: one strong jolt and everything would fall apart.

The admiral interrupted Jason's thoughts. "Boomer's here; wants to talk to you."

"Boomer?"

"That's what Mollie goes by these days. It's just a phase, I'm sure."

"Daddy?"

"Hey! I miss you, little one."

"I miss you, too. When you coming back? I have a lot to show you—you've been gone way too long," she said, sounding as bossy as ever.

"I'm almost done, Mollie. If everything goes well in Asia, I'll be back tomorrow."

"I'm called Boomer now, Dad. I'm tiny, sneaky and lethal, like a boomslang."

"What the heck's a boomslang?"

"I think it's a snake. Woodrow says it comes from a place in Africa."

"Woodrow? You mean Chief Petty Officer Woodrow?" Jason didn't know the SEAL well, only that he was a hard-ass and carried a reputation for being a man born to kill—lethal in every way possible. "I don't understand your association with him, Mollie."

"I told you, it's Boomer now, Dad. He's taken over my self-defense classes. He's teaching me not to be a victim again."

Jason heard something in her voice he hadn't heard before. Had he been gone that long? Did he not really know her anymore?

"I just should have been consulted on who you work with, that's all."

"Well, Dad, you're never here. There's things I need to know how to do. Don't you understand that?"

The truth was, he didn't. When she needed him most, when Nan died, he'd left to fight the Craing, the Caldurians ... hell, dinosaurs. The reason he wasn't relating to his little girl on the other end of his comms signal was that she was doing what was necessary for her own future survival: mentally, physically, and emotionally.

"I'm sorry, Mollie ... Boomer. Work with Woodrow. I trust you, little one. And more important, I love you. You know that, right?"

"Yeah, Dad. I know that."

Jason cut the connection and leaned back in his seat, his mind replaying his conversation with Mollie. *Boomer?*

From the rear seating area of the shuttle, Dira leaned in close and whispered in his ear, "You okay in there?" She had removed her battle suit saying she needed to let her skin breathe. Jason's eyes took in her violet skin and her skimpy, formfitting tank top.

"Can you scratch the middle of my back?" she asked, leaning forward in her seat, using her thumb to point over her shoulder.

"Sure." He reached over and scratched her backbone until she smiled and leaned back.

"Much better, thanks. Tell me about your home. Where you grew up."

Jason's mind went to the collection of old cars, buses, and assorted scrap metal that comprised his backyard—the scrapyard. His cheeks flushed. "Well, there's not much to tell. You've seen where I grew up."

"The scrapyard. I've seen it on *The Lilly*'s display. But what was it like to grow up there? Did you have a lot of friends?" she asked, her face turned toward his, mere inches away.

"When I was young, Mollie's age, it was magical. I loved it. Getting older, though, it was anything but magical. I guess I was embarrassed living at a junkyard. That's probably why both my brother and I left as soon as possible, joining the service. How about you? Tell me about your home."

"It may not be what you envision it to be, Jason. Where you lived, at a scrapyard, you had freedom to explore and do as you wanted. I was never alone. A Jhardian girl, especially one of noble heritage, must conform to certain dictates. The clothes I wore were selected for me the night before; other than family members I was never alone with someone of the opposite sex. I only spoke when spoken to."

"Sounds very formal. Terrible, actually," Jason said, sympathetically.

"Don't get me wrong, I was loved. It was a nurturing, loving environment. But confining, stifling, to the point I was miserable. Wealth beyond your imagination, and a world filled with natural beauty. I've never seen its equal. But I would have loved your childhood existence—your freedom."

Jason watched her lips as she talked. He'd never wanted to kiss a woman as much as he wanted to kiss her right then. A slight smile spread across her lips.

"Are you even listening to me?"

"Yes, I'm listening ... for the most part." His eyes met hers and held there. He felt her move in closer, saw the flesh of her upper arm press into his battle suit.

"Captain," came Grimes' voice from the cockpit. "We're closing in on the coordinates for the last drone."

Chapter 40

With the last drone to be paired taking up space in the limited cargo area, the three rhino-warriors were forced to stand up in the now overly cramped passenger compartment. Jason made his way forward and knelt down at the open entry to the cockpit. Ricket had his locator equipment laid out on his lap, with the holo-display of the terrain below represented in ultra-real, high-definition. The vista below broadened in accordance with the shuttle's movement. Seeing Jason, Ricket widened the locator's perspective, revealing the final drone's pulsating icon.

"China?" Jason asked.

"More west, more like Uzbekistan," Grimes chimed in.

She eased up on the controls, and bringing the shuttle to a standstill, hovered high above the wide open plains below.

"Cool! *1215* ... in China that would be the Jin dynasty," Rizzo said, sitting in the shuttle's front row and directly to the right of Jason's squatting back.

"What can we expect to encounter in Uzbekistan, Rizzo?"

Rizzo peered around the open bulkhead to Ricket's holo-display. "My guess, Genghis Khan has just invaded the Khwarezmia E*mpire. The* location of the icon looks to be at Samarkand."

The shuttle slowly descended while still making forward progress. Up ahead was a settlement of sorts, or some kind of community. As they approached, it became more evident the structures below were somewhat like cylindrical tents.

"Those dwellings are called gers ... or are they yurts? I always get the two mixed up," Rizzo said. "They're made out of a felt-like material, derived from compressed matted wool. Warm in winter months, cool in summer."

As nighttime descended on the landscape below, too many campfires to count billowed up smoke into the night air. Hundreds of the tent-like structures were spread across the wide valley. But it was the spectacle beyond the yurts that got everyone's attention. Tens of thousands of men and horses. Looking through the windshield, Jason lowered his visor and used his HUD optics to zoom in. The soldiers were dressed in leather and bronze. Thick fur collars were attached on some of their cloaks. More tent structures were on the perimeter, different from the others. They would be the soldier barracks. These troops, beyond a doubt, were the conquerors.

"You got a specific location on the drone?" Jason asked.

"Just like the others, it could be anywhere here, within a mile or two radius. Once we get on the ground and start moving, we'll get a better directional bearing," Ricket replied.

"That won't be necessary, Captain," Grimes said, pointing a finger toward the horizon.

In the distance, a long line of horse-drawn carts were lined up, single file, on a dirt road. Each cart held several prisoners in an open-barred cage. The centermost cart held a large, black, spherical object. Even from a distance, it was clearly evident it was the last drone.

"How the hell did they get close enough to grab it?" Billy asked.

No one had an immediate answer.

"So where to now, Cap?" Grimes asked.

"Let's keep our distance, circle around the camp perimeter."

Grimes banked the shuttle to the left and steered a wide circular course to the far side of the encampment. Closer to the drone and soldiers, something else, something in the darkness invisible to them earlier, rose twenty-five feet into the air. It was a pyramid of circular objects.

Grimes brought her fingers up to her mouth. "Don't tell me those are ..." She leaned forward in her seat. "Those are heads, aren't they?"

"Yep," Jason answered, equally repulsed by the sight.

"Yeah, I've heard about this," Rizzo said. "Genghis liked to show his intolerance toward any who confronted him in battle by exhibiting trophies. Heads. For the most part, the heads were taken from the elderly and children."

"A monster," Grimes spat.

"That large tent is empty of humans from what my readings tell me, Captain," Ricket said, pointing toward the barrack-like tents on the outskirt of the settlement.

"Well, it's certainly big enough. Phase-shift us in there, Grimes, before we're noticed hovering around up here," Jason commanded.

In a flash they were no longer high above the encampment, but within the dark confines of what Rizzo had referred to as a yurt.

"Big! It's like a circus tent," Grimes said, looking around.

"I think it's an arena," Rizzo added. At the far sides of the tent's open area were rows of roughly-hewn timber boards staggered upward, like steps. "Looks like a grandstand for spectators," Rizzo added.

* * *

The center of the arena, where the shuttle now sat in near-total darkness, was evidently not visible to the handful of Mongol soldiers who entered the huge yurt. One brought in a nomad peasant woman and had his way with her; another soldier wandered in, did a cursory look around, and quickly left. A third soldier came all the way into the arena, right up to the shuttle, and had to be killed.

Rizzo was most interested in the man's weaponry: a long, crudely-made knife, worn on a hilt at his hip, and a short, curved, composite bow that he'd worn over his shoulder. Holding up the bow and pulling at its draw, he remarked, "Strong pull. You know, it's estimated these little bows were more accurate, and could deliver a shot nearly twice as far as European bows."

Jason was only half listening to Rizzo as he walked the fifty paces to the yurt's entrance flap. Careful not to draw unwanted attention to himself, Jason peered out into the night. Many of the Mongol soldiers he'd seen moving about earlier were gone. He presumed they had turned in to their own yurts for the night. His eyes followed the rocky dirt road into the distance and found the line of carts, still parked where he'd last seen them. The only difference was that the horses were gone, perhaps put into stalls, or put out to pasture for the night. There was just enough firelight and glow from the moon above to see the outline of the drone's cage. *Damn, how am I going to get that thing out of there?*

Turning back to the shuttle, he saw Traveler, Born Late, and Few Words huddled together. Their low-voiced words were indecipherable at this distance. Jason held up a hand and signaled Traveler to come closer. When he was ignored, Jason remembered rhinos had terrible night vision. He walked toward the three rhinos and cleared his throat as he grew closer.

"I need your help. Come with me."

Jason walked slowly, knowing the three rhinos needed to keep his silhouette in sight to guide them across the arena. He opened the flap and pointed to the distant line of carts.

"You may not be able to see it from here, but a hundred yards up this road are several carts. The drone is locked inside one of them. Without bringing attention to ourselves, we need to roll that cart back here."

"It's very dark, Captain," Traveler said.

"We only need one of you to do this. And Billy and I will be right there with you."

Traveler spoke up first. "I will go."

"We'll wait a little longer; hopefully the road will be more deserted within the next hour or so."

* * *

Jason ordered all team members not helping retrieve the drone back into the shuttle.

"Grimes, I want you to get everyone off the planet if anything happens to us." He turned his attention to Ricket. "What's our timeframe?"

"We have two hours, five minutes and thirty-three seconds to pair the two drones, Captain. If we're unsuccessful, the drones will complete their synchronization and lock down a new time realm."

"Be well away from here by then, Grimes. You got that?"

"Yes, sir."

"Captain, I should join you. I am the only one who can interface with the drone," Ricket said.

"You're needed soon on another crucial mission, Ricket. We simply can't risk anything happening to you."

Jason gave Dira a quick nod and a wink, and headed for the yurt's exit flap. Traveler followed close behind, along with Billy and Rizzo. The four of them hesitated before rushing out onto the dirt road. The men had turned off their helmet lights beforehand, and their black battle suits were virtually impossible to see in the darkness. But Traveler was another matter entirely,

Jason thought. He saw that the rhino's seven-foot-tall stature and grey hide stuck out like a Macy's Parade float on Thanksgiving Day.

Jason found he needed to ignore his HUD life-icon indicator. So many Mongols were close by he was tempted to turn back. This was crazy. A bonfire blazed up ahead to their right and ten or more Mongol soldiers were huddled close together against the cold. Right now they were most vulnerable. Anyone looking in their direction would certainly notice Traveler, and probably himself, Rizzo, and Billy. *What's that?* Crap, he hadn't thought about Traveler's thousand pound footfalls. Jason slowed down their hurried pace and immediately the ground shaking subsided.

Three men came into view ahead, walking along the same path. Fortunately, they were going in the same direction. Jason drew his sidearm and, as they drew closer to them, one of the warrior Mongols turned and looked back over his shoulder. Jason fired three times: silent bursts that killed all three Mongols instantly.

Billy and Rizzo ran forward to collect the fallen bodies and deposited them off the road, into the darkness. By the time they'd reached the carts, Traveler was huffing and puffing, with steamy snot billowing forth into the near-frigid air. At their approach, there was movement in the closest cart. Three men dressed in rags sat and stared at them with wide eyes. Iron bars kept them locked into the small caged space. Jason held a single finger to his mouth, hoping that as a symbolic gesture, its meaning was timeless. Apparently it was. The captives returned silent nods and quietly watched them move past. The same thing happened with the next cart, and the cart after that.

The fourth cart held the probe. Barely fitting within the constraints of the bars, it was evident why it hadn't flown off when approached by the Mongols. No longer perfectly circular in shape, a section of the drone was damaged; a jagged opening revealed its internal circuitry. The only positive indication the drone still functioned was several blinking lights on the sphere's far side.

Traveler stood at the back of the cart and was examining a large metal lock that kept the cage gate secured. He crushed the mechanical device in the grip of one hand.

"Can you lift that, Traveler, and carry it back to the shuttle?"

Comprehension spread across Traveler's face and he stepped forward to the rigging at the front of the cart. He lifted the large wooden pole that normally tethered the cart to one or two horses. The cart moved easily, as if it had a three hundred horse power engine under the hood. Traveler pulled the cart forward several feet away from the cart stationed behind it. He then moved to the rear of the cart and opened the gate. He slipped his two beefy hands around the sides of the sphere and lifted it backwards, away from the cart.

"Heavy?" Jason asked.

"Yes."

Traveler turned and headed back down the road toward the shuttle. Several times their movement on the path drew the attention of those sitting by open fires. Faces briefly turned in their direction, then turned back to their conversations. Jason surmised it was too dark for them to see beyond the bright firelight. Thankfully no one stood—no one moved to stop them.

When they had made it back to the shuttle, they had less than an hour to pair the two drones.

Chapter 41

Traveler deposited the drone several feet from the shuttle's stern. Ricket had worked feverishly over the past hour to try to bring it back to life. He was about to phase-shift to the *Minian* to gather better tools and equipment when the drone shuddered and reinitialized.

"It's trying to sync, Captain."

"That's it then, we're done here—now things will revert back to the correct time?"

"I'm hoping so. Truth is, I've never had to reset one. If memory buffers are still accessible from its prior condition, then yes. If not, there's no telling what it will do, or how long it will take. In all likelihood, the drone will revert back to the state it was in just prior to becoming disabled and deactivated—"

Ricket's words were cut short by a flurry of activity at the front of the yurt. Ripped from the pliable wood framing, the fabric covering the front of the yurt was torn away in a single, dramatic motion. Horses and riders filed in and encircled the inside perimeter, coming together from opposite directions. By the time they came to a standstill, completing the circle, there were over a hundred horse-mounted archers poised to loose arrows in their direction.

Jason's impulse was to simply fire his multi-gun and be done with them. The crew's battle suits were practically impenetrable. But he quickly dismissed the idea when he saw Traveler and the two other rhinos standing off to his side. They would not survive the attack.

Jason hailed Traveler via his NanoCom.

"Yes, Captain."

"I want you three to phase-shift back into the shuttle."

Jason saw Traveler turn his massive head in his direction, "Hide? Like a coward?"

Jason knew even making the suggestion was an insult to the warrior, and he regretted he suggested it as soon as the words left his lips. "Forget I mentioned it. We'll find another way."

Three more torch-bearing riders entered the yurt and moved directly toward the shuttle. At the center was a man who appeared to be of mixed heritage. Even in the dim torchlight, it was evident he had bright red hair and light eyes.

Jason's and the team's faces were visible behind their backlit visors and the red-haired man, the apparent leader, was spending a prolonged amount of time taking in their mixed appearances. The rhinos grabbed his attention first; then Ricket; then each human; then Chameli; and finally Dira, with her violet skin and long lashes. The man began to speak and it took several seconds for Jason's nano-tech to start translating his words.

"What clan do you derive from, disgusting peasants?" he asked, dismounting. He took several long strides before stopping. Placing hands on hips, he raised his head and glared at those before him.

Jason, in turn, sauntered several steps closer while keeping his weapon pointed directly at the man's head. The encircling army fidgeted and brought their combined aim over to Jason.

"My name is Captain Jason Reynolds. We are not your enemy. This device," Jason gestured toward the drone lying on the ground, "is ours. Once we've secured it, we'll be on our way."

The Mongol smiled and shook his head. "No."

Jason heard Rizzo in his comms.

"Captain, I'd suggest you negotiate. Life in this time period often revolved around making a trade."

Jason felt the seconds ticking by, and the chances narrowing of returning Earth, and themselves, back to the twenty-first century. They didn't have time for this crap.

"Who am I talking to?"

An expression of astonishment crossed the Mongol's face, which quickly turned to one of anger. "I am Genghis Khan, ruler and king of all lands. I will take pleasure slicing off your heads and lobbing them onto my growing mountain of decrepit flesh and bone." Turning to Traveler, he added, "We will feast on the bodies of these bloated cows with horns. We will feast for a week."

Traveler, his nano-devices able to interpret the Mongol's insults, reached for the heavy hammer hanging from the leather thong at his side.

Jason held up a restraining hand toward his friend and shook his head. He looked back to the Mongol leader.

"Well, good luck with that. Listen, I need to make this quick. I have little patience and no time to screw around. Get back on your horse and ride out of here, or I'll embarrass you in front of your little army."

Jason spoke slowly, giving himself time to reconfigure his HUD settings. Before Khan could utter another word, Jason phase-shifted behind him, grabbed him up by his fur collar, and phase-shifted again.

It took several seconds before the circling Mongol army could find them, now atop the shuttle. Jason dangled the frenzied, writhing Khan in the air by the scruff of his neck.

"Drop your weapons or I'll snap his neck. Do it now or he, and the rest of you, will die."

Confident that the rhinos were no longer being targeted, Jason opened a channel to the rest of his team. "Stun-level. Take them out."

Plasma fire erupted as Billy, Rizzo, Myers, Chang, and Mead spun and continuously fired. Only a handful of Mongols were not caught off-guard and twenty of their arrows flew before they also fell. Every horse was made riderless. The rhinos had one or more arrows buried into their thick hides. Two arrows jutted from Traveler's upper right thigh. Jason cringed, remembering back to HAB 12. The rhino-warrior had suffered similar wounds to the same area.

Jason let Khan fall to the ground below. As Khan scurried to his feet, enraged, Billy stunned him point blank in the forehead.

Dira, moving to attend to Traveler and the others, yelled, "Billy, why'd you do that?!"

"He'll live. Probably," he replied.

Jason shifted to the drone and Ricket's side. "Status?"

"Promising," Ricket replied. He had both hands and most of his head inside the jagged probe opening. "If I can reconnect at least one of the internal phase ports, it should start talking to the others."

More Mongols were streaming into the yurt—some on foot, others on horseback. Billy quickly arranged the SEALs in a circular formation around the shuttle, while the wounded rhinos, much to Dira's overriding objection, stood at the entrance flap and took out entering Mongols, their heavy hammers connecting to flesh and bone.

Jason leaned against the back of the shuttle and felt exhaustion setting in. The lack of sleep, and the fate of the world riding on his shoulders, was taking its toll. But, one way or another, he thought, there would be plenty of time to rest when this was over. That's when the roof fell in.

The yurt tore apart from all sides as outside Mongol riders pulled key side-support poles from the ground, untethering ropes. Within seconds, the team was left standing in the open.

Dawn was upon them. There was just enough light to see the gathering hordes of Mongols preparing to charge them from all sides.

"Into the shuttle. Now! Everyone!" Jason yelled.

The SEAL combatants did as they were instructed, but the rhinos held their positions. Traveler, Few Words, and Born Late fought on, heavy hammers in one hand and plasma pistols in the other. Born Late fell first, as a group of sword-yielding Mongols rushed him, beating him to the ground. Jason saw spurts of blood as his body was hacked apart with knives and swords.

"Ricket, stop what you're doing! Phase-shift the living rhinos onto the roof of the shuttle."

Jason probably could have done it himself … accessed their phase-shift devices remotely, but certainly not soon enough. Traveler and Few Words had their location changed in a flash. Disoriented, they both swung their hammers into open air. Standing upon the shuttle's roof, Traveler angrily bellowed some expletives into the air.

Thrusters were winding up and the shuttle was slowly rising off the ground.

Billy, leaning out from the open back hatch, yelled out to Jason and Ricket, "They're almost on top of you! Get the hell out of there, Cap!"

Jason tore his *eyes away* from Ricket, who was still halfway emerged in the disabled drone. Too many Mongol warriors to count were rushing toward them. He and Ricket had gone unnoticed for the most part, huddled by the side of the sphere, but that had changed.

The Perilous, maneuvering around above them, was firing its primary plasma cannon. Grimes did all she could to keep the attacking hordes at bay, but there were too many.

"Ricket, we need to go. I'm sorry, but we're out of time."

Jason was firing non-stop, no longer caring to use the gun's stun setting. One after another, dozens more Mongol warriors fell, but even with the bodies stacked high, more Mongols kept coming. Arrows flew past Jason and Ricket, ricocheting off their battle suits, while others drove several inches into the dirt at their feet.

"I think I have it," Ricket said.

Jason didn't wait one second longer. He grabbed Ricket by the shoulder, pulled him out of the *drone, a*nd phase-shifted to an open spot on the shuttle's roof. Grimes slowly moved the shuttle higher and away from the drone. The army below watched; some tried to follow on horseback. As they ascended, the drone's pair emerged from the back of the Perilous and hovered for several seconds. Jason and Ricket, crouching on the shuttle's roof, never took their eyes off the hovering sphere.

"Go on, pair up, you piece of shit!" Jason yelled.

Ricket watched the drone, then looked up at Jason. "We should leave now. We need to get above Earth's atmosphere, away from the effects of the drones' influence on time."

"It hasn't paired yet."

"Unless you want to get stuck here, we need to go *now*."

About to protest, Jason watched as the hovering sphere suddenly dropped to ground level and swooped in next to the other drone. Slowly, it settled itself onto the ground and became stationary.

Jason ushered everyone down into the top hatch of the shuttle. "Go ahead and phase-shift into high orbit, Grimes."

She'd been ready to do exactly that and it took her less than three seconds to phase-shift them up into Earth's high orbit. They watched and waited for something, anything to happen. And then it did. There was a spectacular flash of blue light and, as if the whole world had phase-shifted away and then reappeared, they were no longer above Asia.

Ricket shook his head. "Captain, it looks like much of the Allied fleet is here in Earth space. But the *Minian*'s gone. Perhaps we should contact the admiral."

Jason let out a long breath. "Not now. Take us back down, Grimes. Earth is our first priority. Hell, who knows what we'll find down there."

Chapter 42

The quiet stillness on board the *Perilous* was full of anticipation. No one wanted to speak, to break the silence. The shuttle's passengers waited for the time realms across the landscape to merge and settle into what, inevitably, would become the new reality for planet Earth.

Jason sat next to Grimes in the cockpit. Turning away from the view below, Jason scanned those seated behind him. Most were gazing out a porthole, as Dira attended to the two injured rhinos in the rear cargo area that was now freed-up to hold their bulk. Ricket sat quietly by himself, not looking outside and not looking particularly hopeful. Jason got up and moved to the open seat next to him.

"Hey … Talk to me. What's going on, Ricket?"

"Captain, when I said *I think I have it*, that didn't mean that I actually *did* have it."

"What are you saying?"

"There's little chance the Earth you know, your old timeframe, will ever be returned to you. I'm very sorry, Captain. I needed more time, perhaps a few more seconds. I failed you—I failed all of you."

Ricket spoke just loud enough for the others in the cabin to hear him. Heads turned and shoulders visibly sagged; their expressions of hopefulness turned to worried puzzlement.

"Welcome to the twenty-first century!"

It was Billy, shouting through an open comms channel. His voice was overly loud—making everyone cringe. Jason's eyes moved to the time reference display on his own HUD. Sure enough, the current year had locked in—time was advancing in a steady, second-following-second progression. There was a collective sigh of relief. Billy and Rizzo stood and high-fived, while Chameli watched them with a confused, albeit amused, expression.

"Looks like you got to finish in time after all. You got that beat-to-crap drone operational, Ricket," Jason said, smiling.

"No, Captain, I didn't. What's happened is nothing more than an unimaginable stroke of good luck. There may be some technical factors at play that brought us so close to our own time realm, but we'll never know."

"What are you talking about, close to our own time realm?"

"Our HUD's time reference indicator is showing today's date: May 4th."

"So?"

"Today actually is April 14th. It is three weeks earlier, Captain."

Jason thought about that and although it wasn't perfect, the date discrepancy was certainly close enough that life on Earth wouldn't be overtly affected.

Jason shrugged, "Close enough, Ricket. You have to take the wins in life as they come."

Looking up, Jason saw that all heads had turned in his direction.

"What? What the hell's wrong with you people?"

Jason stared blankly back at their concerned faces. Billy was the only one not looking back at him. He was looking toward the cargo area. Jason spun in his seat and saw that Dira had stopped working on Traveler's wounds and was looking back at him. There was concern—and something else—in her eyes. Then she mouthed the words that would change everything. "Nan is still alive ..."

He still didn't connect the dots. "What do you mean—"

Then it hit him. *Oh my God.* Today is the day Nan and Mollie were attacked by Captain Stalls. The day Nan was mortally injured, later to die in *The Lilly*'s MediPod.

Jason was on his feet and moving toward the cockpit. "Grimes! Set a course to Southern California."

Grimes turned in her seat as Jason sat down next to her. She glanced back at Billy, questioningly. Billy moved forward and crouched between them.

"Hey, man, let's think about this, okay? Just for a second."

"There's nothing to think about. Do it, Grimes."

"Maybe you do have to think about it. There may be repercussions, if you save her. Things we may not even be aware of yet. You'd be changing the natural course of events for that timeframe."

"What do you think we've been doing this last week?" Jason asked.

"None of that had an actual effect on our own timeframe. This is completely different."

Jason saw the concern on his friend's face, and the faces around him.

"What would you do, Billy? What if it was Orion? What if she had died and you had the opportunity to revisit—to *change*—that course of events; to have her back in your life again?"

Billy didn't answer. Jason's eyes locked on Dira's. She looked away, obviously hurt.

It was Ricket who broke the silence. "If the captain saves her, or doesn't save her, there'll be complications, or consequences, either way. Captain, there will be two Mollies, two Brians, and probably others ... depending on who was off the planet at the time. I'm with you, Captain, on this one. Save her, if you can."

Jason nodded. "Get us there, Grimes. Phase-shift the shuttle in just as soon as we get close enough."

* * *

Teardrop was on the move, its energy weapon protruding from the open plate at the center of its body.

"Warning! Outside security perimeter has been breached. Weapons fire detected. Plasma turret has been destroyed."

"Mom! Can't you get it to shut up?" Mollie screamed above all the racket. "How many times does it have to say the same thing?"

Nan and Mollie huddled together as they watched the multiple security feeds up on the TV monitor. Once Stalls walked around the outside perimeter of the house, he returned to his shuttle. Several minutes later he exited, wearing a battle suit and holding a large energy weapon.

Stalls moved from one window to the next, pulling and prying at the metal security shutters. Eventually, he concentrated on the largest window shutter at the back of the house. Using the butt of his weapon he continued to pound on it over and over. Having little impact on the shutter, Stalls took several steps backward and fired; plasma bolts shook the house and left blackened scorch marks. The firing stopped as Stalls moved in to check the damage.

Nan watched as the tall pirate became more and more enraged. He began to use the butt of his rifle repeatedly. He stopped, out of breath, and looked up to the roofline. He raised his rifle and fired. Shingles flew into the air, some of them catching on fire.

The outside sounds heard inside the house were deafening.

"Teardrop!" Nan yelled. "He's shooting at the roof. The roof is coming apart!"

Teardrop, now behind them, was also looking at the security feeds.

"He will soon find that the sub-roof is covered in metal plating," Teardrop said, moving about the great room and rising up toward the ceiling. "No structural breach detected."

With a large section of the roof shingles blown away, exposing the metal plates beneath, Stalls stopped firing and stood back. Then he was gone, heading back toward his shuttle.

"Is he leaving, Mom? Has he given up?" Mollie asked.

"I don't know, Mollie. Maybe."

In seconds the shuttle was back airborne and hovering over the pool. Its primary energy weapon came alive, concentrating its fire on the security shutters at the back of the house.

"Structural breach in process, structural breach in process."

Both sliding glass windows shattered as the security shutters went from a glowing amber color to bright white. Intense heat emanated in waves into the kitchen and back out into the great room. The large metal shutters disintegrated. Nan and Mollie ran for cover, seeing the shuttle hovering outside, behind the now-open rear of the house.

Nan watched as Teardrop moved with amazing speed, taking up a defensive position at the rear of the house. Nan, who had felt unsure if the drone would be able to defend them against the pirate's shuttle assault, now felt some hope. Teardrop fired a continual barrage of plasma bolts into the belly of the hovering craft. The shuttle fired back, but Teardrop was so quick, darting from one position to the next, that the only thing Stalls could accomplish was further destruction to the house itself.

Teardrop rose into the air and moved in closer to the craft, concentrating its fire power on a singular spot on the hull.

The shuttle continued to fire back and Teardrop was struck multiple times, destroying one of its arms, and then it suffered a direct hit to its energy weapon. Several more energy bolts struck the drone and Teardrop fell from the air into the pool, where it immediately sank to the bottom.

"Mom!"

"I know, I saw," Nan said back, never taking her eyes off the hovering shuttle. Both Nan and Mollie crouched low, hiding behind the wall next to the fireplace.

"What's he want, Mom? Why's he doing this to us?"

"I don't know. He's a bad man. But we're going to show him he can't get away with it, right?"

"AI, are you there?" Nan yelled above the sound of the hovering shuttle.

There was no response.

"Bag End, Mom, remember?"

"Are you there, Bag End?" Nan tried again.

"Yes, I am here, Nan Reynolds."

"What can you do to help us ... to defend us against the intruder?"

"Security deterrents within the premises are active and functional."

"What about outside? Is there anything else you can do?" Nan asked, taking another quick peek around the corner.

"With the destruction of the plasma turret, there are no additional external weapons available."

The shuttle was on the move again. Nan and Mollie listened as it moved over the house and landed on the driveway.

Nan reached over and pulled the small energy weapon from the holster at Mollie's side.

"You remember how to shoot this, Mollie? You remember what Orion taught you?"

"I think so. But those were targets, not a real person."

"I know, sweetie, but you saw what that bad man did to

Teardrop. We're both going to have to be brave. Can you do that?"

"I think so," Mollie replied, not sounding all that certain.

Crawling on hands and knees they backed away from the wall to get a better look at the security feeds on the TV monitor. The shuttle's gangway had been deployed and it took several seconds for them to see where Stalls had gone.

"There he is," Mollie said, pointing to one of the outside camera feeds.

Nan pulled out her own pistol, ensuring that the safety was off and set to its maximum charge. Mollie watched and did the same thing on her own weapon.

"He's coming around to the backyard," Nan whispered. "Bag End, as soon as you have a clear shot of the intruder, shoot that fucker. Don't stop until he's dead."

Mollie looked up at her mother with wide eyes and then nodded her head in silent agreement.

"Security defense mode has been set to lethal," the AI replied.

They heard his footsteps before they saw him. It became apparent Stalls was carefully making his way around to the back of the house, not taking any chances.

"He's right there, Mom," Mollie whispered, never taking her eyes off the exposed back of the house.

"Okay, shhhh, be very quiet now."

His shadow moved across the deck like a stealthy black cat. When he finally came into view, he was no longer wearing his battle suit. Nan knew why. He wanted her to see him. His inflated ego had taken precedence over basic common smarts. Wearing snug-fitting black trousers and a dress shirt, he looked ridiculous. His long black hair, set loose, cascaded down his back. He was poolside looking down at Teardrop; she guessed he wanted to make sure the drone was truly out of commission.

Satisfied, Stalls stood up tall and turned toward the direction of the house. Smiling, he brushed his long hair back one more time and headed for the broken sliding glass doors. Safety glass crunched under the soles of his boots. He hesitated, peered inside, and took a tentative step forward.

Nan felt Mollie tense, her breathing had increased and she knew her heart was about to beat right out of her chest. Nan held a finger to her lips and put her attention back on Stalls. Her mind raced: *why doesn't the AI just shoot him?*

Stalls, now more relaxed, let the muzzle of his rifle drop several inches. Realizing he was on his way into the great room where they would be instantly seen, Nan pointed for Mollie to hurry and crawl backward out of sight. Nan stood and held her weapon at the ready.

He entered the great room twenty feet away and smiled when he saw her.

"Hello, Nan. I am happy, so very happy, to see you again."

She didn't respond, only held his stare and waited for him to get a little closer. She had practiced, alongside Mollie, getting better at hitting the center zone of targets, but ... as Mollie had pointed out ... those were only targets.

Stalls slowly shook his head and said, "Nan, you have no need for that weapon. I could no more hurt you than I could hurt myself. I've gone to considerable lengths coming here. Finding you. I'm hoping my actions speak for themselves. I'm hoping that you realize I love you. That I want to make you mine."

He took a step, and then another. A new sound emanated from outside, in the distance. Nan recognized the sound; it was another small ship, or maybe a shuttle. *Just ignore it, Stalls*, she said to herself. She wanted him to move in closer—closer to where the AI could blast him back to hell.

Stalls stood still, cocked his head to the side, and listened.

He took a tentative step backward and held there. A quick glance over his shoulder and he saw what Nan had already spotted. Definitely a shuttle, one she hadn't seen before. When he turned back to face her, she was smiling. The cavalry had arrived, somehow. Stalls was no longer looking at her. His attention was on the walls—specifically high up, where there were dozens of small security panels.

"Clever, Nan," he said, smiling. "I would have expected nothing less from you. This only proves how perfect you are for me. Strong, cunning, and beautiful. Come to me now, Nan, and your daughter goes unharmed. I promise you."

Nan's confidence left her in an instant. *Did he know Mollie was mere feet away?*

He raised his weapon and pointed it behind her. He fired, blasting a three-foot-diameter hole midway up, into the side of the chimney. Mollie screamed, while flinging herself clear of the rocky debris falling from above her. Nan rushed to her side and pulled her into her arms. Several small cuts along her cheek were bleeding. Mollie's arms encircled her neck. Nan felt Stalls' presence at their backs, and then his hand was on her shoulder.

"We're together now. We're a family."

Chapter 43

Jason took in the scene below. He was home. The scrapyard appeared the same as it always had, but there was now another far more modern structure nearby, with an adjacent swimming pool. There was also what looked like a demolished gun turret, as well as a small space vessel parked on the driveway. As the *Perilous* approached, it was evident the structure, the new home Nan had built for them, had been fired on. Blackened scorch marks pocked what looked like metal storm shutters. *She'd fortified the place.*

Jason stood and set a phase-shift location for directly below, via his HUD.

"I'm coming with you, Cap," Billy said, getting to his feet.

"No. I'm doing this alone. Hang tight here."

Ricket was also now standing. "What about the bin lift?"

"What about it?"

"It had already entered Earth's lower orbit by this time."

"What does that mean? Why would we care?"

"It would have flashed into existence right along with everything else on Earth. Within the next few minutes, it will drop from the sky and demolish that house, along with Stalls and anyone else who's left in it. We have no way to contact your brother for him to change course."

"Then I guess you'll have to destroy it," Jason said, expressionless.

Billy shook his head. "You'd kill your own brother?"

"To save Nan? You bet. And don't forget, there's already another Brian in upper orbit—a sacrifice we'll need to take." Jason looked down at Grimes. "Can I trust you to do what needs to be done?"

She hesitated, looking from Jason to Billy, then back at Jason again. She nodded and Jason phase-shifted away.

* * *

"Up. Get up."

"Can't you see she's hurt?" Nan spat, not wanting to look up at Stalls.

"She's fine. Come on, up up," he said, impatiently. His grip tightened on Nan's shoulder as he pulled her to her feet. Mollie, still on her back, glared up at him.

"You, too, Mollie," he said, holding out an outstretched hand.

She ignored it and got to her feet on her own.

"Unless you want your little girl to die here I suggest you have the AI disable whatever kind of weaponry you have installed."

Nan looked toward the back of the house. *What was taking them so long?*

Stalls tightened his grip on Nan's shoulder again. "I don't like having to repeat myself."

"AI, disable—"

"Mom, it's Bag End."

"Right," Nan said. "Bag End, disable all security measures. Do not fire on the hostile intruder."

The words had barely left her lips before Stalls was ushering them both through the great room toward the front door. Mollie stumbled and he tightened his grip around her waist.

"Stop it! I'm going—just don't touch me."

Stalls pushed Nan forward to open the front door. She felt whatever hope she had associated with the other ship rescuing her fading fast. Perhaps it was one of his own ships.

She reached for the doorknob and pulled, but the door held fast. "Bag End, retract the security shutters and unlock the front door."

It took several seconds before she heard the high-pitched whine of the security shutter motors raising the metal panel, and then the definitive *click* of the front door's deadbolt being retracted.

"Open it. Now!"

Nan had never wanted to kill someone more than at that particular moment. She knew once they were locked into that ship of his, they were as good as dead. Or worse. Ready to make a stand, she straightened and faced him. "No. We're not going anywhere with you."

He slapped her with an open hand, then slapped her again, bringing his hand back across her face a second time.

"Stop! Don't hurt her!" Mollie yelled up at him, tears in her eyes. "I'll open the door. I'm opening the door, see?"

Mollie reached for the door and turned the knob. The door cracked opened and light poured in from the outside.

Startled, Nan pulled Mollie back into her arms. Nan, Mollie and Captain Stalls stared into the black cold muzzle of a multi-gun. The man holding the gun was Captain Jason Reynolds.

* * *

Jason froze. Seeing Nan alive was simply too much to comprehend. His heart constricted. Emotions overwhelmed him. *It's actually her.* He'd already said his goodbyes; he'd come to terms with the fact that she was gone forever. The mother of his little girl was dead. But it was the trickle of blood at the corner of Nan's lip that brought him back to the present. Rage filled his mind. This time he'd have the pleasure of killing the bastard himself.

He was too late. Stalls, already making a move, brought up his own weapon and was poised to fire. Jason adjusted his aim, pointed his multi-gun over Mollie's head, and just to the left of Nan's ... Yes, he had him this time. Jason felt his trigger finger tighten, but Stalls fired a fraction of a second sooner.

Jason's visor took the near-pointblank blast with little effect—other than to snap Jason's head backward from the driving force of the plasma blast. Off balance, Jason took three quick steps back. Two more blasts to his visor followed. Stalls strode after him firing, continuing to pound one blast after another into Jason's visor. Nan and Mollie stood in the doorway watching in horror as Jason was continually pummeled backward.

Chapter 44

"I'm going down there," Billy said, setting phase-shift coordinates on his HUD.

"Absolutely not," Grimes said. "You heard him, he's doing this on his own."

"Well, if you haven't noticed, he's getting his ass kicked down there," Billy said.

Grimes had maneuvered the shuttle to the other side of the house and they'd witnessed Jason being repeatedly shot at, barely able to remain on his feet.

"Incoming!" Ricket yelled, pointing at the shuttle's holo-display. "Directly above us—it's the bin lift."

Grimes reached for the controls and brought the shuttle into a steep climb. "There it is. Locking on target."

"Wait! Are you sure? There are two people on board that vessel. Two living, breathing people ..." Dira yelled from the back of the cabin.

Grimes hesitated, looking down at her holo-display. "I also see two life forms still in that house. Someone's going to die. I'm sorry." She fired into the clouds above.

"Bin lift's still falling," Ricket exclaimed.

Grimes didn't let up. An endless stream of plasma fire lit up the sky.

"Still coming," Ricket reported.

"What the hell is that thing made of?" Billy asked.

Ricket shrugged. "A solid, heavy mix of various exotic metals."

The bin lift was now visible with the naked eye and falling fast.

"I'm not going to be able to stop that thing. Maybe *The*

Lilly could take it out, but not a shuttle's single plasma cannon," Grimes said, exasperated.

She adjusted the position of the *Perilous* and watched as the bin lift grew in size, came even with the shuttle, then continued on its downward trajectory. Billy was the first to say the obvious: "No one's alive on that thing. Not anymore."

The bin lift had been reduced to a molten heap of hardened metal, and like a meteor, nothing could stop it from impacting below.

Grimes and Billy were on their comms. "Get away from the house, Captain!"

It was too late. The bin lift hit the house with an explosive, devastating impact.

* * *

Jason withstood eight direct blasts to his face visor before regaining enough footing to charge back at Stalls. Somewhere along the way, he'd lost his multi-gun. He no longer needed it. His two hands were all that was necessary. Jason plowed into Stalls a second time and knocked him flat on his ass. To Stalls' obvious surprise, Jason stood tall and systematically unlatched the clasps securing his battle suit. By the time he stepped out of it, Stalls was back on his feet, had a knife in his hand, and was smiling.

"I will enjoy this. You see, I'm going to gut you from your scrotum to your chin." He gestured toward Nan and Mollie standing in the doorway twenty paces away. "Your daughter and ex-wife will replay this scene in their minds over and over until their own dying breaths."

Neither Jason nor Stalls would have time to charge the other. Jason was positioned perfectly to see the house erupt into a ball of fire and disappear into a smoldering crater.

* * *

The shuttle landed nearby and everyone filed out. Billy had removed his helmet and was puffing fiery life into a fresh cigar.

"We're going to let them go at it like that?" Rizzo asked.

"You want to get in the middle of the fray, Rizzo?" Billy asked back, taking in another smoke-filled breath.

Grimes and Dira were the last to come down the gangway and join Billy and Rizzo.

"We can't just let them fight on like that, can we?" Dira asked them.

Jason and Stalls continued to fight. Stalls no longer had his knife and seemed to be getting his ass kicked.

"Too bad about the house. I'm sure that just pissed Jason off that much more," Grimes said.

"At least it was the older house that took the hit."

Dira rushed forward, arms outstretched, and embraced Nan and Mollie. The three hugged for a long while.

"I guess it's time we break up the fight," Billy said.

"Yeah, good luck with that," Rizzo answered.

Chapter 45

"Captain! Don't you think that's enough?"

Jason released another hammering blow to Stalls' solar plexus and watched the bloodied pirate fall to the ground, holding his stomach.

Billy joined Jason at his side and together they watched Stalls gasping for air. "I know you've wanted to do this for a long time, but there's two people over there who would like to see you."

Jason was having a hard time staying on his feet. Even before fighting with Stalls, he'd been ready to topple over. He looked back over Billy's shoulder toward the *Perilous* and his crew standing around Nan and Mollie. Nobody would have told them yet ... told Nan she had died weeks earlier, told Mollie there were now two Mollies. Then his eyes went to Dira; her arms were wrapped around Mollie and they were all laughing at something Mollie said.

"Sorry about your house, man," Billy said.

When Billy and Jason turned back, bringing their attention again toward the crater, they caught Stalls backing into Jason's battle suit. Before Billy could pull his own sidearm, Stalls finished latching the helmet and was running toward his own small craft, parked on the driveway.

"I'll get him," Billy said, following in quick pursuit. But Jason knew he was too far ahead to catch. Already at his ship, Stalls gave a perfunctory wave and moments later the little ship was fleeing into the sky.

"Sorry, Cap. He was too far ahead," Billy said, jogging back.

"Let him go. I have a feeling that's not the last we'll be seeing of Captain Stalls."

Jason headed over to the *Perilous*. Halfway there, Mollie and Nan began running toward him. He held his arms out wide and they engulfed him. Jason kissed Mollie's forehead, and pulled Nan into his arms and kissed her on the lips. Pulling slightly away, he held Nan's face in his hands and looked at her ... looked at her small, upturned nose, the faint freckles on her cheeks, and her eyes, which held a strange mixture of intelligence and mischief.

"For God's sake, Jason, it hasn't been that long," she said, brushing the hair out of her eyes. But the smile on her lips disappeared when she saw the seriousness on his face, his tears.

"What is it? What's—"

Jason put a finger to her lips. "Not now." He hugged them both again and stood back. "How about you show me the new house?"

"First of all, Dad, it's called Bag End. The AI won't talk to you unless you call her that."

"Okay, I can do that."

"And we have to get Teardrop out of the pool." Mollie grabbed her parents' hands, pulling them toward the house.

* * *

"Let me get this straight. Today, Mollie and I are actually living three weeks in the past?"

"Yes. But that's not the ... um ... thing that I need to explain."

"Well, just say it. What's wrong with you?"

Jason watched Mollie in the backyard through the shattered rear window. Bossy as ever, she was pointing into the pool and telling Teardrop something about a missing arm.

"Nan, three weeks ago, what's just occurred here, also happened then. But I wasn't here to help you and Mollie. When Stalls came for you ... You were mortally injured."

"You're saying Stalls killed Mollie and me?"

"You died later on. Mollie was fine. At least physically. But the emotional toll has been significant. She's changed. All that's occurred has changed her."

"So wait up. I'm dead?"

"Mollie took it very hard. Hell, she chose the music for your memorial service."

"So how's this going to work, Jason? There's two Mollies! You're telling me there are now two Mollies?"

"Yes."

They were sitting on the floor next to each other. Nan leaned back against the wall and watched Mollie. She was obviously happy. She stopped yelling at Teardrop just long enough to look in their direction and wave.

"Would you rather I'd just let things unfold the way they had before?"

Nan thought about that a moment before looking back at Jason. "Hmmm," she said, holding two palms up as if weighing both possibilities. "Let's see ... dead or alive, gee, that's a tough one." She smiled. "You did just fine, Jason. We'll work this out. I'm glad you saved me and I'm not going anywhere. How many people get a chance to live life again?" She took his face in her hands and kissed him hard on the lips.

Jason had ignored a persistent NanoCom hail for the last ten minutes. He held two fingers up to his ear. "My father's been trying to talk to me. I have to get this."

"Go ahead. I need to talk to Mollie, anyway."

Jason watched Nan as she got to her feet and headed toward the pool.

"Go for Captain."

"It's about F-ing time!"

"What's going on there, Dad?"

"We've lost her! That's what's wrong," the admiral said, sounding furious.

"Lost who? Is Mollie all right?"

"What? No, Mollie's fine. I'm talking about the *Minian*. Granger found a way in, somehow. The ship's gone. No doubt he's taken her right to the Craing."

Jason thought about that, but the pieces weren't fitting together. Doubtlessly, he'd been out of the loop too long.

"We need you and Ricket to return to *The Lilly*, now! Brian's poised to get *Her Majesty* underway. You're holding everything up."

Jason had to laugh. "Well, thank you, too, Dad. Sorry I took so long saving the planet."

"You can pat yourself on the back later; right now we're preparing for battle—we're planning to attack."

To be continued...

Thank you for reading this fourth book in the Scrapyard Ship series, Realms of Time. If you enjoyed this book and would like to see the series to continue, please leave a review on Amazon.com – ***it really helps!***

To be notified of the soon-to-be released next Scrapyard Ship book, ***Craing Dominion****, contact markwaynemcginnis@gmail.com, Subject Line:* ***Craing Dominion List.***

Books by Mark Wayne McGinnis:

Scrapyard Ship
(Scrapyard Ship series, Book 1)

HAB 12
(Scrapyard Ship series, Book 2)

Space Vengeance
(Scrapyard Ship series, Book 3)

Realms of Time
(Scrapyard Ship series, Book 4)

Craing Dominion
(Scrapyard Ship series, Book 5)

Tapped In
(a Novella - Part 1)